ROUGH PAGES

BOOKS BY LEV AC ROSEN

THE EVANDER MILLS SERIES
Lavender House
The Bell in the Fog
Rough Pages

OTHER FICTION
Depth
All Men of Genius

FOR YOUNG ADULTS, AS L.C. ROSEN
Emmett
Lion's Legacy
Camp
Jack of Hearts (and Other Parts)

FOR CHILDREN
The Memory Wall
Woundabout (with Ellis Rosen)

LEV AC ROSEN

ROUGH PAGES

TOR PUBLISHING GROUP
NEW YORK

ROUGH PAGES

Copyright © 2024 by Lev AC Rosen

Endpaper art by Colin Verdi

A Forge Book
Published by Tom Doherty Associates / Tor Publishing Group
120 Broadway
New York, NY 10271

www.torpublishinggroup.com

Forge® is a registered trademark of Macmillan Publishing Group, LLC.

The Library of Congress Cataloging-in-Publication Data is available upon request.

ISBN 978-1-250-32244-9 (hardcover)
ISBN 978-1-250-32245-6 (ebook)

Our books may be purchased in bulk for promotional, educational, or business use. Please contact your local bookseller or the Macmillan Corporate and Premium Sales Department at 1-800-221-7945, extension 5442, or by email at MacmillanSpecialMarkets@macmillan.com.

First Edition: 2024

Printed in the United States of America

0   9   8   7   6   5   4   3   2   1

For Dan,

who taught me how to write books—

and how to survive them

ROUGH PAGES

ONE

"You ready for this?" Elsie asks. We're standing over her car—a gold Jaguar convertible—both of us looking down at it like it's a body laid out for viewing in church and not just sitting in the garage under her bar. "It's been a while."

"I wanted to give them some time without me," I say. "I'm bad memories."

There's no body here, but if there were, we'd be bringing it back to life.

"Nine months is a longer time than some. I thought you were never going back, honestly," she says, sliding over the door and into the driver's seat, the pants of her sapphire-blue suit not even catching on the edge. I don't tell her I never thought I would, either. I figured they'd be happier without me, that the invitations were just out of politeness. But now I need to return. Not for the family, though—something I can't tell Elsie.

"I guess it's just been long enough." I try to get into the car like she did but my foot catches and I tumble in, my head landing in her lap. She bursts out laughing. That's Elsie, she's always laughing. She makes for a good landlord in that way.

"Really don't want to go, huh?" she asks, tucking her black bob behind her ears.

"Just my feet," I say, righting myself. "The rest of me can't wait."

She smirks and pulls out fast, leaving the garage under the Ruby and heading out into San Francisco.

"I hope they don't think of death when they see me." I'm surprised when I say it. I hadn't meant for that thought to escape my head.

She laughs in the wind like I'm being funny. Around us the buildings are rising up like the fingers of a closing fist, the sun low enough on the horizon the sky is going yellow.

"Don't be so dramatic," she says. "They don't remember you with death. That was Alice. She was the murderer. You were the one who caught her." They—the whole family. The one Elsie is a part of, even if she doesn't live there. I met them nine months ago, spring of '52. A queer family out at a private estate, safe from the world, they thought, until one of them was murdered.

"I was there for one of the worst parts of their lives."

"You helped them get through one of the worst parts of their lives," she corrects. "And now you get to be there for some of the good ones. You earned that. They believe it, even if you don't. I believe it."

I don't say anything. Maybe she's right. It was my first case, the case that saved me, showed me what living a real queer life—even if a secret one behind closed gates—could look like. I found the murderer in their midst, saved the Lamontaine soap empire. But that meant dredging up a lot, picking at everyone's lives, all while they were already in pain. I wouldn't want to remember me, if I were them. And now they have a new baby—adopted by Henry and Margo to the outside world, who thinks they're the couple. But really, adopted by all of them—Elsie, Margo's girlfriend, and Cliff, Henry's boyfriend, and Pearl, Henry's mother, if not by blood. It'll be a strange life for the baby, keeping that secret. If it doesn't get out before she can talk.

Elsie reaches forward to turn on the radio. Eddie Fisher is crooning "Anytime." Elsie starts singing along.

"For someone who runs so many musical acts," I say, "people would think you have a better voice."

"I don't sing around people. Only friends. And how about

you, big shot? You can identify any song from the first few notes, spend all your money on records, and I've never heard you sing."

I blush. "I'm worse than you."

"Sing with me," she says. And what the hell, I do. We're both terrible, howling over Eddie, as she drives us across the bridge and out of the city. We keep singing with the next song and the one after that, until I feel hoarse. Then I just watch the ocean go by on my right, the sun sinking into it like a copper penny thrown in a wishing well. I wonder how much they've all changed. I wonder if they all really want me there, or if it's just Pearl again, extending an invitation for everyone without asking them.

And I wonder why Pat, the family butler and now my good friend, called me, and said he needed me to come, his voice a hushed whisper into the phone, scared, before he said not to tell anyone.

When Elsie pulls up to the gate, I get out to open it, and the smell of flowers hits me, familiar and comforting and sad all at once. Even in February, they bloom.

I was so worried about them being ready to see me, I realize I never wondered if I'm ready to see them. I pull the gate open, wait for Elsie to drive through, and close it again, making sure to lock it. The estate looks mostly the same. Flowers everywhere, glowing in the pink light of sunset. They sway toward me, and I don't know if it's a welcome or a warning. This is where my story started, after all. Well, my latest story. Lavender House, Pearl hiring me for my first case, meeting Elsie, becoming a PI over her gay club, starting to try to have a real life again. This was even the case I met Gene, my boyfriend, on. So much started here, and I'm grateful to it, but looking out on it, I wonder if this is somehow a bookend. If now it's going to take back everything it gave me.

"Stop staring and get in," Elsie says from the car. I follow her order and she drives us down to the roundabout. The house seems the same—a beautiful, huge art deco thing, surrounded by flowers of all colors, especially lavender. The driveway is white stones, which look silvery in the dark. The fountain at the center of the roundabout isn't scorched anymore; they must have fixed that. It gleams and sprays arcs of water in every direction, like a flower. I never got to see it working before. It's pretty. The sound of the water is peaceful.

Pearl comes out of the house first, her arms wide, a smile on her face. She looks the same: sixties, short, with short black hair, in a yellow blouse and white skirt.

"We finally got you here," she says, hugging me before I'm even done getting out of the car. I glance up at the windows of the house. They're curtained, but light shines through. No shadows standing in them this time.

"It's good to see you," I say.

"Elsie says you're doing well, and I appreciated your Christmas letter," she says. "But you should have come sooner."

"I wanted to give you time, and then the baby—"

"Oh, don't be silly, Andy."

"He's worried you'll look at him and see death," Elsie says, from the other side of the car.

Pearl's face goes blank with shock for a moment, and I almost want to turn to Elsie, glaring, and tell her to take me back home. But then there's a flicker of honesty, relief on Pearl's face—yes, she does look at me and see death. After all, her wife died less than a year ago. She blinks, shakes her head.

"I see more than that, Andy." She doesn't lie, at least. "I see a new chapter for all of us. You included. And I see someone who looks like he hasn't had a good meal in months. Elsie, what are you feeding him?"

"I don't feed him," Elsie says, headed to the door. "I just water him."

Pearl throws her head back and cackles at that one.

"Well, come in, come in, come in . . ." She turns, waving me toward the door. Pat is standing there, waiting.

"Can I get a minute to say hi to Pat?" I ask, keeping a smile on. "I know he's about to go help in the kitchen, so if this is my only moment . . ."

"He'll be with us after dinner, he's practically our nanny," Pearl says as we walk to the door. Pat gives me a tight hug. "Oh, but sure, it would be rude if the first time he spoke to you he was serving you dinner."

She goes inside, and Elsie follows, giving us a curious look. Then it's Pat and me standing outside. The landing in front of the door has a beautiful art deco curve over it, and it casts both of us in shadow. Pat's always been slender, but he seems thinner than before, his pale skin gaunt in the dark, his eyes wide. He's in his fifties, but handsome, with high, delicate cheekbones and usually a wry smile. Not tonight, though.

"What's going on?" I ask in a low voice.

"Thank god you're here," he says, barely a whisper, as he fumbles in his pocket then takes out some cigarettes. I get out my case and light one for him before he drops them all on the ground.

"Pat? They're going to be wondering."

Pat was probably the first real welcome here. Pearl was kind, but she was hiring me for a job. Pat was honest—about my past, what people thought of me. He was sympathetic, and welcomed me despite everything; my being a cop until just a few days before meeting him, and my having been cold to him at the bars, cold to everyone in the community unless I wanted to be alone and naked with them. Hell, even then. Pat taking me under his wing was more than I deserved. He was funny, too, often singing and always smiling. That all seems gone now though, replaced with the kind of raw fear I've seen in the faces of clients before.

"You in trouble?" I ask.

"Maybe," he says, looking at the ground, then at his cigarette. "But worse, if I am, then so is everyone in this house."

"What?" I ask, my body cold.

He doesn't say anything and instead inhales deeply on the cigarette, then coughs. I realize I've never seen him smoke before. He coughs for a moment longer, while I wait. Finally, he looks at me.

"You know how I like to read," he says, and I nod, thinking of his room upstairs, every wall a shelf filled with books, every table covered in them. "Well, on my day off, I usually help out at Walt's, the bookshop up in North Beach."

I shake my head; I don't know it. "Help out?"

"The owners are gay. Howard and DeeDee, old old friends, both loved books, so they opened the place years ago. They stocked a lot of gay titles, so I got friendly with them, and last year they decided to start a book service, you know, sending members one book a month that's hard to get otherwise, or maybe trying to publish some new ones themselves."

"A book service?" I say, wondering how that could be so much trouble.

"There's a publisher who's been selling gay books through the mail for years, Greenberg. Sold over a hundred thousand copies of *The Invisible Glass*. People want queer books, Andy. Donald Webster Cory, remember, who wrote *The Homosexual in America*—he started his own book service with the same idea, and so Howard and DeeDee thought, why not us, too? Just in California, for people who came into the shop, people we knew . . . at first."

"Isn't Greenberg the one being sued by the post office? Looking at jail time, maybe." The smoke curls from his cigarette, fading as it reaches out to the garden outside our little alcove, like it can't escape.

Pat looks down at his hands again. "Yes. But that's why it's so important, Andy. These are our stories, and we need to read them, no matter what the government says. We need to read them so we know there are more of us out there, a community waiting. One guy wrote in, some college kid in Fresno, said he found a slip to sign up in a book in another store, and he signed up immediately. He's never met another homosexual, and these stories are . . ." Pat dabs his eyes. "Howard wrote him back. He writes all of them back, so they don't feel alone."

I nod. "Okay. I get why this is important." I've never been much of a reader, but maybe if I'd read more when I was on the force, I wouldn't have felt quite so alone. "So what's the danger?"

"The shop has been closed for at least a week and DeeDee and Howard haven't been answering their phones, either. I went by on my day off, and no one was there. I'm worried. They hardly ever close this long, and never without telling me." He takes another drag on the cigarette and looks at it as if he thought it would taste better.

"Maybe there was an emergency?" I ask.

"I don't know. That's why I'm talking to you. I'm worried that the government found out, the post office told them, and . . . sending obscene material through the mail is a federal offense, right?" He lets the cigarette fall from his hand and it lands with a splatter of red embers. He stomps it out.

"Sure, but how would that be bad for you, or the family?"

He swallows and looks up at me. Pat is usually so filled with mirth and mischief, but now he looks truly scared. "Don't you get it? We mail subscribers the books. That means we need . . . their names, addresses . . ." He turns away, steps out of the alcove down onto the roundabout. The stones crunch under his feet and the light from the house hits him, pale and yellow. I follow him down.

"There's a list," I say, realizing. "A list of homosexuals." As we walk from the house, the smell of smoke fades and the flowers' perfume becomes stronger, overwhelming.

Pat nods. "Hundreds. And I'm on it. And I mail the 'illicit material,' too. If the government finds out and decides to investigate . . ." He stares up at the sky.

"They could figure out everyone here. And then the adoption . . ." It hits me all at once. Adoption is tricky. The government investigates the families. The Lamontaines must have had to play pretend for a long time just for the adoption to go through. If the government finds out the family employs a homosexual, even if they pretend they didn't know . . . I swallow.

He nods, looking back at the house and then walking along the side of it. There are bare trees here, with long, thin branches. I remember they bloomed pink, once. When we've reached the side of the house, he steps off the roundabout onto the grass and kicks it. "They'll take her away. I'm so sorry, Andy. I just . . ." He looks down again and starts crying. I reach forward to put my hand on Pat's shoulder.

"Okay, Pat. I'll look into it. And if they do have the list, I'll figure out how to make sure the family stays safe."

He reaches out and clutches my hand tightly in his. "Thank you, Andy. I'm so scared. What if I've ruined everything?"

I don't say anything. I don't have the words to tell him that maybe he has.

TWO

"What took you so long?" Elsie asks, when I come inside. She's holding two drinks and hands me one. I take a long sip. The house is warm and bright, more than I remember it being. The shadow that was over the place last time seems to be mostly gone, as much as a murder can be. The only thing that's the same is Irene's portrait hanging over the landing. I never met the woman, but that portrait was always there, Irene always looking out, severe.

"I know," Elsie says, following my eyes. "We did change it to the one Pat painted of all of us, but while the social worker is still checking in from time to time . . . she's back." Elsie throws back some of her drink. The other portrait had been in Irene's office, showing all of them. Henry and Cliff, Pearl and Irene, Margo and Elsie, real couples' portraits, all in one. It shocked me when I first saw it. "But Pat said he wanted to work on the one of all of us, anyway," Elsie says. "Add Rina to it."

"Rina? That's her name?" I ask.

"Yeah." Elsie's eyes crinkle with joy confirming it. "Short for Irene. Pat said she was family now, too, needed to be in it. What did he want that took so long?"

I stare at the painting. Irene stares back down, judging. She was so protective of the family. Like an iron wall.

"Pat wanted to smoke," I say. "So I finished the cigarette outside."

"Still nervous?" Elsie asks, eyebrow raising.

"Well, well, well," Margo says before I can answer. She comes out from the door that leads to the lounge. Margo, too, isn't quite how I remember her. She's in wide-legged pants and a sleeveless blouse, almost pajamas, her hair held back by a patterned scarf tied as a headband. "Look what the cat dragged in."

"The cat is your girlfriend," I say, smiling at her. I don't go for a hug, I know she wouldn't like that. She leans forward and pecks me gently on the cheek.

"Indeed she is."

"You're looking more casual than I remember," I say as she leads us into the sitting room—all white, but with vases filled with flowers in all colors. Pearl is at the bar, mixing drinks. "The baby make you switch to more comfortable clothes?"

"I can still doll up like the perfect housewife for the papers," she says. "But after everything that happened . . . I decided to just be myself around the house more. No one can see. And besides, it's not like Cliff was wearing any clothes. The standards around here were always low."

"Hey," Cliff says, walking out into the room from a side door. "I wear clothes." And he is more covered up than I'm used to, in a purple polo shirt and slacks.

"Rina started pulling on his chest hair," Margo says. "That's when he became interested in shirts again."

I snicker.

"Oh, you're just angry you won't be getting another show," he says, coming up to me and giving me a tight squeeze. "Though Elsie says you have a boyfriend?"

"I do," I say, blushing a little. "Gene. He's the manager at the Ruby."

"You should bring him next time," Pearl says, ushering me farther into the sitting room. "Cliff, put on some music. Do you need another drink, Andy?"

"Sure," I say, handing her my now empty glass. I drank fast. They don't know the danger they're in, and I can't tell them. Their perfect little family, that was so hard to make, that they work so hard to protect, it could all be gone soon. "Whatever you're having."

Pearl takes my glass and refills it as Cliff turns on the record player. Perry Como singing "Don't Let the Stars Get in Your Eyes" comes on.

"Henry is changing Rina's diaper," Margo explains as Pearl hands me a fresh martini.

"No nanny?" I ask, sipping.

"We thought about it," Pearl says. "But finding the right sort of nanny would be hard, and we all like spending time with her. We're big enough to split the work up, and Pat loves her, too. So far we haven't really needed one."

I nod, and try not to flinch at Pat's name.

"Evander," says a voice I recognize as Henry, coming into the room behind me. "I'd like you to meet Irene."

I turn around and smile. I don't know if I've ever been a baby person. As a cop, my encounters with kids were usually them crying because something terrible had happened, or not crying for the same reason, which was worse. But Rina is smiling like a sunbeam, in a lavender dress that looks a little too big for her, blue eyes wide and searching, over cheeks so round she looks like she's trying to store something in there. The joy everyone in the room is radiating looking at her, maybe. Smart idea, saving that for when she'll need it.

"Why, hello," I say, looking at the baby, not so sure how I'm supposed to respond to Henry. He looks different, beaming in a way I never really saw behind his calculating exterior before. "Nice to meet you."

"Rina, this man saved our family," Henry says softly. "So pay attention to him, and if you're ever in trouble, and you can't find us, you go to him, okay?"

Rina gurgles and a thick strand of drool comes out of the left side of her mouth as I laugh to hide that I teared up a little at that. Maybe I'm not only a reminder of death to them, like Pearl said. Except they don't know why I'm back.

"Oh, enough of that," Cliff says, taking Rina from Henry. "Let's dance!" He holds her out as he spins and shimmies and everyone watches, laughing. Rina has a huge grin on her face the whole time and is staring widely at everyone, toothless mouth open in some kind of joy I think we forget as soon as we can talk. I sip my martini, feeling part of it, but not, too. It's their family, after all.

"See?" Elsie says, sidling up to me. "Everyone wanted you back. You shouldn't have stayed away so long."

"Yeah," I say. "You're right." She is. That almost makes the reason I came back, how I'm only here to save them again, hurt more.

"Next time you can bring Gene," she says.

"Then who would watch the bar?"

She frowns. "Good point. Think I should fire him so you can bring him?"

"No."

She sighs.

"So how did it all work?" I ask. "The adoption? Was it hard?"

Margo rolls her eyes. "Convincing social services to let a family of homosexuals adopt a child? No, Andy, that's very easy these days."

I snort a laugh. "I just mean, how hard was it?"

"Very," Margo says, frowning. "More than we expected."

"I had to stay away for two months," Elsie says. "Some social worker overseeing the adoption."

"Mrs. Purley," Margo says. "Terrible old woman. Wore dresses from last century, I think."

"I've heard a lot about Mrs. Purley," Elsie says, looking at me.

"She was awful," Margo says, turning to Henry. "Wasn't she awful?"

"She was, um, very devoted to her job."

"Do your impression," Margo says, grinning.

Henry blushes a little and shakes his head.

"Oh, come on," Cliff says, putting his hand over Henry's. "It's very good."

Henry smiles a little, then sits back up, and raises his face slightly, his nose in the air. "'The child,'" he says, his voice high, shrill, and every vowel too long, "'the child must be taken care of appropriately. For this child was born of unfortunate circumstance, and all traces of her mother's upbringing must be shunted out of her for her to have a proper life.'" He sniffs slightly. "'A home such as yours, while it may be grand, is not necessarily the right place for such a child. We shall evaluate you to deem you worthy.'" He leans back and Cliff claps.

"It sounds just like her," Margo says. "That was the first thing she said when she met us. Word for word."

"I couldn't help but memorize it," Henry says.

"I offered her some soap, a whole set, all the scents, and she . . ." Margo looks over at Henry, who straightens out, nose in the air again.

"'Scented soap is like perfume,'" Henry says in the voice again. "'And I am *not* the sort of woman who would sully herself with perfume.'"

"What does that even mean?" Margo asks.

"Oh, I know," Elsie starts, but Margo puts her hand out over Elsie's mouth.

"I know what it means," Margo says. "I just think she's terrible."

"And thorough," Cliff says. "These new investigation standards for adoption . . . She thought it was improper for Pat to change Rina's diaper. Thought it was odd that Margo sometimes talked to Henry about business—so we stopped doing that around her. And I had to live in the servants' wing on the top floor. So did Pearl."

"I said I was the house manager," Pearl says with a shrug. "It wasn't so bad. She didn't mind it when I changed diapers."

"*I'm* the house manager," Cliff says, sitting down and bouncing Rina on his lap. "And I'm very good at it."

"Yes you are," Pearl says, patting him on the knee, then taking Rina from him and making a funny face at her. She giggles, and Pearl smiles before turning to me. "Cliff handles menus, shopping, all of that. And Margo handles the scent formulation and advertising," Pearl says, sounding very proud. "She's like the new Irene."

Margo scoffs. "I am not."

"You kind of are," Elsie says, putting her arm around Margo's waist. Margo blushes ever so slightly.

I laugh. "I'm so glad to see you all so happy," I say. They all look at me, their expressions suddenly a little ashamed at that. Because I accidentally did exactly what I knew I would—reminded them of reasons not to be happy.

I get up and go to the bar cart, taking time to finish my drink and make myself a fresh one, turned away from all of them, so they can have a moment to find their happiness again.

"Speaking of menu planning," Cliff says, "I think it's nearly time for dinner!"

Everyone rises, Pearl taking my arm, and walks across the hall to the kitchen. It's all laid out, the table set, silver gleaming. It's picture perfect for their perfect family.

"So Mrs. Purley approved you, though?" I ask as we sit down.

"We had to keep up the charade for a while," Pearl says, sounding tired, "but yes."

"We were the model family," Henry says. "That's, um, what she needed us to be."

"But she didn't want us to be," Cliff says. "I swear she would have rather Rina stayed in that orphanage." He takes Rina back from Pearl and presses his face to her belly. Rina kicks and giggles in the air. "But you came home with us, didn't you?"

"We only have one more check-in, and it's not for a month," Margo says, relieved. "And then we'll never see Mrs. Purley again."

THREE

We eat and drink and talk, Rina being passed around, giggling, but my mind is only half there. If Pat's right, and the government is onto him, then it's an easy jump to questioning if Rina is safe here—allowing a homosexual around your child probably counts as unfit parenting. And from there, probably more investigation from this Mrs. Purley—especially into books. I know Margo has some queer pulps. Pearl has a Sappho quote framed on her office wall. It wouldn't be hard to figure out what sort of a place this is once she knew what to look for, and then it would be the end: a business ruined, probably people imprisoned for fraud, and Rina back up for adoption. A family destroyed.

"So then Andy here takes the drink from Gene, shoves it right up against the guy's mouth, and says, 'I think this is what you're asking for,'" Elsie says, recounting a story from last week. Everyone laughs loudly.

I make eye contact with Pat as he pours Cliff more wine. He looks away.

"He was just confused," I say, remembering the story. The guy had been asking for a kiss from Gene over and over. It happens sometimes, and I'm not the kind of boyfriend who gets defensive and punches a guy for it. I asked him for a kiss once, too, before we were together. But this guy was persistent and Gene gave me a look asking me to step in, so I just took the drink and gave it to him. He was the one who fell face forward into it.

"Manly," Cliff says. "I hear you punched out a cop, too."

I shake my head. "I just took a punch the cop meant for someone else. For Gene. I wanted to protect him, not make things worse."

"Oh, don't be so honest," Elsie says. "That rumor has been drumming up plenty of business."

She's right about that. That punch I took, and returning some blackmail photos gratis, turned my reputation around a little. I went from untrustworthy-ex-cop-doing-tail-jobs to he-might-be-okay-or-it's-all-a-scam, and my jobs upgraded—lots of blackmail out there. Sometimes I still get a tail job or two. Sometimes I get someone being harassed by an old trick, and worried they're going to be blackmailed or something. Lots of people who want to make sure they're clean before applying for a job they know will do a government check, and know how to hide who they are going forward. I've even made a healthy business as a matchmaker, helping folks who need dates and cover stories for outings with the company or family.

And these people, at this table, also need me to keep them safe, even if they don't know it.

"Rina has dinner with you every night?" I ask. She's in a bassinet between me and Margo, put there when the salad arrived. She fell asleep almost immediately.

"Every night," Margo says, looking down at the baby. Her face turns softer than I've ever seen it, and she reaches down to caress Rina's cheek. Then she seems to remember I'm watching and looks up, the softness gone. "We rotate the bassinet to different positions every night so everyone gets to feed her."

I stare down at Rina's small form, sleeping now, but still in her dress, her thumb firmly in her mouth. She looks so peaceful. She is so lucky to have this family. I can't let it get taken from her.

"So," Cliff says. "Tell us about the boyfriend. Gene. He's Elsie's manager?"

I nod, feeling myself blush slightly as everyone watches me. "Bartender, manager, nurse. He was the one who took care of me when the police . . ."

I see Pearl frown slightly, and look down at my food—pork chops. They taste delicious. The cook, Dot, has really outdone herself. She'd lose her job, too.

"Anyway," I continue, "he's smarter than me."

"A lot," Elsie says.

"He and Elsie have a book club," I say, the words creaking out of me as I think about what it means, knowing what I know now.

"A book club?" Margo asks. "Without me?"

"You won't read the Narnia books," Elsie says with a grin. "Just your dirty pulp store novels."

Margo chuckles. "I like my gay pulps. Why read about straight people?"

I smirk to hide my worry—where does she get her books? Through Pat? He would have mentioned that, but she's also too clever to get caught buying anything queer in public.

"Well, the Narnia books are about kids," Elsie says. "And centaurs. And a talking lion."

Margo shakes her head. "I'm glad you can have your book club with him, then. And read those stories to Rina," she adds, softer, as though the thought just struck her.

"But what does Gene look like?" Cliff asks, turning back to me. "Handsome, I assume."

I blush slightly. "Very. He's Filipino, five eight, black hair, brown eyes."

"That's not very romantic." Cliff laughs. "It sounds like the description of a suspect. I was hoping for something like Pearl's poetry."

"I'm no poet," I say.

"Henry, how would you describe me?" Cliff asks, fluttering his eyelashes.

Henry's eyes go wide with panic. "Oh, um, well . . . handsome," he says. "Though, um, I wouldn't use that word outside the house, of course. Dark wavy hair. Hazel eyes."

Cliff sighs, looking at Pearl. "You raised him with poetry, and this is how he describes me."

Pearl laughs. "You're very good-looking, Cliff. And I'm sure Gene is, too. You should bring him next time. We can all write sonnets together."

After a dessert of baked Alaska, we return to the drawing room, and Pat joins us, still half as a butler, mixing everyone drinks, but also playing charades with us, and moving Rina to the nursery when she starts to cry in her bassinet. He seems less worried now, but that's probably a façade more than faith in me. Or it could be trying to savor every moment with them before something terrible happens. That's how I'm feeling, saying good-night to Rina, laughing at Henry's attempt to act out a scene from *Niagara,* enjoying the feeling of Pearl's hand on my shoulder as she stands behind me, squeezing, happy to have me there. I try to take it all in, in case this is the last time.

We leave sometime after midnight, everyone giving me a warm hug and telling me to come back soon. Pat hugs me last, and I can feel his nervousness in the way his hand squeezes my shoulder.

"I'll go by tomorrow," I whisper in his ear. "I'll call to let you know what I find."

"Thank you," he whispers back.

I get in Elsie's car, and everyone stays outside waving as we leave the estate, locking the gate behind us. On the highway, the smell of the ocean is strong in my face.

"See, that wasn't so bad, was it?" Elsie says.

"No. It was pretty good, in fact." I smile, trying not to think about Pat. "Hey, your book club—if I were finally going to join, but maybe wanted to keep it secret from Gene until I caught up . . . where do you get your books?"

"Oh, easy, Walt's. North Beach. All us gays who read go there. I think Pat even works there on his days off."

I nod. It's what I expected her to say, but it doesn't make me feel any better. Worse, if anything. Like the chill you feel that lets you know you're getting sick. "That sounds familiar. I'll try to stop by sometime."

"Oh, if you do, can you pick up an order for me? They should be in by now, though no one has called me about it. Just some of the pulps, for Margo. She's already got so many flowers, I like bringing her books instead."

"Sure thing," I say, smiling so it doesn't look too suspicious. So she's on the list, too, or at least in their records. But having another reason to go there is a good cover, in case she hears about me up there, or sees me bringing home a book from this book service he mentioned. I could probably trust her, she likes Pat, but it would be asking her to keep a secret from her family, too. "You ever read books like Margo does?"

"Sometimes," she says. "There are quite a few. Most of them are sad, though. I don't like books that are too sad. I like stories with adventure and magic. Pirates. I love books about pirates." Her eyes go wide. "I should get Rina a pirate costume!" She tilts her head. "Or do you think she's too young?"

"Not for the costume, but I'd keep her away from swords for a little while."

"Ah, see, you're smart, too, in your way."

I shake my head, chuckling, and look out at the dark water.

FOUR

The Ruby is packed by the time we're home. The band is in full swing, Lee singing "The Lady Is a Tramp," and the dance floor is overrun with couples, their bodies moving to the rhythm. I spot Gene—he's manager now, but still tends the bar. He likes that part of it. It's just now he also oversees the other bartenders, checks stock in the morning, helps the band load in, calls for replacements if a singer drops out last minute, makes sure there's enough waitstaff, and orders supplies. It's been a few months of training for him—a lot he sort of knew how to do, but didn't know the details of. Turns out, despite Elsie never seeming to take much seriously, it's a serious job, with a lot of hard work. He's been coming by early and going up to her apartment where they go over when to buy, when not to buy, how to deal with drunk customers and angry suppliers. It's strange to think what the story of his life would be if someone hadn't sent photos of him and another man to the medical school he was enrolled at. I watch him pour a drink and wonder if his hands would be better off sewing someone shut, if he'd be happier. Then he looks up at me and smiles, and I hope not. I hope this is the happiest he can be, because it's the happiest I've ever been, and so much of that is because of him.

"Hey," he says, stepping out from behind the bar. "How was it?"

"Oh, he was a hit," Elsie says, lighting a cigarette. "They missed him, they loved him, they want to meet you."

"Me?" Gene looks shocked.

"They asked him to describe you, and there was talk of poetry."

"Talk, but not creation of it, apparently," I say.

Gene grins and takes my hands in his. They're cold, he handles ice and glass all day, but I'm used to that. I like it, even, the slight shiver I get when our fingers interlace. He peers up at me, and I smile back and I can tell he's reading me. Not too many people can do that. Usually I'm the one reading them—when I was a cop, I was proud of that, how I could hide my secret so well I knew how to spot other people's. But Gene can see through me sometimes. Or maybe it's just that I can't stand hiding myself with him. It makes me tingle to be so revealed, kind of like I'm nervous, but not scared. Just . . . there. Being seen, under a spotlight in the dark. That's intimidating, even if it is him.

He squeezes my hands, then turns to Elsie. "Well, poetry or not, I'm glad everyone was happy to see you. And since you're back, boss, you mind if I take five to dance with my boyfriend here?"

"By all means," Elsie says, hopping on a barstool and surveying her kingdom. "Dance, kiss, be happy."

Gene comes out from behind the bar and leads me to the floor. I'm about as good a dancer as I am a singer, but I like the feeling of his arms around my waist, mine around his neck, our bodies close. I just try to sway a little, let him turn me around.

"So?" he asks, quieter, leaning in. "What's wrong?"

I pull him closer but don't say anything at first. I want to tell him, want to tell someone, because I hate keeping this secret from Elsie, and sharing it with Gene would feel better. But then he'd have to keep it from her, too.

"You can't tell Elsie," I say. "Would you be okay with that?"

"Is she in trouble?"

I nod.

His thumb rubs the side of my neck. "But she doesn't know?"

"It's someone else's trouble."

He's quiet for a moment, staring at the rest of the dancers, and then refocusing on me. He looks like he won't be happy knowing or not knowing. I couldn't tell him which is worse, though. We dance quietly a moment more, his hips swaying under my hands.

"Tell me," he says finally.

"Pat," I say. Gene knows Pat, he stops by the bar sometimes.

"Is it bad?" Gene asks.

"Could be. You know the bookstore, Walt's?"

"Sure. I go there all the time."

I feel my hand squeeze his a little tighter. "It's been closed unexpectedly for a week."

He frowns. "A week? I was in there just . . . yeah, two weeks ago, I guess. You think something happened to Howard or DeeDee? Both?"

"I don't know. They have this . . . book service. Books in the mail. Queer ones. A list of folks who they mail these books to every month. And the post office has been cracking down on obscene materials lately, so if they found out about and decided to end the book service, they could have threatened Howard and DeeDee with jail . . . but it doesn't make sense the two of them would just up and vanish. There'd be a trial. Feds could have intimidated them into closing up maybe, or even thrown them in jail to await trial, though that seems unlikely . . . lots of things could have happened."

"Because of books?" His expression looks like he's been punched.

"Sure," I say. "Books aren't above the law."

He sighs and pulls me a little closer. "It's unfair, the things we're not allowed."

"Yeah," I say. "But we take them anyway, right? Dancing isn't legal either. We're doing that. Or at least you are."

He smiles. "So even if they're not legal, publishers still print them?"

"I think so. I don't know much about it—some laws are federal, not state, but I don't remember ever raiding a publisher. I think the First Amendment protects them—but selling the books, advertising them, sending them through the mail . . . that's what they can criminalize. Were you part of this book service? Pat says there's a list of the subscribers, and that's what I'm most worried about."

"Worried about me?"

"Aren't I allowed to be?"

He grins. "Allowed? It's required."

"Well then, I'm just doing what I'm supposed to."

"Yeah." He frowns slightly. "And yes, I'm part of the book service. Howard asked me to sign up a while back, and I did. But don't worry about me, there's nothing anyone can do that hasn't been done already, remember?"

"Yeah," I say, but I don't point out he's wrong. A list of homosexuals, and Gene on it—even if he can't get kicked out of med school again, and the cops already see him at work, there's his landlord. His parents stopped speaking to him after the medical school told them why they'd cut him, but he might have other friends. And depending on who got the list, it might just be someone who wants to check off every name with a bullet, or a fist. I swallow.

"Your hands are getting sweaty," Gene says. "You're worrying."

"Does your landlord know about you?" I ask.

Gene looks confused by the question at first, then realizes, and shakes his head. "But there are always other landlords, right?"

"Still . . ." I hold his hand tighter.

"Worry about Howard and DeeDee, not me."

"I can do both."

He smiles at that. He seems so unconcerned. Maybe he hasn't thought about the guy checking off the list.

"You should tell Elsie."

"I want to, but Pat . . ." I hold him closer and sway.

"I understand. Maybe it'll be nothing and then you won't have to tell anyone."

"Maybe."

"You're going to go by tomorrow?" he asks.

"That's the plan."

"Maybe I can stay over tonight and walk you there in the morning, then. Make sure you find the place."

"I think that would be very helpful," I say, pulling him closer.

The next morning after breakfast, Gene walks me to Walt's. The wind is strong as we get closer to the water, and all around us, the crowds seem younger, kids in their twenties, smoking, chatting, in black clothes. It smells like salt and smoke, and a little of reefer, though no one is smoking that openly.

"Why is it called Walt's?" I ask. "If the owners are named Howard and DeeDee?"

"Walt Whitman," Gene says. "Their favorite poet. He was queer, too. At least, I think so. Howard told me once he wanted to call the place Galahaut, but DeeDee said no one would trust a store with a name like that."

When we finally reach the store, it's closed up, like Pat said. It's a small building, unassuming, between an antique store and a record shop. My eyes dart into the window of the record shop, but everything on display I have already.

"You're here for the books today, remember?" Gene says with a laugh.

"Maybe I was hoping to point out a gift you could buy me."

"What makes you think you deserve a gift?"

"I mean, I'm pretty heroic."

"Are you?"

"I'm taking this case, helping the innocent."

"A hero never asks for a reward. That's in all the books."

"I've never heard that."

"You should read more."

"I would, but the store is closed," I say, gesturing at it. The windows are glass, but there are blue curtains in front, so we can't see inside. WALT'S BOOKS is printed in gold letters on the left window, NEW AND USED on the right. I look through the small gaps in the curtains behind the windows, but all I can see is darkness. I try the door, but it's locked.

"So . . . is that bad?" Gene asks, his joking tone gone.

"Maybe," I say, walking around the block. There's an alley in back, a few cars parked along it, and each of the stores has a back door. Walt's back door has a glass window on top, but it's been shattered. No glass outside, and the matching blue curtain hung inside the door has been pulled out slightly, to cover the broken window. The door is even locked. But it's easy enough to reach in through the broken pane and unlock it.

"Should we be doing this?" Gene asks.

"No," I say. "You want to go?"

He looks up and down the alley. It's empty in the morning light, some steam coming out of a vent in the sidewalk. There's the faint sound of music coming from the record store—Anita O'Day, I think. "Lover Come Back to Me."

"Okay," Gene says. "I mean, we're just checking no one is hurt—a broken window could mean someone cut themselves and needs help, right?"

"Maybe," I say. "Stay behind me just in case, though, all right?"

He swallows. "All right."

I open the door and go inside. It's a back room of some kind, an office with a few small windows looking out on the alley, dingy white walls. No broken glass here, either—someone cleaned it up. Maybe just an accident? There's a torn, empty box on one side of the room, which is otherwise strangely bare. On the other side is a desk, some books on it, and a dolly cart in the corner, for moving lots of books at once, I guess. Nothing looks too out of place, aside from the box. It smells sort of odd, though. Fishy. On the desk are piles of books, wrapped in brown paper and bound with twine, notes stuck on them—one is marked *Elsie Gold*. I'm not shocked, but her name just being out here makes me cold. Has anyone seen it? Is she on someone's list now, too?

There's a door to the front of the store, and through that is a whole other world. Shelves of books high as the ceiling, not just on the walls, but in the middle of the room. Where there aren't shelves, there's a blue wallpaper, old-fashioned damask, with an image of two knights, one standing already without his helmet, the other kneeling and taking off his. Looks like it's from a fairy tale, but not one I recognize. Same image over and over, but only on slivers of wall that show between the shelves. A lot of trouble to wallpaper a place you knew was going to be covered in books.

The lights are out, but some dim sun comes in through the curtains, with bright lines of it on the edges. There's a small counter and register. I check the till, and there's some cash in it. No one robbed the place. It looks like they just closed up and didn't reopen. Which is exactly what could have happened if the feds decided to go after them at home. But even then, you'd expect the place to have been tossed. And they wouldn't have just broken in with a smashed window in back. They would have gone in the front door—with a key they took off Howard or DeeDee. Maybe they knew exactly what they were looking for, though, and the broken window was an accident, unrelated.

I open the door again and wave Gene inside. He looks around the office, studying it.

"Never been back here?" I ask.

"No. I mean sometimes I caught a glimpse through the door

when they went to grab a book, but usually everyone was in the store."

I let him look around in the main store. "Anything look off, different than it usually does?"

He shakes his head. "Same as usual."

"The queer books, those have a particular section?"

"Uh . . ." Gene looks around. "Not really. I mean, a lot of them they kept in the back, the office, just in case."

"The office?" I ask. "But it was empty."

"I know." His voice wavers slightly as he says it and I reach out to stroke his shoulder briefly.

I go back into the office and look around more closely. There's no sign of any books, aside from the reserved orders already wrapped on the desk. Maybe they were in boxes, like the torn one on the floor, all carried out by the feds. Or just stolen. I go through the desk and find an accounts book, but no list of addresses. I look over the numbers—they weren't doing great, but they were making a little profit. They'd just invested in something big, though—one large payment to a printer, and one a check made out to cash. My math isn't great, but it looks like they were about to have a very bad few months unless they made the money back—selling their new book, I guess. Or go bankrupt.

I keep searching the desk and find some scraps of paper it takes me a little while to figure out—betting slips. Dated a little over a week ago. They're both marked with a stamp—the Shore Club, a mob-owned gambling joint in Fisherman's Wharf I remember from my cop days. Could be one of them got into trouble with the mob, but I don't know why they'd just break in and take some books. Could be they broke in to take the pair of them, but then they'd have emptied the register, too. Could be nothing. Without knowing the code the club used, I'm not even sure what these slips are betting on, or if the amounts were worth killing over. I pocket them and keep searching, but all I come up with is a stack of paper slips, all of them identical—a letter. At the very top, in fancy type, reads *Walter's Book Service*, and below that:

DEAR READER,

Did you enjoy this book? Are you looking for similar titles, but are unable to find them on the shelves of the everyday book shop? We also find that sometimes our tastes are not catered to, which is why we've started WALTER'S BOOK SERVICE. We work with publishers and printers to bring you the highest quality stories featuring difficult-to-find characters and plots. Books such as The City and The Pillar, Hemlock and After, and The Invisible Glass. Or, if you'd prefer stories for ladies, we have selections in the vein of Spring Fire, Women's Barracks, and the English translation of Olivia.

For three dollars a month, we'll send you one of our personally selected books of fiction or memoir, one that's difficult to find on the shelves. If you subscribe for a whole year, we'll throw in a bonus book every fourth month--that's fifteen books for only thirty-six dollars! A real value!

If you would like such books shipped to you, simply fill out the coupon at the bottom of this letter and mail it in with your check or money order.

Cordially Yours,

Walter

Below that is a form asking for a name and address, and whether the reader would prefer stories for ladies or gentlemen, and an address to mail the slip to—same as the store. Risky. Would have been too easy to figure out who was running this. The letter is vague enough it doesn't break any laws, and I don't know the books mentioned in it, but I'm guessing a lot of queer readers would—and so would anyone keeping track of immoral books. To the feds, this could practically be an invitation for a raid. And if they're just sticking them in books, like Pat said, it would be an easy invitation to find.

I'd asked Pat last night for more about Howard and DeeDee, about their lives, but he hadn't known much—no addresses, no phone numbers aside from the bookshop. This is where they lived, he said. Except there's not much sign of that now.

I do one more tour of the place, but don't find anything else. The torn box bothers me. The empty side of the room. Something was there, and it was taken. The only thing that makes sense is the feds, clearing out the queer stuff. But then why the back door, the subterfuge? Why not scour the shelves in the main room for other dirty books? And what is that smell?

"So?" Gene asks.

"A lot of leads, but nothing certain," I tell him, picking up the packaged books marked with Elsie's name. I'm worried about the label—someone seeing it. "I'd better call Pat. Walk back to the Ruby with me?"

"Sure," he says, and before we leave the empty shop, he pecks me once on the cheek. Outside, we stand a little over a foot apart, hands in our pockets, not too close. I close and lock the door from the outside, and pull the curtain so it's hanging same as before we went in. I light a cigarette and we walk out of the alley. After the soft blue light of the bookshop, the late-morning sun seems too bright.

"Were either of them gamblers, do you know?"

"I don't know . . ." Gene shakes his head. "I mean, I bought books from them. Howard was always fun to talk with, but . . . when I think about it, I don't know what I really knew about them. Just the books. You think they're all right?"

"I don't know. Could be they were grabbed for some reason,

or the feds have them locked up for peddling smut or some-thing . . . but then you'd think they'd have reached out, gotten a lawyer. Maybe they did, just didn't tell anyone. I can check that, if I need to."

"There wasn't any blood in there, that's good."

"Yeah, at least there's that."

The sunlight is cold on my back as we head back to the Ruby. Something about the bookshop doesn't feel right—too many leads, but also not enough. And worst of all, no sign of the list.

FIVE

Back in the Ruby, Gene gives me another kiss before getting to work, checking stock and washing all the glasses. Elsie is probably still upstairs on the top floor, in her apartment, so I leave her books on the bar and walk up to my apartment and office, on the second floor, right next to all the female and male impersonators' dressing rooms. It's still morning, so none of them are in yet, but evidence of them is always here—sequins and feathers in the hall, the smell of perfume and lipstick. I didn't know lipstick had a smell before I moved in here. But it does; same smell, no matter what shade.

I unlock my office and sit down at my desk. It's sparse in here—I try not to show off too much of myself; people who hire me value that kind of discretion. But I'm the only one most of them can come to, the only one they can be honest with. So I'm honest with them, too—I don't have a PI license, but I was an inspector in the SFPD, so I have the skills. I can do this, if they just trust me.

I take down some of the law books I have up on the shelf, the kind with laws I don't know well and sometimes have to refer to, and I read about adoption long enough to go through a couple cigarettes. It's not good news, especially with the way they were talking about Mrs. Purley. I pick up the phone and dial the house—the servants' line, since there are two of them—and wait. Pat picks up after a moment.

"Hello, Lamontaine residence, this is the butler speaking."

"Hey, Pat. I stopped by that bookstore today."

"Oh, thank god. Is it all right?"

I pause too long.

"Oh no. Andy, tell me, what did you find?"

"Nothing," I say. "That's what worries me. Someone had broken the back window, probably let themselves in, but the place was clean, nearly. No sign of a struggle, but I found some betting slips, and maybe some books were missing—did they keep a lot of books in the back?"

"Yes," he says quickly. "Yes, that's where new stock lived, or anything they thought they'd need large amounts of—books for the book service, too. They waited there until we mailed them out."

"Okay, and when did you last do that?"

"About a month ago. The new ones should have gotten in last week. Howard was so excited—it was a new book, and they were publishing it. Wouldn't tell me what it was about, just said it was a true story and no one was going to believe it. DeeDee wouldn't tell me either, said Howard was keeping it a surprise."

"This is for the book service. Queer books?"

"Yes. Do you think that's why the feds came for them? Because of this new book?"

"I don't know that the feds came for them at all."

"Did you find the list?"

I sigh. "No, sorry, Pat. No sign of the list."

"What list?"

I look up. Elsie is leaning on the doorframe. I frown. The door had been closed a moment ago.

"You listening at my door?" I ask her.

"You've been acting weird since dinner yesterday. You even gave me that Old Andy smile. The one that was all about hiding."

I want to scowl, but it's almost nice to be seen through that way. She's the only one who saw my transformation, the only one who could spot it.

"Elsie . . ." I say. "I have to have some privacy."

"If it's about Pat, it's about my family. You don't get privacy if it's about them, about me."

"Please don't tell her," Pat says into the phone.

Elsie is staring at me, an eyebrow raised. I think about everything I just read about adoption. "I think you should," I say to Pat. "She deserves to know. They all do."

"That's Pat?" Elsie asks, walking closer. "I knew you didn't just finally decide it was time to go back. Is he in trouble?"

"Why don't you talk to her, Pat?" I say into the phone. "You can trust her, you know she cares about you."

He sighs, and I hand the receiver to Elsie, and watch her face as he talks. She nods, then frowns, and finally she goes pale and fumbles out her cigarette case.

"You need to tell them, Pat," she says finally. Her voice is calm but her face is shaking between expressions—scared, angry, sad— like watching flowers fall out of a tree until it's bare. "We can fix it, but Mrs. Purley is still sniffing around. They have one more meeting with her. You . . ." She tilts her head, cradling the receiver between her ear and shoulder so she can open her cigarette case. I stand and help her, lighting one as she continues to talk. "What'll happen is we'll tell them, and then I'll tell them I'm going to put you up for a while. You'll stay on my guest bed. They'll tell Mrs. Purley you're on vacation—unless she knows about it. Then they'll say they fired you, because they found out and didn't want her to know because it might endanger the adoption. I think she'd buy that . . . right?"

She looks at me and I shake my head. I don't have an answer beyond handing her the cigarette, which she takes gratefully.

"I know, Pat, I know," she says, and takes a deep drag. "But this is the safe way to do it. For Rina, right? I stayed away for months . . . you can too. Until Andy figures this out." Her eyes stay on mine, pleading. I nod this time. What else can I do?

"Okay," she says. "Yeah, please, Pat, you'll stay here. You can help around the bar, if you want. I know you can mix drinks." She takes another drag. "Yeah. I'll be there soon. We can tell them together."

She hangs up the phone and stands for a moment, just smoking. Her eyes go to me, then the wall, then the ceiling.

"You're going to fix this, right?" she asks.

"I'm going to do everything I can."

"That's not what I asked, Andy, and you know it. This is bad. You need to solve this. For Rina."

"I will," I say.

She slumps down in the chair across my desk and shakes her head. "If Mrs. Purley does find out, she'll buy that story, right?" She doesn't wait for an answer. "But then she'll still investigate more. Turn stuff up . . . I'll make sure they hide everything when I go there tonight. But even then . . . I couldn't be around the place for . . . a long time, maybe, depending on how often Mrs. Purley was checking. I'm too notorious. People might ask about Cliff living there . . ." She swallows. "This would change everything."

"I know."

"I'm angry you were going to keep it from me."

"I'm sorry, it's just that Pat—"

"Yeah, he apologized, too. He's scared, and you were protecting your client. I get it. But I'm angry anyway."

"You all take chances," I say.

"I know. They let me through the gate—that's a risk itself, but . . . we all know about that. Keeping it from us . . ." She shakes her head.

"I think he's embarrassed. Ashamed he's the one putting everyone in danger."

"Mortified, more like. I know. I heard it in his voice. I'll get over the anger. I understand. I just . . . How bad is this? I mean, can they just bribe their way out of it?"

"Did Mrs. Purley sound like the type who could be bribed?"

She shakes her head.

"If she knew the family consorted with a known homosexual, she'd consider that child endangerment."

She frowns. "I hate the way it sounds when you say it."

"Even if he's just the butler, even if the family claims not to have known . . . they'd investigate. And they'd investigate especially looking for queer stuff."

"So what's your plan? What's next?"

"I'll head down to the DA's office and poke around, see if I can find out if they were arrested. If so, we can figure out what to do next. And if not, well, then I'll keep looking. I'll find the list."

She leans forward and clasps her hands. The cigarette between her fingers is mostly ash now. "What if it's too late? What if Mrs. Purley is already writing up a report to take Rina back?"

I don't have an answer, so I don't give any. I reach out and take the cigarette from her before it singes her fingers and put it in the ashtray, where it crumbles into dust.

"Even if it means I have to stay away for a while . . ." she says, looking at the floor. "How long do you think it takes for a kid Rina's age to forget someone?" Her voice is quiet. The band isn't here yet; the whole building aches with silence, wanting to be full of sound.

"Could be this is all nothing," I say. "Could just be someone's sick in bed, or had a slip and fall in the shower."

"Both of them?" Elsie says.

"Maybe," I say, though I don't believe it.

She nods, her eyes still on the floor. "But you'll make sure Rina gets to keep her family?"

I nod, thinking of the baby, her squeals of laughter. "I'll fix it."

"Good." She looks up. "If there are any expenses Pat can't pay, bill me, okay?"

I shake my head. "I'm not charging him. Or you."

She smiles slightly. "Still. If there's expenses."

"Thanks."

Behind her, Lee appears in my door, holding a newspaper. He's in a red polo, with beige jacket and slacks that set off his dark brown skin, and a matching fedora. No lipstick, so not a lady, not at the moment.

"We have some kind of meeting and I wasn't invited?" Lee asks.

"What are you doing here?" Elsie asks. "You're not on for hours."

Lee nods at me. "We have an appointment. Virginia Henry, from the astronomy lab, looking for a boyfriend."

I flinch. I'd forgotten. Lee helps me out with the matchmaking side of my business. We go fifty-fifty on them. When a client comes in, I ask them about what they need, who they're trying to fool, all that. Then I tell Lee the kind of person we'd need and he finds someone who would be a match. Then I bring everyone together in my office, where I help them hash out a backstory—how they met, what they do. It's all the same kind of job as I always tried to do on the force. Keeping people safe. But this time it's my people.

"Andy," Lee says. "I am happy to be your girl Friday, but I am not your secretary."

"It's fine, I have time, it's still early."

Elsie raises an eyebrow at me.

"Really," I say. "This shouldn't take more than an hour, and the DA will be out for lunch soon anyway. You know I want that case solved, too."

"Another case?" Lee asks, walking farther into my office. He sits in the chair opposite mine. Lee may be a female impersonator and singer by trade—and one of the best—but after singing, what he loves best is mysteries. It was why he was nice to me when everyone else gave me the cold shoulder: he wanted to hear about my cases. And since he's useful on them, I tell him.

"Pat's in trouble," Elsie says. "And I want to make sure it doesn't blow back on the family. Could be really bad. But Andy is going to fix it. I'm going to head up there now, get everything sorted." She nods at both of us, and walks out, hands in her pockets, which she does when she's nervous.

"What kind of trouble?" Lee asks.

"Pat was part of this book service, run out of Walt's—you know it?" I ask.

"Oh, sure," he says. I'm not sure why I asked. Lee knows every homosexual in the city, or close to it. "I buy my mystery magazines and novels there."

"Well, they ran a gay book service, too—with a list of folks to mail these gay books to."

"Yeah, I think Howard mentioned that. Is it legal?"

"Not really. Lewd materials through the mail, that kind of thing . . . Federal law was never my beat, but the post office is already going after one book service, so it's dangerous. And now DeeDee and Howard are missing. With the list."

Lee lets out a low whistle. "That doesn't sound great. You sure Howard isn't just chasing some young fella? He's a romantic type, grand gestures, y'know?"

"The store looked like it had been broken into. And DeeDee is gone, too."

Lee nods. "She's the responsible one. And a talker. If she were going to close up, or there was a break-in, we'd have heard about it. Do you need to cancel on Virginia, then?"

"No." I shake my head. "Really, this should be quick."

Lee looks at me across the desk. "She should be here in five minutes. We really can cancel, though. She'll understand."

I shake my head. I've only just got this business up and running, got the trust of the community. I can't go playing favorites. If Howard and DeeDee are locked up, there's not much I can do. And if they're not, the trail isn't going to get any colder than it already is after a week. "This will be quick."

Lee nods and sits across from me, putting his newspaper down on the table. He points to a story about Christine Jorgensen, the American GI who a few months back made headlines by getting an operation in Denmark and emerging as a "blond beauty."

"She just came back to New York, hounded by reporters," Lee says. "They say she might do a nightclub act. You think she'll end up here?"

"And compete with you?" I ask, glad to not be talking about Pat anymore, about Rina. "She wouldn't dare."

Lee smirks. "Good answer." I think he's doing this to get my mind off the case. Trying to get me to smile, ready for a client.

"You want to do what she did?" I ask him. "The surgery, the hormones?"

Lee tilts his head, thinking. "I don't think they'd do it for someone with my skin color," he says. "But if they did . . . I don't think so. Some days, maybe, I think it would be nice to have a body I don't need to pad to fit my dresses right, but some days I really love the body I got. Now if they had a pill or shot that could change me back and forth . . ."

A brisk knock on the door interrupts him and we both immediately turn to it, our backs straighter, our faces more professional. I catch Lee seeing the same thing as me, the way we both went rigid, and he cracks a smile.

"Come in," I say, both of us standing to shake the hand of the woman who enters. "Virginia?" We've only talked on the phone before now.

"Yes." She looks around the office, appraising, but her expression reveals nothing. She looks nearly thirty, smartly dressed, with glasses and hair pulled back in a tight bun.

"I'm Andy, and this is my associate, Lee." I nod at Lee, who's leaning on my desk. "Please, sit." I motion at the chair, and she does, tucking her skirt under her legs instinctively. "So, you need a boyfriend?"

"That's right." She nods, and looks at both of us for a moment longer, considering. "I work at the astronomy lab. I love my work. But it's federally funded, and lately, some of the people I work with have been asking questions—why aren't I married? Why don't I have a boyfriend? Some of the men even hit on me, and one . . ." She shudders. "Asked me out. I've managed to keep them at bay with the usual devoted-to-my-work nonsense, but I've noticed a certain iciness of late, and I worry there's suspicion. I can't very well tell them my girlfriend of seven years is a cocktail waitress. Someone told me about what you've been doing—these fake relationships."

I nod. "Absolutely. We can find you a gay man who is in a similar situation, and work out a story about how you met, and a timeline for your relationship. He'll go to a few work events with you, you'll go to some with him—or maybe meet his family, whoever is giving him a hard time. You can keep it going as long as you like, even get married if that's convenient, or we can work out a hard end date and a reason for the breakup."

"Well, definitely not marriage. But perhaps something that could last several months, almost a year? That would keep them quiet for a while, right?"

"Yes. Though after the breakup, it'll start back up again a while later."

"Will it? I'm practically an old maid. Past marrying age, surely."

"If you don't mind my saying so, you're younger than you look, and very pretty. That'll make people wonder why you're not married, and you'll need an excuse."

She nods. "That makes sense. You really have thought about this, haven't you?"

"For the better part of a decade," Lee says, smirking at me.

I laugh. "He's not wrong. I hid myself while working for the police for years. I'm good at knowing what people will expect. But, if the breakup is devastating and you can pull off heartbreak, they'll probably leave you alone for a few months afterward. And then we can do this all again."

She tilts her head, thinking. "So a relationship of . . . let's say thirteen months, plus another six afterward. How long, do you think, until I'm no longer dateable?"

My eyes widen, a little shocked. "I couldn't say, but certainly by forty."

She sighs. "Nine years. I'll have to do this . . . five point six eight times. Six, really; I suppose I can't do this by fractions. Well . . . six fake boyfriends isn't so bad, I suppose."

"Did you just do that math in your head?" Lee asks, impressed. "I could never."

She nods, not especially proud or ashamed of it. "It's simple arithmetic. I use much more complex equations every day at work."

"But do the others in the office do that as quickly as you?"

She smirks. "Most of the men have to use calculators."

Lee laughs. "Oh, we'll have to find someone funny for you."

I nod, but don't say anything—I prefer not to talk about the kind of person we'd match our clients with in front of them.

"I think we can help you," I say. "For one fake boyfriend or six."

"Should I pay for all six at once?"

I chuckle. "No, no. We'll find a man we think will work, you two meet, and if you like him, you pay us. We handle it from there."

"We do the relationship for you," Lee says.

"That sounds worth every penny," she says, standing. "Thank you. I'd better get going, though. I told them I would be in late because I was having breakfast with my mother, but they probably have figured out by now I don't like my mother that much."

We shake hands and she leaves. Lee grins at me.

"She's funny, right? I feel like Jimmy Parsons might work, he's funny?"

I shake my head. "Funny isn't important. We need someone smart. You heard her, she's the smartest one in the room, and everyone she works with knows it. If we match her with anyone who seems less bright than she is, it'll just make her look more like the man in the relationship, and when they break up, the rumors will be stronger than before. Funny is good, but we need someone with a sharp mind to make her seem matched and feminine." I shake my head at the ridiculousness of the job.

Lee nods. "Oh, that's clever, I wouldn't have thought of that—but that's why I need you, I guess." He smiles.

"Like you said, no one knows how to hide being queer like me." I say it half-proud, half-ashamed, because that's what I am. "So look for someone brainy. Doesn't have to be charming—if he's cold it might even help explain why she doesn't go out with anyone from the office—she prefers stoic. But confident. Someone who will correct her when she's wrong."

"You think she'll be okay with that?"

"I think if I explain why, she'll understand it. I'll come up with something intellectual they could have met doing. Fighting over a chess set at an antique store maybe . . ." I start thinking about that, then remember Pat, and put it to the back of my brain. "You start looking for the man."

"I will," he says, standing. "You need any help? With the Pat thing? I want to help, too, if I can. Howard and DeeDee are good people."

"You know their last names?"

Lee stares off a moment, trying to remember. "Howard Salzberger, DeeDee Lamb."

"Thanks," I say.

"That all?"

I nod. "Still need to figure out what's going on. But if you want to ask around, see if anyone has talked to them lately, that could be useful."

"Sure." He nods. "I can do that tonight." He glances at his watch. "I'll walk out with you, I have a shift at the music store."

We leave together and I head down Mission to the civic center, all the while aware of how close this brings me to the police station and my former colleagues. The federal DA's office doesn't worry me too much, though—as cops, the DA and courthouses we went to were usually state, not federal. I was only in here a few times, talking to the DA about cases I worked that related to the mob. Most people here probably won't recognize me, unless some local PD is stopping in for the same reason I used to.

It's not lost on me that the building also houses the post office, the other agency that would be going after the book service. It's a big building, from about fifty years back, the outside white stone cut with horizontal stripes all around it like you're seeing it through venetian blinds. Inside is like a palace: marble walls, an elevator in a gold cage dotted with eagles, and floors and ceiling tiled in complex patterns—green, white, diamonds, crosses, as if the idea was to make an oriental rug out of stone.

There are courtrooms in here, and judges' chambers, but the DA is on the second floor, at the end of a long hall, like they wanted to keep it away from everything else. Inside is unassuming. The room is still marble, but there's just a few chairs, a rug, and a desk. A few people sit in the chairs, waiting to talk to someone, maybe to report a federal crime, give a statement. Behind the desk is a young blond woman with thick glasses who looks up at me curiously as I approach her.

"Hello," I say, putting on my best smile. She's not the secretary I used to report to, but the last one I remember was getting up in years, so maybe she retired, or she's on vacation. "My name is Andy. Chauncy said I could get some information on the Salzberger and Lamb case?"

It's a risk dropping the DA's name like that. I've really only met him a few times.

She tilts her head at me. "Which case?"

"The bookstore owners."

She keeps staring at me. "Well, Mr. Tramutolo didn't mention anything to me, I'm afraid, so I don't know anything about it. But if you show me your lawyer's ID, I can pull the case file."

I shake my head. "Oh, no, I'm not a lawyer."

"Oh, then . . . your badge?"

I shake my head again. This isn't going how I'd hoped. I'd hoped she'd confirm or deny there was a case before asking for ID. "Sorry, I'm a PI, not a cop," I try.

"Then your private investigator license?" she asks, narrowing her eyes.

I sigh. I'd love a PI license, but getting one would require the okay from my old place of employment, and if they saw I even applied, well . . . They didn't kill me when they caught me in the bar, or a few weeks later when they beat me bad enough to break a rib, but that doesn't mean they wouldn't mind trying again.

"You know you can't legally operate in the state of California as a PI without a license, right? What did you say your name was again?"

"I have one," I lie, "I just never need to use it . . . I'll go grab it from home."

She smiles in a way that feels like a glare. "You do that."

"Thanks." I turn around, trying to keep my face level and not look as defeated as I feel. I was cocky. Thought this would be a lot easier.

As I'm walking for the door, one of the folks waiting on the benches stands up as I pass, bumping into me. She's reading from a notebook, not looking, and she drops it.

"Oh, gosh," she says, smiling at me. "I'm so sorry."

"No problem," I say, kneeling down to pick up her notebook and hand it to her.

"Say, don't I know you?"

I look at her. Forties, maybe fifties, with a round face, bright eyes, and dark hair pinned at the nape of her neck. She's wearing a red jacket and skirt, and a matching red cap. She does look familiar, but I'm not sure why.

"I'm Rose Rainmeyer, with the *Examiner*," she says, putting out her hand with a big smile.

A reporter. I shake her hand, hoping it's not sweating. "Andy," I say quickly. "I don't think we've met."

But we have. I need to leave. Now.

"That's it," she says, not letting go of my hand. "Inspector Andy Mills. Evander. The Westman case."

I nod. I shouldn't even have said my name. She was a good reporter, asked smart questions. That's what worries me—I'm not in the business of answering them for her anymore. Reporters were a little trouble when I was a cop, but now . . . if they got curious? She could write me a death sentence in the form of a headline.

"Yes, yes," I say politely. "I remember now. Good to see you again." I pull back my hand and nod, walking away.

"You working on a big case? Something federal?" She walks

alongside me, and when we get to the door, I'm obliged to hold it open for her.

"No, no, nothing like that," I say, walking a little faster down the long hall. She keeps pace.

"Those names you mentioned—Lamb, I think. And a bookstore? Which one?"

"I really can't talk about it," I say, trying to smile.

She laughs, and smiles back. "Sorry, sorry, I know. It's just my nature. I see a cop on a case and I want to know everything."

"It's nothing, really."

"Except you told the secretary you weren't a cop," she says, narrowing her eyes. "You said you were a PI."

We're at the stairs now, and I start down them, but she follows. "Yeah, I left the force a little while back. Just felt like I could do more good this way."

"Really? But weren't you one of the shining stars of the department? I remember I thought so. When I interviewed you, and you spoke about the victim with such insight and compassion, I thought to myself, 'Now, that young man is going places. He's the kind of man our police force needs.'"

I blush slightly. Her article had been flattering. "Yeah, I read what you wrote. It was very kind."

"It was the truth, Mr. Mills. I only report the truth. I love the truth." I stop on the landing and look at her. She's smiling so widely, so sincerely. I remember that smile. She made me more comfortable than any of the other reporters. I was almost chatty with her. But while her love of the truth is probably good for her, and makes her fun to talk with, it could be really bad for me, for my clients, for the Ruby. If she reported on where my office was, the cops wouldn't stop raiding, no matter how much Elsie paid them off.

"Still," I say, "it was a very kind truth."

She laughs, a tinkling bell sound. "Well then, why did you leave? Don't tell me the boys gave you trouble after my article came out? I couldn't forgive myself if that were it."

"No, no." I shake my head. "Everyone was happy with your story, Mrs. Rainmeyer."

"Miss," she says. "Divorced."

"Sorry."

"Oh, don't be," she says with a wave of her hand. "He didn't like me being a reporter, and I didn't like him being a bore. Wanted me cooking when he got home. Can you imagine? I can barely fry an egg."

I laugh. "Well, you're a fine reporter, so I'm sure it was for the best."

"Thank you, and it was."

I start walking again, and she finally doesn't follow me.

"But Mr. Mills," she says when I'm a few steps down. I stop and turn. "I'm a good enough reporter to spot that you never told me why you left." She raises an eyebrow. "And a good enough reporter to know that when someone doesn't want to tell me something, there's usually a story there."

I take a step back up toward her, and she opens her notebook, which she's been holding this whole time. A pen is clipped inside and she takes that out, ready to write. She's above me, because of the steps, and I feel like I'm kneeling before her, begging her to stop.

"There's really no story, Miss Rainmeyer. I didn't like the hours." I shrug. "I wanted to be my own boss. Really."

She sighs and closes the notebook with a roll of her eyes. "Well, I guess not everything is news?"

"Sorry to be a bore," I say.

"Oh, don't worry. You've got nothing on my husband."

She grins, and I tip my hat at her before turning around and walking down the rest of the stairs and heading outside. As I'm opening the door, I glance back up at her, and she's watching me, one hand on her hip, the other still holding her notebook. I hope I threw her off, because otherwise, she's a whole new type of trouble.

SIX

Outside the air is cool and I take a deep breath of it, like I've been underwater. That building is stuffy, and Rose's questions didn't help, the same way a tightening noose wouldn't. Worse, I didn't find anything out. But if I can't follow the government lead, I have another—criminals. I fish the betting slips I found out of my pocket. The mob likes to know where their money is. If Howard or DeeDee were regulars, they could have an idea of where they'd be. Though if the mob decides not to answer my questions, they might do more than just politely ask me to leave.

Fisherman's Wharf is up north, but first I grab a quick burger at a soda shop for lunch, and go over what Rainmeyer might be able to find out about me, and how. My number is unlisted, so she can't get my address that way. Same with my office. Only way she'd be able to find me is if she happened on one of my business cards. They were Elsie's idea—hand them out at gay bars, drum up business. There are two kinds: one that says *Amethyst Investigations, above the Ruby,* but no name, and then ones with my name, but just a number, no address, not even "PI." We were very careful about that, making me both easy and hard to find. Sure, Rose could ask around, maybe even find out the reason I left. But no editor is going to let her go to print without more than "gay cop fired, might be a PI now . . . somewhere . . ." are they? I've got to hope I threw her off the scent of a story. There's nothing else I can do at this point, aside from keep working the case. So I hop on a trolley to Beach Street.

Fisherman's Wharf is almost cute. It was probably more authentic fifty years ago, when it was where the commercial fishermen sold their catches from little stalls set up around the docks, or right off the boat. But that grew into Italian seafood restaurants, and stories of the fishermen and their picturesque little boats lined up along the docks brought in tourists, too. It's something between a neighborhood for locals and fishermen and a sight-seeing spot now. The restaurant signs are all painted with bright colors, with fish jumping, or fish in nets, or maybe a shrimp, all of them grinning, happy to be eaten. But down an alley you might still find something less colorful, like the very demurely marked Shore Club, which you would only notice by a shingle on the door with the name, and under that, another shingle: MEMBERS ONLY.

I've been here a few times before. The thing about cops and the mob is we don't just fire on each other every time we lock eyes, like a constant showdown. It's more like a game for them—seeing what they can evade, knowing their rights, how to skirt laws and then smile to our faces about it. Usually it was the guys with me who were the brutes, eager to beat something out of a suspect. But the Mafia boys would always just nod politely, even answer your questions—though often with lies, or at least half-truths. So, because I wasn't trying to beat information out of them, but instead talk to them, and trust my gut to spot their lies, some of these guys might call themselves my friends. They would say it with a knowing smirk, but they'd happily say it. It's good for them to have friends like me. Makes them look like they're not criminals.

I walk into the small room at the front of the club. It's painted a dark blue, with a tan rug, and there's a pair of large blue doors I can hear faint music coming from. In front of them is a very large man whose frown lifts slightly when he sees me.

"Andy," he says. "Haven't seen you in a while."

"Been working a different beat," I say. "I like you guys too much to try to put any of you in prison."

He smiles, though we both know it's a lie.

"Bridges here?" I ask.

"Every day," he says, opening the door for me, and nodding as I go through.

Inside is the real club. The Mafia runs a nicer joint than the Menlo Club that used to be around the corner, until we shut it down a few years back. I was part of that raid, helping out the feds. Shabby place, beige walls, lots of sad middle-aged men sitting around. Bones Remmer didn't have style. But he wasn't really Mafia, he just set up clubs with their permission. Bridges is real Mafia, and he has style.

There are no windows, but there are curtains, long velvet drapes, again in dark blue, usually framed by potted palms, so the whole place feels lush. The walls are still a deep blue, and the only light coming in is through skylights or the nice lamps set up around the place. At the far end of the room there's a small stage, with a quartet and a blond tenor in a tux singing "Pretend." He sounds good, too. Good enough some patrons are watching him and not focusing on what lies between me and the stage— gambling. Card games at polished wood tables, dealt out by men in plain suits. A roulette wheel—that wasn't here last time, an upgrade. And a craps table. On one side of the room, toward the back, near the stage, is a bar, painted blue and black. And all around us are gamblers—men and women of different ages, some looking like this is just an illegal amusement for them, some desperate for a winning streak. The air smells like smoke and nervous sweat. And presiding over it all from his stool at the end of the bar is Michael Parisi—Bridges.

When he sees me, he lights up and waves, like we're old friends. He's in his fifties, with salt-and-pepper hair, and a tall frame that looks narrow until you see how big his hands are. He's called Bridges because that's what he likes to dangle people off of when conversation fails. I put on my best smile and walk over to him.

It's funny, how I feel less afraid here than I did talking to Rose. Maybe it's because here I know what I'm dealing with. If they knew about me, the only interest they'd have in my sex life is blackmail, and there's not much they can squeeze out of me these days. I can't help them with the cops, I'm not making much money. I'm a poor mark to them. Though, they don't know that yet. They probably still think I'm SFPD.

"Inspector Mills," Bridges says, confirming it. "I haven't seen you in such a long time. What a pleasure. Here, sit." He snaps his fingers and the man behind the bar comes over. "I believe the inspector's drink is whisky soda, am I right?"

"I'm not particular," I say.

Bridges laughs and claps me on the back so hard I flinch. He's got a deep voice, and a laugh like a drumroll. When he leans back, I spot the gun holster under his jacket.

"And I'm not an inspector anymore."

"Oh? Has your absence been because of a promotion? We should drink to that."

"I quit the force," I say.

His eyebrows shoot up in what I would normally say was surprise, but I know Bridges. He keeps his feelings under lock and key, then displays what he decides, like a magician holding the real card behind his back. It's not that he's unreadable, it's just that he chooses exactly what you're reading—and it's usually fiction. Once you know that, though, it becomes a whole new game. "Well, that's even better to drink to."

"You knew," I say, keeping my voice friendly.

His gray eyes are unreadable; his small smile never slips. "If I did, let's drink to your telling me."

The bartender puts two drinks in front of us. The glasses are dripping. Gene would never allow that.

"Do you know why I left?" I ask, taking my eyes off the glasses and looking back at him.

He shakes his head. "I noticed your absence, and I asked around, and heard you were no longer a member of San Francisco's finest. Why? No one would tell me. I hope you haven't gone to work for the feds."

"No." I shake my head. "Just myself. I'm a PI now."

His expression remains neutral for a moment, before he decides what to do with it—mildly impressed, the jutting lower lip, the slow nod as he takes a sip of his drink. "I like it."

"You like it because I can't arrest you."

He shrugs, not denying it. "I like it for you, too. You seem . . ." He waves his hand, gesturing up and down me. "Happier."

The side of my mouth tips up at that. "It's good to be in control, let's say."

He turns to watch the crooner on stage and I take a sip of my drink, then do likewise. The singer is a slip of a thing, hair so blond it's nearly white, pale as fine china, and looks as breakable, too. But his voice is strong, aching as he sings.

"My sister's kid," he says.

"Who?" I ask. "The guy with the mic?"

He nods.

"He's good. Really good."

He smiles. "She married some Frenchman. They named him Merle, if you can believe it. He inherited too much of his dad, he's not really fit for the family business, but he sure can sing, so I put him up here. Hoping some record label might come in here one night and hear the talent. He actually tried to go out on his own, auditioned for an agent, but . . ." He shakes his head, sighs. "Kid fainted during the audition. Too nervous. Had to find him an agent through my connections, but . . . I don't know if he has the chops to make it. So I take care of him. He might be a little soft, but I love the kid, would do anything for him." He's quiet and we both watch Merle sing. "My Maria, she never could have any, y'know?"

"I didn't," I say, surprised by the admission. "I'm sorry."

"Now that you're not a cop, we can talk like real friends," he says. "I always liked you. Smart. I like smarts, even when they're across from me, but then you've got to be careful. But you never pushed more than you needed to, or tried to go after anyone big when we let you have some small fish who had fucked up. Smart."

"I only went after who the evidence pointed me at," I say, which is a half-truth. I only went after the ones the evidence would stick to, and the way he says it, like I was an obedient little kid, feels like a smack across the face I need to smile through. My last big case before I got caught, the one Rose interviewed me about, that was the mob. Some low-level kid had gotten his girlfriend hopped up when she said no to taking dirty pictures, and then took them anyway. Technically, it was all for the Mafia, but they didn't sign off on anything that stupid. So they were happy to be done with the kid, and I was happy to send him across the bay. I couldn't go after Abati with that, or add to Lima's charges, couldn't pin anything on the big bosses. I was ambitious, but not a fool.

Sure, I could have always come in here, declared I was shocked to find illegal gambling, and then taken them all in, but they paid the chief well enough that he would have kicked them loose and fired me. I remember once listening as a pair of uniforms came back from checking out this place after someone had claimed there was gambling here. The chief had asked them if the reports were true, and without even blinking, the senior of the two of them said, "We went down there and asked the owner if there was any gambling going on, and he said no." That's how you police Fisherman's Wharf.

"And what evidence are you looking for now?" Bridges asks. "Or are you just here for a little gambling?"

I shake my head. "I was never lucky enough for that. But I am here on a case. I'm just wondering if you knew a guy named Howard Salzberger, or a woman named DeeDee Lamb? I found some betting slips at their shop, your seal right on top."

He nods, slowly, still watching his nephew sing, then turns to me. "I know Howard. He in trouble?"

"That's what I'm trying to find out. I can't arrest you either way, so I'd appreciate you being straight with me—did a collection go wrong?"

He grins, widely, not a planned expression but genuine amusement. "Howard? No. We all like Howard. How long has he been missing?"

"About a week," I say.

He shakes his head. "That's a shame. He's a very nice gentleman. I didn't know him very well myself, but he was friends with Joe. And then Merle here, Howard was a big fan of his. Always clapped the loudest after every song. Do you know what happened to him?"

"Not yet. There's a lot going on. Could I talk to Joe?" It's not a name I recognize.

"No, no, Joe left."

"Left?"

The tenor, Merle, comes to the end of "Pretend," and Bridges starts clapping loudly, his heavy hands coming together like stones. I join in, and watch Merle as he takes a small bow before walking offstage and coming toward us. Up close, I can see his eyes are red, and he's sweating. The bartender gives him a glass of ice water and he presses it against his neck.

"The lights are so hot up there," he says to Bridges. His speaking voice is a little higher than his singing voice, but softer, too. Almost flimsy.

"You want me to tell the guys to dim them?"

"No, no . . ." Merle shakes his head. "Spotlights should be bright." He almost sounds sad saying it, and takes a long drink of his water. When he looks up, he stares right at me, then quickly looks away. His eyes are gray like his uncle's, but too large for his slim face, like a pixie's.

"This is former inspector Evander Mills," Bridges says. "We're just catching up on old times."

"Former?" Merle says nervously.

"Just a PI now," I say. "You sing real well, kid."

"Thanks." He smiles, and looks down demurely, his long eyelashes reaching down his face.

I turn back to Bridges. "So, Howard."

"Mmm." Bridges nods, then looks at the empty stage. On his other side, I see Merle stiffen slightly, his eyes flashing to me, then to the bar again.

"When did you last see him?"

"Oh, I don't know," Bridges says. He sips his drink. Merle is still frozen, like a cat caught in a car's headlights. "Merle, you know Howard? When did you last see him?"

Merle thinks for a moment, before saying "Who?" unconvincingly.

"You know, your biggest fan—the old guy who always sits up front and claps."

"I don't . . ." He looks at me, still thinking. He's like the opposite of his uncle; every thought in his head shines in his eyes like a movie screen. Right now they're playing panic, and deciding how much to lie. "Oh, him," he says finally. "I don't know. I haven't seen him in here in . . . eight days."

I nod. "That lines up."

"With what?" Merle asks.

"He's missing, and some folks have asked me to find him."

"Oh," Merle says, drinking his water too fast, all the ice clanging in the glass like someone dropping all their change on the bar.

Bridges nods. "So there you go. Eight days."

"Eight days," I say with a nod. Not a week, more specific than that—eight days. Like Merle has been counting. "And you said he was friends with Joe?" I ask, wondering if I can get more out of him about that.

"Yep. They were always chatting, drinking, laughing. Good friends, I'd say."

"And where is Joe?"

"Like I said, he left."

"For where?" I ask.

Bridges shrugs. I take a long sip of my drink. I'm not going to get anything else out of him.

"I'm going to go outside," Merle says, standing suddenly. "Cool off."

"Don't forget, that radio host is coming in today. Take it easy on yourself until he shows up."

"I will," Merle says, walking away. He doesn't look at me.

"I'm doing the best I can for him, you know?" Bridges says when Merle is out of earshot. "I just don't know if he has the stamina to be a star."

"He's got the talent," I say.

"Yeah." Bridges smiles, proud.

"So you won't tell me about Joe," I say, and pause, but Bridges says nothing. "So can you tell me about Howard? How much was he into you for?"

"Oh, hardly anything. He wasn't unlucky, he wasn't lucky, so he usually ended up paying us a little every week, but he was never more than a week or two late, and it was never so much money we were offended by his withholding of it."

"Could he have gotten a loan from someone else?" I ask.

"It wasn't more than a dollar or two a week," Bridges says, shaking his head. "Maybe five, if he went for a round of craps. He really just liked socializing, I think. Listening to music, betting on some games, talking with friends . . ."

I need to find out who Joe is.

"All right," I say, standing. "Well, if you see him, let him know his friends are worried about him, would you?"

"Of course, of course."

I take out my wallet to pay for my drink but he pats my hand.

"Andy, no, on the house. You're welcome here any time."

"Well, thanks," I say with a nod.

"And, perhaps . . . since you are a private investigator now . . . you might be willing to do some work for me? I'm sure I can pay your hourly rate."

I swallow, suddenly feeling warm. You don't say no when the mob asks you to work for them, but I also really don't want to work for the mob . . . or have them coming around my office. The amount of blackmail they could get on my clients would be like a gold mine.

"I'm still building myself up," I say carefully. "It's just me, working from home. Even this case is really just a favor. But when I'm up and running, and can handle bigger cases, like I'm sure you'd have, I'll be sure to stop by."

He smiles, and I can't tell if he's angry, which scares me. He claps me on the back. "Sure, sure, get set up first. Then come by again. The offer is standing. Like I said, you're smart. I like smart."

"Thanks," I say.

"See you later," he says with a slight nod. I turn and weave my way back out through the card and dice tables, back to the alley-way outside, where the air smells like fish, but at least it's cool.

"There you are," says a soft voice. I look up. Merle is standing at the corner, peeking into the alley. He puts out his hand and gestures at me, a soft curl of his fingers toward himself, and I walk over. "I've been waiting for you."

SEVEN

"Waiting for me?" I ask. Merle turns around the corner, out of sight of the club. We're in an even narrower alley now, and the fish smell is stronger, rotting. There's a trash can just behind him, and shadows fall over his face. He's undone his bow tie, which on someone else might look like a man who's had a long night out drinking, but on him gives the air of a girl trying on her mother's necklace.

"I want to know about Howard," he says, his voice shaking a little. "He was . . . a good fan."

"Really?" I ask, taking out a cigarette and lighting it. "You didn't seem to remember who he was a few minutes ago."

"I know, but I was . . . thinking about it out here. I remembered him once my uncle described him. I worry. I care about . . ." He swallows. "My fans."

I turn away and walk more into the light and he follows, letting me get a good look at his face—pale, eyes red; from crying, I think.

"You know what kind of a man Howard was?" I try.

He quivers like a plucked bass string that doesn't make a noise. "Older?" he says finally.

I smile. "His friends are my friends," I say carefully, looking into his eyes. "That's why I'm looking for him. They're worried. Like you."

"Like me," Merle repeats, sounding confused. He looks down at the ground.

"You want a cigarette?" I ask.

He shakes his head. "They make my throat sore, harder to sing."

I nod slowly. "Howard liked to listen to you sing."

"Yes." His eyes go off someplace, and he smiles. "I sang to him and he read—" He stops suddenly, realizing something, his eyes back on me, hard, then soft again, confused. "When you said, like me . . ."

It hangs between us with the cigarette smoke, and I realize he has a lot more to lose than I do, so finally I nod. "Like me, too," I say.

"Oh," he says, and I can see the goose pimples break out on his neck. "Oh." He shakes a little, then takes a few steps back, falling against the brick wall in the shadow, slumping slightly. His hands come up to his neck and he holds them there, like he's keeping his head from falling. "Oh," he says a third time, and I have to work not to laugh. "I . . . a detective? Really?"

"Really," I say with a nod.

"And you know Howard?"

I shake my head. "No, I'm sorry. But I knew his friends. You're his friend, right?"

He nods, his eyes locked on me.

"Are you more than a friend?"

After a moment, he nods again. Then, his feet light, he takes a few quick steps so he's closer to me again, and reaches out, takes my free hand. "He's a wonderful man. He reads to me. I . . . can't really read well. The letters, they get all turned around and dance when I look at them. But I love stories, and Howard brings books. I sing to him from stage, and then afterward, when my set is over, he leaves, and then I go meet him at his place, and he picks out a book and we lie in bed and read."

"Just read?" I ask.

He blushes, bright rose pink, and doesn't say anything.

"Sorry, none of my business. But you care for him, that's clear."

He leans in close, his lips hovering next to my ear. He smells like salt water and daisies. "I love him," he breathes. Then he takes a step back and looks around, like a deer hearing a hunter.

This poor kid. Queer, but part of the Mafia. In an outsider like me they'd find it distasteful, maybe amusing, but being in the mob is all about masculinity. Merle already fails enough on that front that he's just singing in their club, and not part of the real business. But if they found out he was queer . . . That might be a stain on the family. And stains get rubbed out.

I look at his eyes, the way they widen and glance both ways, over and over. I remember doing that myself, when I was a cop. The feeling of always being watched, always being so close to being caught. I'm surprised he told me, but with Howard gone, and no one to tell, maybe he was even more scared, more desperate for help. He looks it. He seems off, somehow, a teetering vase. When I was a cop, I just cut myself in two: gay, cop. Two half-lives that couldn't make a whole. But Merle seems like a whole—a whole that's about to shatter. I get why. His life is terrifying. Howard was his only safe haven, and now he's gone, and he's probably wondering if his uncle did that—if his uncle will do it to him next. But if Bridges really loves his nephew, then it's easier to take out his lover and hope the kid never finds another one. Even if that means Merle will probably shatter into a thousand pieces on the floor.

"How did you meet?" I ask him.

"Oh." He smiles, dreamy again. "He came into the casino a lot. Listened to me sing. One day, afterward, he told me I was good, and asked if he could buy me a drink. I said just water, and he laughed, thought that was funny. He said he ran a bookshop and I liked that—I told him, I like stories. My mother used to read to me from a big book of fairy tales. I liked those. But . . . I told him I wished I read more. He said he could bring me books, if I wanted—instead of the drink he wanted to buy me. And I don't know why, but I told him." He lifts a hand slightly, like he's reaching out to someone. "I told him reading was hard, that I'd failed out of school, and I was only really ever good in the church choir, so . . . I became a singer. But I couldn't do anything else. I'm . . . useless aside from music."

"Music is important," I tell him.

He smiles, but it's sad. "Anyway, he told me that he knew other people like me, and if I wanted, he could read to me. I was embarrassed, but excited, too. He gave me his address, and that night, I went to his place and he read to me. It wasn't . . . untoward or anything like that. He's a gentleman."

"Do your parents know about this—your uncle? Just about the reading, I mean."

"Oh, no." Merle shakes his head quickly. "No, no. I tell them I like to go walking, to clear my head, and rehearse where no one's around, learn songs. Really it doesn't take me long to learn music. I just listen to the radio. But they let me wander off. I'm twenty-four now. I should have my own apartment, but Mother likes me staying with her."

I nod, thinking about what Bridges said, about how he tried to go off on his own, and fainted at the audition. I wonder if that was because he knew it was his only way out—too much pressure. Or if they asked him to read some new song.

"So how long has this been going on—the reading?"

"Oh . . . the reading started nearly eight months ago. First it was once a week, then twice, then every night. And after a month of it, I thought I had a sense of him, and . . ." He looks around again.

"I understand," I say, then take a drag on my cigarette. "Had you known? Before?"

He shakes his head. "I just knew what I didn't like. But there was one book Howard read me, an old story from the Knights of the Round Table. Galahaut."

I frown, confused. "You mean Galahad, like in the movie serials?"

His eyebrows turn to a deep V and I can see him clench his jaw. "No. Galahad was Lancelot's son. This is Galahaut. He was a half giant, and he fought Arthur and Lancelot, but he's so impressed by Lancelot in battle that he stops fighting them, he saves Lancelot, and they all talk and become friends. He and Arthur were like brothers but he and Lancelot . . . Howard told me that they were . . ." He whispers, "Lovers." He turns his head to make sure no one is listening. "I never knew about that. That that could be. And suddenly . . . I knew. I knew what I wanted. I wanted Howard. My Galahaut."

I nod. "That's very nice," I say, not sure how else to respond to the look in his eyes, so desperate, so detached from the world. "So when did you last see him?"

"Eight days ago, like I said. I've been counting. He was coming in almost every day before that, but that day, he said he'd be busy one night, so he'd be back the day after tomorrow. Six days ago. I know something must be wrong, oh, I just know it."

He leans back against the wall again and starts to cry, putting his hands to his face like a mourner.

"Relax," I say, walking toward him and putting my hand on his shoulder. "We don't know what's going on yet. It could be the feds arrested him, for dirty books."

"Dirty books?" he asks through his hands. "That's illegal?"
"Yeah."

He lowers his hands and stares at me with those big gray eyes. He's pretty; I can see what Howard saw in him.

"He was going to save me," he sighs. "Like a knight."

"Save you?"

"He said he was going to make money soon. A lot of it. Enough that he and I could just . . . go away somewhere. A beach maybe, down in Mexico, or some island . . . I'd sing at the bar there, he'd run a little bookstore. Start over. Far away from . . ." He looks at the end of the alley. "I don't belong here." He looks back at me. "He promised."

"Did he tell you where the money was coming from?"

Merle shakes his head, his white-blond hair swaying like feathers in the breeze. "He wouldn't break his promise . . ." He looks down again, his hands falling to his sides. He looks weak, like he could faint any moment.

"Look, I'll find him, okay? That's what I'm doing."

He doesn't look up. I'm not sure he's even heard me until he takes a deep breath. "Good. Please find him. I need him. I need him to keep his promise. This life . . ." He shivers. He's terrified, but the kind of terrified where it's every day, so it bakes into your bones. I remember it. I wonder if being gay and part of the Mafia—even on the edges—is worse or better than being a gay cop. Both gangs of men, filled with machismo, happy to turn on you when they find out your secret. I squeeze Merle's shoulder again.

"I know it's rough," I say. "If there's anything I can do . . ." I hope he doesn't ask me to hide him away. Because I would, if he asked. His fear is too familiar. But I'd probably end up dead for it.

"Just find Howard," he says.

Around the corner, a door creaks open and then closes.

"I need to go," Merle says, his face pale. He pats the skin under his eyes and then combs his hands through his hair. Then he looks at me again, his eyes confused, like he still doesn't understand who I am. And then he walks away. I watch him, wait for a few minutes before I grind out my cigarette with my heel and walk back out. The street the club is on is empty. I walk past it, back to the streets along the water, with their happy fish signs, and families pointing at boats, reading menus to decide where to have an early dinner.

I didn't learn anything about DeeDee, but Howard is a clearer picture now—an affair with a mobster's nephew. Friends with another now-missing mobster. Coming into some money soon, and planning to run away. He was playing with a lot of fires; it's a wonder the bookshop isn't rubble and ash.

But none of this tells me where he or DeeDee are. Or where the list is. Which means I haven't helped Pat or the family at all. And I'm not sure what else to do.

By the time I make it back to the Ruby, the sun is just starting to set, giving everything that golden glow. Inside, people have started to turn up for drinks after work, letting their hair down, dropping the masks they use around their straight coworkers, families, friends. A few nod at me, and say hello. I say hello back. One of the female impersonators, Stan, is onstage, singing "Why Don't You Believe Me." He's not as good as Lee.

Gene is behind the bar unloading a crate of alcohol onto the shelves, Elsie sitting by the bar, watching the crowd. She spots me and tilts her head, slightly worried behind the smile she has pasted on for the crowds.

"So?" she asks as I get closer.

Gene stops unloading the drinks to stand close to us, reaching his hand across the bar. I squeeze it briefly.

"I don't know," I say finally.

Elsie frowns. "What does that mean? Did you get the list?"

I shake my head. "I can't find either of them. The DA was a bust, won't give me any information without a real PI license. The other lead was gambling at a Mafia bar, and I found out . . . a lot about Howard. But nothing about where he went."

"You think the Mafia killed him?" Elsie asks. "Because if they have the list, that's not much better. Back in New York, they're running half the gay bars in the city, and they do it so they can snap photos and blackmail anyone rich and stupid enough to get caught on film. They love to blackmail us, Andy."

"I know," I tell her quickly. "But . . . I didn't get the sense they knew about Howard. So I don't think they have the list . . ." I think back to Bridges, and his careful, polite expressions. He could know. He could have killed Howard for screwing his nephew and found the list on him. But would he know what it was? Did he know about the book service? I shake my head. "I don't think the Mafia has the list. Or if they do, they don't know what it is."

"So what's the plan, Andy?" Her voice has an edge in it, and Gene squeezes my hand. We both know she's worried about her family. So am I.

"I want to talk to Pat again," I say. "Find out more about the book service. Then . . . I think I'll have to hire a real PI to find out if the DA has them locked up. That's the best play."

"You're a real PI," Gene says.

"A licensed one, then," I say with a small smile. "I'm really sorry, Elsie."

"Well, Pat is upstairs. You can talk to him right now," she says, crossing her arms. "I helped him pack up last night."

"How did telling the family go?"

"Not great. Cliff was the most upset, which surprised me— started crying, said we should take Rina, all change our names, run away. Henry talked him down. Pearl was the most supportive. But . . . he's out now. Took a bunch of gay books with him, not just his, either. My apartment is filled with boxes of them now. The family portrait, too. We'd just put it up yesterday, but now Irene is back. Can't keep that woman down." She frowns a little and sighs. "Whole place is changed."

"I'm sorry. But that's good, right? It means they're ready for when Mrs. Purley comes by. A little act, like they normally do when straight people visit. If the worst does happen, and they're investigated, they're prepared now."

"I have a whole box of Cliff's muscle mags," Elsie says. She tries to make it sound funny, but she looks too worried.

"They can handle it," I say. I almost believe it.

"Can they?" Elsie says. "Mrs. Purley doesn't sound understanding. They could lose their kid because of what . . . books?" She shakes her head. "It feels like a joke. They've managed so long and now . . . books." She runs her hands through her hair, tugging it slightly. I've never seen her do that before. "And even if it does work, and they manage to hide everything, how long does that investigation go on? How long do I have to stay away? Does Pat?"

She looks up at me, her face suddenly older, gaunt. Elsie is good at hiding her nerves—she runs a gay bar, she's notorious, she has to be. But right now, she looks genuinely terrified. Then someone laughs in the crowd behind her and she flinches, quickly puts a smile back on.

"Rina won't forget you," I say, moving my hand from Gene to take one of hers. "No one could ever forget you. You make sure of that."

She laughs, one brief bark, and some color comes back to her face. She looks down at our hands, and squeezes mine before pulling away. "All because of books," she says, still trying to wrap her head around it.

"It's the stuff you take for granted you stop being careful about," I say. "I'm going to go talk to Pat, okay?"

"Okay," she says. I give her hand a squeeze.

"You need anything?" Gene asks me. "Before you talk to him?"

I reach across the bar and he takes my hand again. "After," I say. "Make me something sweet?"

"I'll have it waiting for you when you get back," he says.

I walk slowly up the stairs to Elsie's apartment. I wonder how long it really does take kids to forget people. My dad died before the war, and sometimes I feel like my memory of him is fading off somehow, like there are blank spots I'm filling in. But Rina is so young. Would it be blank spots she can't fill in, or would she just not remember Elsie—any of them?

Elsie's apartment isn't like the Ruby. The Ruby is lush and warm with wooden tables and red leather and the red diamond-pattern wallpaper. It glows. But her apartment is sparse. White walls, dark wood floors. A few elegant pieces of furniture. A photo of Margo on the wall. Tidy. At least, it usually is. Now it's filled with boxes. Wooden egg crates, a few cardboard boxes, and some suitcases, piled high, like shaking towers in the middle of the apartment. Pat is building them and rebuilding, moving them into corners of the room as I come in.

And leaning against the other wall, too large for the space, is the family portrait, the one they said would hang where Irene's portrait is now. The one I said they should put there. Pat painted it, and like Margo said, he'd added Rina. It looks finished now—the whole family, all of them in lavender, paired off: Elsie and Margo, Pearl and Irene, Henry and Cliff. Except now Rina is there, too. Henry and Cliff were alone on a loveseat, Cliff leaning into Henry, but now Cliff is holding a baby aloft as he leans, both of them grinning up at her. Irene and Pearl stand behind them, waving at Rina, and on the floor, where once there was Elsie in a suit and Margo in a dress, Margo is kneeling in wide-legged pants and a men's button-down, Elsie sitting next to her, still in a suit, their hands overlapping but also waving at Rina, who seems to be reaching back down to them. Rina is at the center of everything now.

The portrait looks sad here. It's in a corner, the only place it'll fit, and light barely touches it.

Pat doesn't seem to have noticed I've come in. He's lifting boxes, putting them down.

"Hey Pat," I say.

He looks over. Only the lamp in the corner is on and he's cast in shadow and buttery light. He pushes a heavy-looking suitcase against the wall.

"Those are Pearl's Sappho books," he says. "Heavy."

"You need a hand?" I ask.

He shakes his head, then walks toward me. "It's bad news, isn't it?" he asks, looking at me. I look down and hear him sigh.

"I didn't make any headway with the DA," I tell him. "I think I'll need to hire some outside help for that."

"Oh," he says. "All right. So . . . tomorrow?"

"Maybe," I say. "But also . . . now the mob might be involved."

"What?" Pat's voice tremors. "The mob?"

"Howard gambled at a Mafia casino . . . with more than money. He was friends with a guy there, who's missing now. And he was . . . having an affair with the nephew of the guy who ran the club."

"With a member of the mob?" Pat almost screams.

"No, just his nephew. He's not a made man, just sings at the club. But if his uncle found out . . ."

"So he could be dead," Pat says. "And you think then the mob would have the list?"

"They could. But I'm not sure they'd know what it was. But if they did . . . that's blackmail."

"Well, at least the mob probably won't tell Mrs. Purley, right?"

"Not if the Lamontaines pay them. They want to make money off the information, they don't care about adoption."

"I see . . ." Pat says. He looks back at the piles of boxes and walks over to one. I follow him. "They were hard to get up there. I just threw them down when I did. Books are so heavy . . . but I lift them at the shop all the time, so . . ." He picks up a box. "Cliff's muscle mags. Light. I should stack this on top." He puts it against the wall, far from the other box. "I want them to take up as little room as possible, you know, so it's not inconvenient for Elsie. So I'll stack them up in this corner here. Like a Christmas tree . . ." Tears start to run down his face. "I really messed up, Andy."

I close my arms around him, hugging him tightly, like he did for me when I first showed up at Lavender House. "It's okay."

"You should have seen them yesterday," he says, wiping his eyes with the back of his hand. "They were so angry. Cliff, he . . ."

"They're scared, not angry. It just looks the same sometimes. They knew you were gay, they knew you worked at this bookshop, they just didn't think it was going to be trouble. You're part of their family."

He sniffs and laughs at that, pulling away from me. "Am I? I'm the help, Andy."

"Pat . . ."

He shakes his head, and goes to pick up another box. "It's not the same. You know it. You worked for them, too. They're kind, good employers. We're almost family, but . . . I think with Rina, I forgot a little. I'm not. I'm the butler. Stupid thing to forget. To think it was my home, you know?" He lifts the box and carries it over to the wall, placing it next to the first box. "Margo's pulps."

"It is your home. You're their friend. And they care about you."

"Sure," he says with a shrug. "But that's not quite the same. If your family puts you in danger, you worry, you try to save everyone. If your friend puts you in danger . . ." He lifts another box and puts it on top of the last one. "More pulps."

"I think we're all kind of family," I say.

"That's a nice thought," he says, looking at the boxes. "I brought the feds and the mob to their door and took their books and maybe their baby . . . what kind of family is that? I should have . . . I got lazy. No, not lazy. Well, yes." He shakes his head. "I got comfortable. That was the mistake. You know, before Irene hired me, I don't think I stayed in any job more than two years. In any apartment, either. I was a bartender, a janitor, a waiter. I used to sing backup for radio jingles, too, did you know that?"

I laugh. "No."

"Well, none of that work was ever very regular, and then my landlord figured out that all the men I was having over weren't just drinking buddies, so he kicked me out. I wasn't feeling so bad, wasn't the first time I'd been in that situation, but then Henry came up to me at one of the bars, said he'd heard I needed a place to stay. I thought he was coming on to me, honestly. Henry was good at hiding his outside life. Like you, except he really changed the way he looked in the bars: dark glasses, hair in his face, like a costume. I think he liked it, honestly."

"Probably."

"So, I thought this was just some guy coming on to me, asked me to go for a drive with him, but . . . when we pulled up to the house, I thought . . . I thought wow. Some young rich thing wants me? And then I thought no . . . that can't be it. Maybe he's going to kill me. Not that there was much escape possible at that point. And then Irene walked out, all severe and appraising, and I had no idea what was going on." He lifts another box of books, and moves it to the wall. "I thought maybe they were religious nuts trying to save me or someone was paying to send me to a sanitarium, but . . . no. It was a job interview. Had to tidy up a study, make a martini, set a table. I knew how to do all that . . . and then she explained everything. The job, the family—just her, Pearl, and Henry, then. I'd have a place to stay and a generous salary. I could go into town on my nights off, live my life—as long as I never brought it back, or told anyone who I worked for. I thought . . . yes. Just until I get some money saved up to rent a new place. Then, after a few years, it was money saved up to buy a place. Still don't have that . . ." He laughs. "Spent it all on books." He puts another box into a stack against the wall, and stretches, leaning back. "I got comfortable. I . . . liked it a lot."

"It's not over, Pat," I say, lifting up a box myself. It's heavy but the flap is open so I can see inside. Leather-bound books in Latin or Greek. I put them in the Sappho pile. "This isn't your fault. It's the world's fault. You told me that, remember? That it's the way the world treats us—"

"*The Homosexual in America*, I remember. Still. It's the way the world is treating me, not them. I should have been more careful."

"I'll figure this out, Pat."

"Do you think . . . with the Mafia . . . Do you think they're dead? Both of them?" He says the words slowly, carefully. "Should I be . . . do I need to go farther away?"

"I don't know," I say. "I think you're probably okay. You weren't on the payroll in their ledger. And I still haven't stopped by their homes, so there's a lot to investigate. It's just that nothing I found out today was very good. Howard was taking some big risks. DeeDee, if she was in the wrong place at the wrong time, could have gotten caught up in that. I haven't found anything else out about her, though. No sign of a lover or any life outside the bookstore."

"DeeDee didn't have much of a life outside the bookstore," Pat says, sitting down on the sofa. "Not since her girlfriend Suzie died.

74 LEV AC ROSEN

They were together forever. DeeDee actually took some time off after that. Let Howard handle everything for a few months. Only came back about six weeks ago. But without Suzie, I don't think she has anything besides the bookstore. Oh, and her sister in Vegas. She'd visit her sometimes. Always talked about her, younger, divorced, works as a cocktail waitress but maybe drinks too much instead of serving. Sounded like DeeDee went there to check up on her a lot."

"Good to know. I can try to dig up her number, call her."

"Thanks," Pat says. "I need to . . . finish this." He looks at the piles of books. "What happens if I don't go back? If it's never safe?"

"You'll find another job. Elsie will hire you."

"No . . ." He raises his hand, points at the boxes. "The books, I mean. What if they never go back? Can the family just . . . never read again?"

"I . . . don't know, Pat."

"I moved around a lot as a kid, you know. Dad was a railway worker, managed train stations. We started in Philadelphia, but as they added more and more stations going west, we moved. Got here just around when I graduated high school. So I never had a chance to make many good friends. Soon as I did, we'd be off . . . I got good at making friends fast, though, being friendly . . ." He smiles. "Always have a joke. That's what I learned. But even then . . . we'd leave. Books came with me. Books were friends. Even if I had to return one to the library, I could check it out again at the next one. And oh, when I found books about queer people!" He looks up, smiling. "*The Sins of the Cities of the Plain.* Filthy novel—and older than I am. A friend slipped it to me one night, maybe he was hitting on me. I loved it." He licks his lips, almost laughing. "Books . . ." His eyes fall to the rest of the boxes and he frowns.

He stands up again, and checks another box of books. "Henry's—he didn't have many really gay ones, but just in case, he packed up all his movie star magazines and biographies of the women of the screen. Said Mrs. Purley might find them suspicious. Thanked me for taking them." Pat shakes his head. "All these magazines and books . . . what if they can never read again? What if they're just too afraid? All because of me."

"They'll read again, Pat."

"Maybe."

He starts moving the boxes again in silence. I don't know what to say. After a while, I realize there's nothing to say, and I leave, shutting the door quietly behind me, as Pat moves more books.

Downstairs, as promised, Gene has a drink waiting for me.

"He look okay?" Elsie asks. Her glass is empty.

"No," I say. "He feels awful. He's moving books around, crying. I think he's lost. I think he feels like he doesn't have a family, or like he took all these books . . . He's blaming himself. Thinks he's ruined everything."

Gene shakes his head. "I can't imagine."

"I'll go talk to him," Elsie says, standing. "It was rough, yesterday. I . . . should have stood up for him more. I was angry . . . but we all take risks. We have to, otherwise what's the point of . . . anything? Margo's risk is me. Mine is Margo, and the club. Pat's is the clubs and . . . well, books. But we all take risks. He shouldn't feel bad that his are the ones causing trouble this time. Could have been any of us. Might still be one day." She puts her hand on my shoulder. "Solve this fast, Andy. My family is unspooling."

I nod and turn to Gene, who smiles at me sadly. I sip the drink. Citrus and rum, I think. Something new. It's always a new drink with Gene. He likes to try new drinks on me. "Thanks," I tell him.

"Did Elsie say something about unspooling?" Lee asks, sitting down next to me. He's dressed like he's come from the record store, in a polo and a jacket.

"I didn't find anything good out today," I say, looking around. The bar is filling up, people are laughing. The band is playing on stage without a singer. Too many people for me to tell him everything. "And Pat has moved into Elsie's place for a while, just in case. He's . . . not doing so well."

"Well, I found something out," Lee says, "but I don't know if it's any good."

"You did? You've been here five minutes."

"I had some downtime at work, so I made a few calls." His fingers dance on the bar as he explains, first two fingers walking forward. "My friend John, lives over in Oakland, so comes into town now and then." The fingers walk back. "I took him to Walt's and he loved the place, Howard found him a bunch of books and signed him up for the book service." All four fingers gather together and then he lays his palm flat. Gene brings him a rum and Coke without asking. "Thanks."

Gene nods before another patron calls out to him and he leaves.

"Did you tell him the list was missing?" I ask Lee.

Lee shakes his head and his hand leaves the bar, scooping up the drink and bringing it to his lips. "Not yet. You're going to find it. But what he said was that he writes Howard, right? And Howard said in his last letter he was working on something big that was going to be mailed soon. Something he'd found, and he was going to publish. A memoir."

I nod. "Yeah, they'd paid for printing, I saw that in their books. Invested a lot. And the boyfriend told me Howard was sure he'd be rich soon."

"Boyfriend?" Lee asks.

I turn away, and look out at the crowd. The music is getting livelier and the place is starting to feel warm, crowded, smelling of cologne and perfume and bodies. I look back at Lee, keeping my voice low. "I can't talk about it down here. Later, in my office, I promise."

"All right." Lee raises an eyebrow. "Have time to talk about Virginia? I've lined up three eligible bachelors."

I look around again to make sure Virginia isn't nearby. There's a burst of laughter from across the bar that ripples through the whole club. It's relaxed now, people have thrown off the stresses of outside. But no sign of Virginia. "Sure." I nod, sipping my drink. The citrus in it is orange, I think. Maybe lemon, too. "Give them to me quick."

"All right." He leans back. "First is Tony. Accountant. Smart, good with the numbers like Virginia. Kind of shy."

I shake my head. "Shy won't work. She needs someone who will challenge her in front of her colleagues."

Lee cocks his head and takes a sip of his drink. "All right, then there's Ralph or Bill. Ralph is smart, funny, but in that kind of biting way. Lawyer. His mom has been pressuring him to get married. He's a little older—almost forty."

"And Bill?"

"Scientist, like Virginia, teaches chemistry at Stanford, down in Palo Alto. Quiet guy, but when he talks the teacher thing really shows—loves to help people understand."

"Ralph," I say.

Lee looks at me, skeptical, maybe because of how fast I decided. "You sure?"

I smile and sip my drink. I am. "Best bet. Older will make her seem youthful and feminine, and I don't know if she's going to take a teacher seriously—if she doesn't, she'll look disdainful, less feminine. I could tell her to act like she thinks he's brilliant, but I suspect she won't like it."

Lee laughs. "That's probably true. Okay, you want me to set it up?"

"If you don't mind," I say. "I know you're not my secretary."

He squeezes my arm. "Yeah, it's okay. Girl Friday, right? Plus, you have a big case. I'll make it for next week. Will you be able to come up with a story for them by then?"

I nod. "Sure. It's easy, have them meet fighting over something—chess set, like I said, or if they don't play chess . . . something."

The band starts up, and we glance over at the stage. Stan is up now and starts singing "Half as Much." He's not great, but he's good enough people start dancing slowly in front of him, and it fills the bar with the sort of gentle communal movement music does. Everyone seems to sway in time, like pages fluttering in a breeze.

"Sounds good to me," Lee says. "And do we need to move the meeting with Oscar and Elena?"

Another matchmaking client, and his potential new girlfriend. We're supposed to meet up and go over their story and how it'll work. I shake my head. "It'll be fine. That shouldn't take long."

"You sure?"

"No. But I don't want to drop these clients every time I have another case. These are important—these make it so no one gets hurt." I take a long drink.

He shakes his head just as Gene comes back over, taking my now empty glass, making sure our hands touch as he does. "You've turned into such a softie, Andy."

I laugh. "Sure." I turn to Gene. "That right?"

"You were always a softie," Gene says, grinning. I want to reach across the bar and kiss him, but he winks and is gone before I can.

Lee snorts a laugh. "Well, I'd better go get changed. I'm on in a while." He heads upstairs. Gene comes back with a full glass, and I sip it. No citrus this time; it tastes like fire.

"You want to stay over again tonight?" I ask Gene. "Since you're working late anyway?"

He grins. "Since I'm working late anyway?"

"Yeah."

He laughs, then shakes his head. "Nah, I only had the one change of clothes there, and I'm wearing them. Gotta stay at my place tonight."

"Oh." I nod, a little disappointed. "Well, maybe you could bring some more clothes to keep in my place."

He smiles, his face too kind. "I think just one change of clothes at your place makes sense." The music seems to get louder.

"Oh," I say, a little surprised.

"What kind of memoir you think could make him rich?" Gene asks.

I stare at him a beat, trying to figure out if the change of topic is because he's interested in the new one, or doesn't want to talk about the old one. He looks down at the crate of alcohol in front of him and takes out a bottle of vodka, then turns behind him to put it on the shelf, reaching up. Maybe he just doesn't want to be too demanding, move too fast, keeping a lot of stuff at my place. We've been together a while, sure, but not half a year. Haven't even said "I love you"s yet. I've thought it, though. I've looked at him, putting on his socks in the morning after staying over, fastening his garters, and I've thought that that's a man I love. Kind, and funny, and warm.

"Andy?" Gene asks.

"Hm?" I realize he's been waiting for me to answer him, it wasn't just wondering aloud. "What kind of memoir could make him rich? Well, it would be a gay one, because it was for the service. Pat says some of these books do really well. *Glass-Something* sold over a hundred thousand copies."

"*The Invisible Glass*," Gene says. "Beautiful, sad book."

"What's it about?" I ask, taking another drink, deeper this time. The fire in the alcohol burns a little.

He leans on the bar for a moment, his eyes on the ceiling, remembering. "This white lieutenant visits a Black company during World War Two. Their commander is a racist, abusive asshole they have to obey even as he shows them no respect, and the white lieutenant falls in love with one of the Black soldiers." His eyes flutter back down to mine and he shrugs, sad. "Shows how awful and racist the war was, how they treated people like us. The ending was kind of brief, they didn't get into the two men's relationship as I would have liked. Felt like maybe it was cut by someone, actually. Sad ending, of course." He turns back to the crate and takes out another bottle, frowning at it before putting it on the shelf.

"All right, so a war book, a race book, a gay book, all in one. Think Howard could have found something like that?"

"You want to read it, maybe?" Gene asks, turning back to me, smiling.

"I . . . could," I say. "Though the only bookstore I know is closed now."

"I bet Pat has a copy." He stares at me a while, analyzing. I sip my drink. "But if you're not a reader . . ."

"You know," I say, lifting my hand out, which he walks over to take. "The boyfriend, Howard's boyfriend, is also not a reader. But Howard read to him. Maybe you should read to me."

He laughs. "You want me to read to you?"

"Yeah, you stay over, we read all night."

He nods, trying not to laugh. "Just read?"

"That's what they did . . . at first."

"You know"—he leans over the bar, close to me—"actually, that does sound sort of romantic. I will bring *The Lion, the Witch and the Wardrobe* next time I stay over. And I will read to you."

"Really?"

"But, if you fall asleep, I will leave you forever." He drops my hand and takes a step back. I watch his face. He's teasing, I know, but I do wonder if maybe I'm not enough of a reader for him. Not bright enough, maybe.

"I promise I'll stay awake," I say. "As long as you don't stroke my hair."

Gene laughs, turning back to the crate and taking out another bottle. "All right. No hair stroking, I promise." He puts it on the shelf. "But we still don't know what kind of book Howard had planned."

"Maybe he has the memoir of a gay soldier. I don't know if that would make him rich, though. So many of us were in the war . . . we all have stories. It would have to be a really good one."

"Or just well written." Gene takes the last bottle from the crate and puts it on the shelf, stretching to place it. I enjoy watching. "Sometimes the story itself isn't as special as who tells it, the way they tell it."

"So maybe the who—could be someone important. Someone high up in the military." I think for a moment of James, my lover during the war, who proved himself duplicitous on many levels when he hired me a few months back. He's probably a rear admiral now.

"Maybe," Gene says, lifting the empty crate to take it to the storeroom. "That would definitely get attention."

"There wasn't even a title in the accounting books," I say, shaking my head.

Suddenly, the lights flash. Everyone dancing splits apart. The music stops, people turn still as statues. A raid.

"Go," Gene says, and I hate leaving him, but I do.

I head upstairs to Elsie's apartment, where I'm safe. I know the way, and my body weaves through the crowd easily—maybe people are even parting for me, knowing why I have to run. I move too fast to look at their faces, to thank them. The world is a blur of people and then stairs until I'm safe. Elsie's payments to the cops have been up to date. This is probably just a routine show of force, and the flashing light means everyone has had time to prepare—standing away from each other, putting on name tags that say their sex so they can't be accused of the crime of trying to deceive. The cops will do a quick tour of the place, maybe say something threatening, and then leave. But we all agree I need to hide when these happen, because if one of my former colleagues sees me, they'll probably drag me out for a beating, or worse. Last time they spotted me, it wasn't even in a gay bar, and they still broke one of my ribs. I hate leaving him alone down there, though.

In Elsie's apartment, Pat is nowhere to be seen, and Elsie is lying on the sofa, hand on her forehead holding a cigarette. She looks up when I come in.

"Pat's asleep," she says. "He's doing better, I think. It's a lot of guilt."

"I'm not here for him—there's a raid."

She frowns, annoyed. "We're up to date . . ." She sits up, then tilts her head, reconsidering. "Gene has it."

I want to run downstairs even more now, make sure he does.

Elsie seems to see my face, how I'm turning toward the door, and shakes her head. "Gene has it," she repeats, and pats the empty space on the sofa next to her, and I go sit. "You're not good at helplessness."

"Is anyone?"

"I don't know. I think it's something we get used to. You can't go downstairs to protect your boyfriend. Pat can't take care of the family. The family can't protect Rina . . . we're all helpless sometimes." She takes a long drag on the cigarette. "But." She shrugs. "That could just be a feeling. Maybe Pat saved the family by coming here. The family saved Rina from something worse by coming up with their story. We feel helpless . . . maybe we're not."

"Maybe," I say, taking out my own cigarette, and lighting it. "You still angry at Pat?"

"No," she says, then nudges me with her shoulder. "And not with you, either. Sometimes bad things happen. Doesn't mean we should pack our lives up into boxes." She gestures at the stack of packed books Pat has made in the corner. He was right, it does look a little like a Christmas tree. "Oy vey, that's a sad sight."

The smoke spirals from each of us like branches.

"You think I should read more?" I ask.

She laughs so loudly I think she might alert the police downstairs. "You're asking that now? On this case?"

I shrug. "Gene reads. You have a little book group. Lee reads. Pat, Margo, Pearl . . ."

"Don't say Cliff. Those aren't books."

"How about Henry?"

She smiles. "Don't tell him I told you, but he loves Shakespeare. I found a notebook once, he has whole dream casts for plays written out, with movie stars. Bette Davis as Lady Macbeth, Lauren Bacall as Viola. Mostly women, of course."

I smile, thinking about it. "At least those aren't gay."

She snorts a laugh. "Okay, yes, I think you should read more. If only so you don't say anything like that again. Plenty of Shakespeare is pretty gay. Plenty of . . ." She shakes her head. "Books. Imagine if they went into every house in America that had one of the books in that pile there, and dragged the occupants out in handcuffs. There wouldn't be anyone left who ever read anything. But . . . maybe that's the idea, you think? First get rid of the queer books, then all the rest of them?"

"I don't know."

"Yeah. Me neither." She stands and goes over to the window and looks down on the street. "They're leaving . . . last car just pulled away. You can probably go back down."

"Yeah," I say, standing. "You coming?"

"In a bit. I'm going to wait for Pat. Make sure he doesn't wake up alone."

When I head back downstairs, it's like nothing has changed. The music is still playing, Gene is still behind the bar.

"You all right?" I ask him.

"Sure," he says. "They just wanted to hassle us. But we're paid up. No trouble."

"You sure?"

He stares at me with a sort of sad smile. His eyes are warm brown, like coffee, and he takes a break before he speaks. "Andy, I promise, I'm fine."

"Okay," I say, feeling a little like he's annoyed with me, but not being sure why.

Lee takes the stage a while later, in a black sequin dress, and bright red lipstick. She starts singing her rendition of "My Foolish Heart," jazzy and slower than she usually sings, her notes long and lingering, wrapping the whole room in velvet, making everyone feel safe, the raid forgotten. I watch her, and by the time she's done, the bar is full, and Gene is done unpacking the case of alcohol, and when he's back from putting away the crate, he's back to tending bar. I wait until Lee's set is over, then say goodnight to Gene. I think about asking him again if he wants to stay, but something holds me back. Instead I just reach across the bar and he gives me his hand to squeeze.

Upstairs, I dream of Gene as a knight in armor, standing over me. He takes off his helmet and then reaches down for a kiss . . .

I wake up to the phone ringing. I squint at my clock. It's just past 8:00 A.M. I used to be up and on my way to work by this time when I was a cop, but now it seems far too early. The ringing is coming from my office, across the hall, so I run across and then realize I'm just in my underwear before coming back for the key. I unlock the door and make it to the phone, still ringing.

"Amethyst Investigations," I answer.

"Mills," says a voice I never thought I'd hear again. I feel my skin break out in gooseflesh—from shock, fear. But as I hear it, and it scares me, the memory of how to respond comes back to me immediately, and I find myself speaking without realizing.

"Yes, Chief."

EIGHT

"We should talk," he says in his gruff voice. He was always no-nonsense, the way a good police chief should be. Gray hair, always combed back, always in a tie, always wore his dress uniform even when he didn't need to. He was somehow distant but hands-on at the same time; sometimes he would come out just to watch the fresh meat in action on some low-level drug bust, but he wouldn't participate, or give orders, just watch. I think he liked seeing us succeed, seeing our boyish excitement afterward for having accomplished anything. That's when I usually caught him smiling to himself.

"How . . ." I swallow, realizing I'm standing in my office in just my jockeys. "How did you get this number?"

"Found the card on a fairy a while back," he says. "Just your name, a number. I thought maybe you were selling your body or something. I didn't ask him about it. Didn't use the police listings to look up the address for the number, either."

"Uh, thanks," I say. The number may not be listed, but he might be able to find it anyway, use his power to intimidate someone at the phone company. I try to swallow, but my throat is too dry.

"But like I said, we should talk. Let's meet somewhere."

"Meet?" I say. It sounds like an order to appear at my own execution.

"Don't worry. I just want to make sure we're on the same page."

"About what?"

"That's why we need to meet." He sounds a little annoyed now. "Look, you pick a place, if that'll make you feel safer. But I prom-ise I'm not trying to hurt you, Mills. If I were, I'd simply find the address for this number, and send some boys to bring you in. Would you prefer I do that?"

"No," I say quickly, every hair on my body standing on end.

"Then pick a place."

I go over places in my mind as quickly as I can—public, somewhere he wouldn't try to arrest or beat or kill me, someplace no one wants to see any violence.

"The zoo," I say finally. Lots of kids there. And I can always jump into the lion's cage if I need to hide somewhere.

He laughs once, almost like an intake of air. "I'll be there when they open."

"It might take me a little longer."

"I'll wait by the giraffes," he says, and then hangs up.

I keep holding the receiver for a moment, still unsure what just happened. I have a meeting with my old police chief by the giraffes.

No one is going to kill, beat, or kidnap me by the giraffes, I tell myself. I can feel my heart racing like I just had to fight someone off. My blood is running back and forth in my body, some sort of endless track, but not like some Olympic marathoner—it's looking for a way out. I cough a few times as my breath comes rushing back into my lungs.

No one is going to kill, beat, or kidnap me by the giraffes. So what is he going to do?

In the shower, I think about just not showing up. But then he'll start looking for me, if he hasn't already, and send guys to collect me. That would be worse than anything that could happen by the giraffes.

I dress in a suit from the old days—gray, with a white shirt, and a navy tie. Back then, I wouldn't even have worn the navy tie. It would have been black. I grab the trolley to the zoo without eating. Nothing would stay down, anyway. The thing about the chief is I always kind of liked him. Even when he fired me, when I was dragged into his office after the bust, my belt still unbuckled and fly unbuttoned, and pushed into a chair across from him. He'd just looked me up and down, like he was disappointed.

"Well, you're fired, obviously," he said. "But because you're a good cop—were a good cop—I'm not going to book you. I'll say you quit. The boys . . . well, they're not happy. They looked up to you. They feel like you tricked them. So, you're going to buckle your belt and follow me out the back way, so they can't get a shot at you. After that—and I mean the moment your feet hit the pavement—you're on your own. So take a few minutes, get yourself together, and figure out your plan, because I'm marching you out of here in five minutes." He got up, left the office. I buckled my belt and pants and let myself cry, trying to choke back how loud the sob was. I knew the other guys were listening at the door. Then he came back in with a glass of water, which he handed me. I drank it, and then followed him to the back door.

"A real shame," he said to me, as he held the door open for me.

And I was so grateful for all that. Because I knew how much worse it could have been.

But now, riding in the tunnel under Twin Peaks, I realize that while it was kinder than it could have been, that didn't mean it was kind. And in the months since I've left, he might have had time to decide it should have been a lot crueler. I can't think of any other reason he'd want to see me.

The zoo is already teeming with kids. Real little ones being pushed in strollers, a line of schoolgirls all dressed in identical uniforms. There's the sound of those high-pitched screams as they gawk at gorillas or reach out toward lions. The place smells like too many things at once, none of them meshing: the green of the plants the animals eat and sleep on, popcorn the kids are spilling, animal manure, cotton candy, vomit. The sun is like a searchlight, hot on my neck. When I find him, he's not in uniform, just a plain black suit, black tie, black hat. He has a small box of popcorn, red and white striped, and he's sitting on a bench, taking out one piece at a time and putting it in his mouth. He chews it slowly, staring at the giraffes, who walk back and forth in their pen, slowly, like some kind of ballet.

He doesn't glance up at me when I walk over to him.

"Mills, sit down."

I sit. He keeps watching the giraffes, eating popcorn. I look around for other faces I might know, people staring at us, but there's no one around except kids, moms, teachers. We might be the only two adult men here.

"I wanted to meet to make sure we're on the same page about things," he says.

"All right," I say slowly. I put my hands together in my lap, like a child. I don't know why.

"You quit," he says, and eats another piece of popcorn. "That's the official line. It kept me from having to explain why you were fired."

"I know." My throat feels dry, and the words come out softer than I mean. I look at my hands, and make myself stretch them out, fingers apart.

"I don't need some newspaper story about how the police department is filled with fags, like the State Department. I don't want McCarthy calling me before the House committee. You got it?"

Newspaper story. I nod, understanding now, and look up at the giraffes, who are positioned so when we look at them, their necks cross, like a giant X. "Rose Rainmeyer, with the *Examiner*."

He nods and turns to me for the first time. "Did you call her? You trying to . . . sell your story?"

I shake my head quickly, and look down again. My hands

have curled into weak fists, turtles hiding in their shells. I stretch them out again. "No, I ran into her and she remembered me. Asked why I quit. I said I didn't like the hours." I look up at him, and he stares at me a moment, then snorts a laugh and turns back to the giraffes.

"Who does?" He puts another piece of popcorn in his mouth, chews it, swallows. "Well, she wasn't convinced. Came into the station, said she wanted to talk to me, asked me questions about you: Why did you leave? Weren't you such a great cop? Why didn't I fight to keep you? I told her you left for personal reasons you didn't tell me, and yes, you were a great cop, and I did fight to keep you, even offered you as much of a raise as our limited budget would allow, but you turned it down. Is that all clear?"

"Yes," I say. I feel relieved, I think. Maybe disappointed, too. I thought there'd be more here. But it's just him checking I won't talk. He doesn't have any interest in me, my life, not even to end it. It's sort of freeing, but sad, too. This was a man I respected and now I'm not even really worth thinking about to him. I lean back and look up at the sky. It's a bright blue, striped with thin, flat clouds, like prison bars.

"Good," he says. "Shake her."

"I'm trying," I say, and take a breath. I turn back to look at him. "But there is one thing that could help."

He stops eating the popcorn but doesn't look at me. "You can't be a cop again, Mills. You can't be a cop and a pervert."

He says it so casually, it almost lessens the sting.

"That's not what I want. I've been working cases. Privately."

He sighs, and his grip on the popcorn box loosens. It tilts in his lap, too empty to spill. "That's stupid, Mills."

"But I haven't applied for a license, because I figure you'd have to approve it, and you wouldn't."

"No," he says. The popcorn box goes straight again as his grip tightens.

"But she noticed that, when she was talking to me," I say. It's only probably a lie. She heard who I was looking for, that I was a PI—she probably heard me say I didn't bring my license. Not hard for her to find out it was because I didn't have one. "She might poke around some more, wonder why I never applied."

He swallows and puts the box of popcorn down on the bench between us. His eyes stay on the giraffes, but his voice grows quieter.

"I could just trace where that number goes. Mention it to some of the boys."

"The boys already found me once, Chief. Cracked a few ribs, but I lived." It comes out angry, and he turns to me.

"What did you expect them to do?"

I don't really have an answer to that, so I don't say anything. Behind him is some kind of bird exhibit, the birds unmoving in small cages until now, when a child hits the chain-link with a stick. Now one raises its wings out, dark red, and flutters them momentarily like an explosion.

"You should have left town, Mills," the chief says. "I thought you would." The bird's wings fold in again, the fire gone. "Going private, talking to reporters . . . you're smarter than that. People find out about you, this Rainmeyer writes a story—'Fairy Cop Turned Private Dick'—you're gonna get killed. You know that, right? Maybe by one of the boys, maybe by anyone else. You become the most famous faggot in town, people will line up to sock you in the jaw and slit your throat. So why do it?"

"I want to help people," I say. "I always wanted to help people."

"Go work in a homeless shelter," he says.

"They'd fire me, too."

"Well, that's not my problem. And you shouldn't be, either. Damnit, Mills." He sighs, and looks at the giraffes again. I follow his gaze. They've turned and seem to be staring back at us. A little girl in a blue coat stands at the edge of the fence, her hand stretched out through the gaps in the chain-link to try to pet one of them. "Don't talk to the reporter," he says finally. "Not for me, for you. Avoid her. Avoid anyone from your old life who asks questions. Disappear. That's the only way someone like you gets to live now. And if you end up on a slab in the morgue, and I'm told I have to figure out who killed you . . ." He stands up. "Well, you know how we handle homo-cides. They all go to cold case. Because everyone understands killing a pervert. It's not even really a crime in the eyes of the public. And we only have so many resources."

"So that's a no on the PI license?" I ask, surprised by my own anger. I know what he's saying is true. But it still annoys me to hear him say it.

He looks at me, and for a moment, he seems genuinely sad. Like I let him down. And I feel bad about it, too, like I made my father cry, something no one should ever see.

"Be careful," he says. It's more of a threat than concern, or maybe it's both. I don't know. He walks away and I look up at the giraffes again, but they've turned away, walking to the other side of their tiny space.

The ride back to the Ruby feels quieter, emptier. Only one other person rides the cable car with me—an old woman, holding a stuffed monkey toy from the zoo. I think about what the chief said, about how if anyone figures out where I am, who I am, what I am . . . then terrible things will inevitably happen to me. And to my clients. And the Ruby, too, maybe. I knew that already, but hearing it from him, in his vaguely disinterested tone, made it feel more concrete, like walls have risen around me, separating me from the world I used to live in. Well, better to be on one side now, instead of split down the middle like I used to be. The problem now isn't really the wall. I can't do anything about that. It's Rose Rainmeyer, who's peeking over it and trying to grab my hand and pull me back. She's the danger now. And if she's calling the chief about me, that means she's still pursuing it. I go over it again in my mind—the only way she can find me is if she somehow got one of my business cards, like the chief did. And she's not picking up queer folks on the street.

It should be fine. The chief stonewalled her, I stonewalled her, and now she can't find me. There's nothing else for her to do. Maybe I can tell Lee, though, make sure everyone knows not to gossip about me to anyone outside the community. Otherwise, I just have to hope I don't bump into her on any more cases.

When I get back to the Ruby, Gene is outside on the sidewalk, talking to a guy from one of the liquor companies. He's in a uniform, leaning on a branded truck—both it and the uniform are green, with a fancy-looking bottle painted on the side of the truck and the lapel of the uniform.

"This isn't what we agreed," Gene is saying to him.

The guy crosses his arms, looking bored. "Maybe you just ordered wrong."

"I didn't order wrong."

"You sure? Your type, I know English comes bewy haad." He smirks at his own fake accent. I swallow, and walk faster toward them. My body shivers. I've never heard anyone talk to Gene that way and I feel sick in some way. Like I've done something wrong just hearing it.

"Do you hear an accent?" Gene says with remarkable restraint. I can feel my fists clenching already. "And I know what I ordered. One crate of the vodka, two of the gin. So let's go inside and call your boss to confirm that."

"What's going on?" I ask. I want to just rush the guy, knock him out.

"It's fine," Gene says, keeping his eyes on the deliveryman.

"You his boss?" the guy in uniform asks.

"I'm security here. Is there a problem?"

He looks me up and down. "Nah, no problem. Just a misunderstanding. Your little Chinaman here screwed up an order."

Again I feel a sickly shiver down my spine, like I should have been able to stop him from saying that before he did. I look at Gene, to see if he's okay.

He frowns, but doesn't look bothered otherwise. "I'm not Chinese." He says it like he's bored.

"Mexican then, whatever." He stands up from the truck and points at Gene. "You fucked up the order and now you're blaming me." He turns to me, then. "If I call my boss and waste his time checking some record because he can't read English right, I'm gonna get chewed out. So take the fucking crates, or I'm out of here."

"He didn't fuck anything up," I say, stepping between them, waiting for an excuse to hit him, begging for one. "He never does. Call your boss."

The man turns to me again, and looks me up and down, then crosses his arms. "Fine. Show me a phone. You watch the crates," he says to Gene.

"I'll show you the phone," Gene says. "Andy, watch the crates."

"Sure," I say, staying put as Gene goes into the club, the delivery guy reluctantly following him. They come out after a few minutes, and now the delivery man's face is red. He takes one of the crates on the street and loads it back into the truck, and takes out a different one, which he brings into the club. Gene watches silently, his arms crossed over his chest, as he brings in the two left on the street, gets in his truck, and leaves.

"Fucking asshole," Gene says finally.

"Yeah," I say. "You okay?"

He looks at me, fury still shimmering on his face, and looks like he wants to say something, but instead turns and goes inside. I follow, getting in the elevator with him. It's not like I've never heard stuff like that before. On the force, the guys would throw around language like it all the time, and I knew it was bad, and always hated it, but it's different seeing it said to Gene. I can't imagine how awful it was for him.

"You okay?" I ask again.

"Fine," he says, his voice flat, lying.

"I had a weird morning," I say, thinking changing the subject might help. I can't stop the deliveryman from saying what he said, but maybe I can help Gene forget.

"Yeah?" he asks. His voice is chilly. "Well, I'm behind because that asshole wouldn't just call his boss to confirm the order, so . . . we'll talk later, okay?"

The elevator stops at two—the Ruby—and he gets out without turning around.

"Sure," I say, feeling like I've done something wrong, but I don't know what. "Later."

The doors close and I rise to the third floor, where my office and apartment are. Pat is standing in the hall, between the two.

"Hi," I say, stepping off the elevator. He's smiling. "You feeling better?"

"DeeDee is back. I've been calling the store every few hours, you know, just hoping and . . . she picked up. Been visiting her sister all week."

I give him a hug. "That's great, Pat."

"But she says Howard was supposed to be minding the store. She doesn't know where he is."

"Oh." I don't know what else to say. I already told him how

Howard was taking a lot of risks. I go into my office and motion him to follow me.

"I told her you'd stop by, maybe figure out where he is."

"Does she have the list?" I ask, sitting down. He sits opposite.

He tilts his head. "Yes. Well . . ." He sighs. "DeeDee kind of rambles sometimes. She's all over the place. And when I asked her she said she thinks she does, said something about how she'd find it. Sounded like she knew where it was kept." I nod. That doesn't mean the list is safe. Howard still could have had it. "I know. But she started talking about Las Vegas and her sister, so I just told her I had to go so I could come find you. You want to go down there together?"

I watch Pat, almost bouncing in the chair across from me. "I think I'll go down alone."

"Oh," he says, confused.

"I just want to meet her and try to ask her questions, get everything straight. Howard is still missing, so we're not out of the woods yet, right? And if you're there it might become more vacation talk, more chitchat."

He nods. "Okay, that makes sense. And I should be helping at the bar, anyway."

"Yeah," I say, thinking of Gene, his face just now. "You should do that. Gene just got a shipment in. I'll head over to the bookstore now, and see what I can find out. It might be that Howard's disappearance has nothing to do with the store. It could be his mob affair that got him in trouble. Or something else."

"Or?" Pat asks. "You don't look as happy as I do."

"Or maybe they just raided the place while she was gone," I say. All we know now is that DeeDee was out of town. We still don't know what happened, or who's in danger.

"That makes sense," Pat says. "So . . . should I stay away from DeeDee altogether then?"

I tilt my head. "Maybe. Just for a little bit. If the feds are watching the place, or Mrs. Purley has your name and is diving into your background . . ."

He nods. "I need to stay out of sight."

"Exactly."

He sighs. "All right. I'll go help unload this shipment of booze. Thanks, Andy."

"I'll tell you what I find out," I say, and watch him go. I think about stopping downstairs on the way out, talking to Gene again. I've never really seen him get angry before, so I'm not sure if I should stay away, but it's what he asked for. And Pat will cheer him up, I hope.

Outside, I walk the way Gene led me yesterday, back to the bookshop. This time the curtains are drawn back in the windows, and a few people are browsing inside. One turns, and spots me outside—and waves with just her fingers, a big smile on her face. Rose Rainmeyer.

As she comes outside, a little bell on the front door chimes as she pushes it open. To me, it sounds like church bells, the kind they ring for a funeral procession. I think about just running, but she already saw me. And then she's in front of me, wearing a pink-and-black-striped jacket and skirt, with a matching hat, and a blouse underneath that ties at the neck with a ribbon. Danger shouldn't look like a candy striper.

"Mr. Mills. I was so hoping I'd find you here."

NINE

"Miss Rainmeyer," I say, tipping my hat slightly, hoping it'll cover my panic. "You knew I'd be here?"

"Well, I remembered the names you'd told to the woman at the DA's office," she says quickly. "So I did a little digging in public records—found they owned a bookstore. Not quite the criminal enterprise I was hoping for, but color me intrigued. What's the case?"

"You know I can't tell you that," I say, walking a little away from the store, out of view of the windows. She follows me. "But even if I could, trust me, Ms. Rainmeyer, there's nothing newspaper-worthy here."

"Oh, newspaper-worthy isn't about the facts—it's in how you write it. I already talked to one of the owners, DeeDee. She seems sweet. No idea what she could be up to, though. Now, the other one . . ." She takes out her notebook and flips to a page. "He could be . . ."

"Ms. Rainmeyer," I say, my tone as polite, but firm, as I can make it, "if a reporter is poking around a case, it could make it very difficult for me to do my job."

"Well, if you were to tell me what you're working on, I wouldn't have to poke around." She smiles. "You're going to say it's none of my business, but you're wrong. Everything is my business, quite literally. I need to find news in order to report on it."

"I appreciate that, but not everything is news, and this case is definitely not." I say it as calmly as I can. I want her to think I'm being sincere. "The truth is, since becoming a PI, my job is quite dull. Insurance scams, cheating wives. Nothing worth the time of a talented reporter."

She beams at that. "Flattery. I like it. It won't work, but I do like it."

"What will work, then? If I go in there to talk to someone, and you follow me, neither of us will get any answers. So I need you not to follow me."

She tilts her head, thinking. "That's true. All right."

I try not to let the shock show on my face, but fail. She laughs.

"I'm a reasonable woman," she says. "You're right. No one will talk to a PI if there's a reporter in tow. You should go in alone."

"Thank you," I say, with a nod, walking back to the bookstore.

"I'll be waiting outside when you're done," she calls, waving at me as I pull the door open. The little bell clangs, but she doesn't follow me inside, so I go behind one of the shelves, out of sight of the windows, and take a deep breath. Between the chief this morning, and now the exact woman he told me to avoid showing up, I feel like I'm being hunted by something—not the usual way, but like someone is setting me up, luring me into a cage with a tiger. This is bad. If she keeps on me, she could expose me, my clients, my location. She might even stumble on the list, and then she could publish it, like they do the names of people arrested in raids on gay bars. Anything she writes about could get targeted, destroyed. Including this case: Pat, the family at Lavender House, baby Rina. Not to mention me. I swallow, but my throat is dry and it sticks on the way down, like swallowing a ball of sand.

"All right, there, dear?" A woman behind the register comes out and walks over to me. "You look very nervous, I don't mean it rudely, though I suppose it comes out that way, but you do look nervous, maybe like you saw a ghost. Do you need a glass of water?

Not that water will help with ghosts, will it?" She laughs. She's maybe in her sixties, with short gray curls and cat-eyed glasses on a string of beads that falls from her face down and around her neck. She's wearing a yellow dress with a blue cardigan over it and a small matching yellow hat, the colors so bold it comes across as childlike, and her expression seems younger than the lines in her face.

"Are you DeeDee?" I ask.

She nods, a little wary. "Dorothea, really, if you can believe it. My mother, though, she thought Dorothy was too plain, wanted me to have a fancy name. Like my sister. Rochelle. She thought that was fancy, too. But I go by DeeDee, just plain DeeDee. She probably rolls in her grave every time someone says it, but it's not as plain as just Dot, is it?"

If I hadn't been warned about her being a talker, I'd say she was trying to cover up a lie—people do that sometimes, talk so much they hope you won't catch what they've buried in the words. But sometimes, people just talk a lot.

"I'm Pat's friend," I say.

Her eyes widen, and she nods slowly, over and over, as she thinks. "Well, let's go in the back, then, shall we?"

I nod and follow her to the back room. She stops once at the register to put out a little bell on the counter, and a sign that says RING IF YOU NEED ASSISTANCE.

In the back, she sits behind the desk, staring at me. The office looks mostly the same, aside from a purse and a stack of unopened letters on the desk, and some paper taped over the broken windowpane. "So you're the detective. The gay one, I mean. I've never met one in real life. Any detective, not just gay ones. Though I suppose you're probably the only one, aren't you? Gay detective, I mean. That can't be a very common job."

"Far as I know, it's just me. Pat says you were surprised to find that Howard hadn't been minding the store? And now you don't know where he is?"

"No idea. I'm worried, but also Howard, he sometimes got these big ideas, and he would sort of follow them and forget about other things. Though never this bad before. At least not since we were children. We grew up a few houses down from each other, you know, our mothers were friends. Everyone thought we'd get married, that's a laugh, isn't it? We almost did, just to make them happy, you know? But being married to Howard . . ." She shakes her head. "It's enough running a business with him. I was very happy living in a ladies' boardinghouse until I met my Suzie, and then we found a landlord who just thought we were a pair of old maids who lived together for company. Marrying him would have ruined all that."

"Sure," I say. "But Howard, this week? Any idea where he's gone?"

"Oh, well, I mean he knew where I was going, knew I was visiting my sister in Vegas. It's a wild town, Vegas. Have you been? I don't think it's the best place for my sister, honestly. But Howard, right, you wanted to know about Howard. I really don't know if I should be worried. He should have kept the store open, but Howard was so easily distracted, caught up in his ideas and plans . . ." She smirks, then shakes her head, remembering what we're talking about. "Pat is worried. Are you worried?"

"Yes, I found some things out that concern me."

She pales at that, and looks down. "Are you sure? I thought maybe it was just one of his little adventures, did that all the time when we were children. Vanished in the woods overnight once. They called the police, made a search party with dogs and everything, but he was just building a tree house out there. By himself! Saw the perfect tree for it, he said, had to do it." She shakes her head, sort of amused, sort of annoyed. I get the impression it's something she does a lot. "Had to do it. That's Howard. Saw an adventure, had to take it. When we got older it wasn't tree houses anymore, of course. It was men. Much more trouble than tree houses. But this one . . . if you're worried . . ." She sighs, and shakes her head, looking suddenly so sad. "It's that book."

She looks over to the empty side of the office. The scrap of cardboard box is gone now.

"A new book for the service?" I ask. "The memoir you were publishing yourself?"

She freezes for a moment, staring at me, then shakes her head. "So you know about that. I told him, I told him it was a bad idea. A gay mobster. No one would believe it, and if they did then we'd be in more trouble. But he went on with it anyway."

"A gay mobster," I repeat, letting the idea of it sink into me. A wild book for sure. But who's the author? Not Merle, I decide quickly. Merle might have been his boyfriend, but Merle is no mobster. And too young to have many stories. But his friend, Joe, the one who Bridges said wasn't there anymore, he was older, he was definitely working for the mob. Could easily be him. "Did you know the author, too?" I ask.

She shakes her head. "Some friend of his. I never met him. I would have run if I had. I would have run if I'd known . . ." She shakes her head again. "Howard thought it would make us all rich, like *The Homosexual in America*, he said, but with crime. Decades of stories of life in the mob, but also life hiding from the mob. Affairs, murder, oh he went on and on, I just . . ." She pauses, again, thinking. "Anyway. It doesn't matter. When I came back, and I saw the book hadn't arrived . . . I knew. Something was wrong."

"Hadn't arrived?" I ask.

"They should have come in on Tuesday. I left on Monday morning, I think it was. Yes, that must be it. It's a long drive, you know, got there well past midnight, should have left earlier."

"But the books?"

"Yes, the printer was supposed to deliver them Tuesday, like I said, and then we'd stack them up over there, like we usually do, and then the next week, yesterday it would have been, Monday, we'd put a few copies on the shelves and mail out the rest to the book service subscribers. We'd need to spend the weekend packaging each of them up, we have a lot of subscribers . . . a lot more than I ever thought we would."

I nod. So the books were probably here, and then taken. Maybe by the mob. Certainly if they knew about the book, they'd want it gone, and probably Joe and Howard, too. Which would explain all of them missing. But if the feds had raided the place, then they would have taken the books too. And the way Bridges talked about Joe . . . it didn't feel like Joe had betrayed them. There wasn't any anger there. And wouldn't Merle have known? I shake my head. Too many things are still unclear.

"Why are you so sure it's the mob?" I ask.

"Who else would it be?"

"The feds," I say. "The post office is cracking down on gay books being sent through the mail."

She tilts her head at me, thinking, her eyes going wider. "You could be right. If they raided the place, then they could have arrested Howard and taken these books right here because they were all waiting to be mailed. But then why not the front of the store, too?"

"Have you checked that all the gay books out there aren't missing?"

Her eyes go even wider and she practically leaps up from the chair and dashes back to the front of the store. I follow her. She flits from shelf to shelf, looking. "The thing is we don't have just one shelf for those kind of books, of course, that would draw attention, don't want that, that's how you get bricks through your window. No, no, we just put them around in different sections, like . . . here's one. And . . . there should be one here, but there isn't . . ."

I nod. "So maybe they were taken, but they couldn't find them all."

"Maybe," she says. She looks around. There are a few customers, but no one who seems to need help. They take down the leather-clad books and flip the pages quietly, the sound like rustling leaves. It smells in here, I realize. Like leather and old paper. It smells good. I can see why people want to spend time here.

DeeDee shakes her head and leads me back to the office, where she sits down again, her breathing heavy. She bends over, her hands on her knees. Her wrists are so thin, I worry she might fall forward.

"I'm sorry about all this," I say.

"Don't apologize, dearie. This isn't you. This is . . ." She takes a deep breath and looks up at me. "This is the world."

I nod. "I'll find a way to check if it was the feds. If it was, you should hide the rest of those books, and be careful, they might have a warrant out for you too."

She nods, solemn. "I understand. But I don't think it's them. I'll keep the store open. With those books gone . . . it's going to be hard for a while. I'll come up with something else to send the subscribers."

"If you do that, then the feds will definitely—"

"I'll pick a clean one," she says, waving her hand. "Nothing unseemly on the page, a sad ending where we're punished for . . . being us. It'll be a safe one."

"I still think it's a bad idea," I say.

Her mouth hardens into a flat line. "Books are important," she says, her voice harder than it's been till now. "Even the ones not about us. Stories, you know, they let us see into other lives, make us imagine how it might be for other people. Howard and I, even before we knew what we were, we read together, traded books, talked about how the characters made us feel. When I had figured out what I was, it was because of a book I just picked up in the library . . . *Imre*. I don't think even the librarian knew what it was. I don't know how it got there. I read it, and . . . so many things became clear to me. It was about men, but if two men could be like that, then, women . . . well, I showed it to Howard, and when he had read it, we met—in that damned tree house, that's where we always met—and we just cried. We hugged each other, and we cried, because we knew what we were and we knew that we weren't the only ones, because this book existed." She wipes away a tear that's forming in her eye and leans back. "And now, now, that McCarthy and Cohn, they say they're going to check for subversive books at the American embassies overseas. I have a friend whose husband works at one, and she wrote me, said that they might burn the books! In Indiana, an old librarian friend of mine says there's a lady trying to ban *Robin Hood*. Too communist to take from the rich and give to the poor, apparently. She says the American Library Association is working on a statement, though. About the freedom to read." She smiles, proud at that. "Well, I'm not a librarian anymore, but I'll keep the shop open, Mr. Gay Detective. That's what I'll do. I'll try to get the stories that deserve to be out there out there . . . as long as I can manage it, anyway." She tilts her head and squints at me. "You know, if Howard were here, he'd probably be trying to get you to write a book. Anonymous, of course, like the mobster's was."

"It was anonymous?"

"Oh yes, didn't even use a name on the cover. Just by 'A Former Criminal.' Though if he was still gay, even if he left the mob, he was still a criminal, I say. But I think that was about selling, about style. Howard was good at that sort of thing, better at it than me.

He could sell a book to anyone who came in. Knew how to make them curious about it." She shakes her head. "I don't know what I'll do without him."

"He might not be dead," I say. "And if it is a lawsuit from the feds, then he could get out soon."

"Oh." She nods, clearly not believing me. "Right. Well, that would be nice, wouldn't it? Still, best to go on without him, can't rely on him for at least a little while, so I'd better get out there and try to sell some books. Did you need anything else from me?"

"Do you know where the mailing list is?" I ask. "I assume Howard had it, if he was here all week getting ready to mail books. Did he keep it in the office, home?"

"Oh, well, he knew a lot of those addresses by heart, he had a very good memory, at least for words, you know, not where he left things, but names, addresses, and he wrote them all back, so many of them, he just answered these letters . . ." She pats the stack of unopened letters on the desk, then looks down quickly. "I don't know who's going to do it now. Me? I don't know if anyone wants to hear from me." Her eyes linger on the letters, getting watery.

"I'm sure they do," I say, though I know it sounds false. "The address list, though . . . did he have it? Pat said you knew where it was."

She wipes her face with her palm and turns back to me. "I know the places it could be," she says, looking confused. "You're worried someone has it?"

"Maybe. And that could be dangerous for a lot of people. What does it look like?"

"Oh, it was just a little brown address book. Normal. No one would know all the addresses in it were . . . well. But I'm sure it's around here. I haven't looked around much yet, only got in a little before you, and some woman came up to me, asked me strange questions about how I was. Very peculiar, didn't like her."

"Yeah, she's a reporter, don't talk to her again," I say, frowning slightly.

She pales and shakes her head. "Oh, I won't. I know trouble when I see it, trust me, and when I see trouble, it's time to go. But I don't have the address book yet. I'll look around, of course. It might be in my car, or apartment, or it might be at his house. I . . . don't want to go there, in case he's . . ." She shakes her head and then opens a drawer, taking out a large purse. She keeps speaking as she rifles through it. "I have a pair of his keys. He had a spare for my place, too, you know. Just in case. Never can be too careful, and we're at the age you start forgetting things. If you find the address book there, please bring it back. I need it, so I can send out the next round of books. I'm not going to stop just because Howard is gone. This is important. And it'll keep the place afloat. Without the book service, we'll go under for sure. Just my savings . . . and oh." She stops rifling and frowns. "Howard's life insurance. I was the beneficiary on that." She laughs suddenly. "Probably shouldn't say that in front of a detective though, should I?"

"He could still be alive," I tell her again.

She shrugs. "Oh, here they are." She takes out a pair of keys on a ring and hands them to me. "If he isn't, I'll try to figure that out then. That could help keep the store afloat. He would have wanted that. He was a generous man, you know, too generous sometimes, I think. Gave away books sometimes, to people who couldn't afford them. Always said books should be free. I said he should go work in a library then, and we laughed. Like they'd ever allow people like us to be librarians. Terrible life, hiding everything like that from work. I tried it for a little while, thought it was a good job after publishing, but then the government started getting nosy . . . I quit pretty quickly. Worked at bookstores. No, no, here was our little place. Even if he did give away books sometimes." She looks at the keys I'm still holding. "Bring those back when you're done," she says softly.

"I will. And I'll tell you if I find . . . him."

"Right down the street, star on the door. He's the back apartment on the ground floor."

I nod, and shift my weight to one foot. The list is still missing. Hopefully it'll be at his place, because I already looked everywhere here. But the idea that Howard might have memorized those addresses means even if I do find the address book there, he could still be somewhere, naming names.

"I suppose I should get back to work, plenty of customers out there, waiting, trying to find a book." She forces a smile, looking at the door to the main room. "You should get to work, too, finding my friend. Terrible job, you have. Though I'm not paying you, am I? So is it a job? Is someone paying you? Pat?"

"Pat's a friend. This is a favor."

She looks back and smiles widely at that. "That's so kind of you, really, such kindness. But I shouldn't be surprised, Pat is so kind, and has so many friends, so many people willing to help him out, you know, because he helps so many of them. He's here so often, just moving boxes, doing inventory, or reaching high shelves, and it's not as though he's much younger than us, he's no spring chicken either, but he's sprightly, and if he can't lift something he can always find some young man to do it, he knows a lot of young men, more than Howard even."

"Did Howard know a lot of young men?" I ask. Merle seemed like the type who could get jealous.

DeeDee blushes and turns back to the book of poetry, not perfectly wrapped, and taps her fingers on it. "Well, I suppose when it's phrased that way it sounds sort of scandalous, but I didn't mean it like that, you know. But he knows many young men, sure, and he's . . . dated some of them, certainly, nothing wrong with that, they're adults, just younger than Howard, but who isn't younger than Howard? Except me, I suppose. He never really settled down, though, if that's what you're asking, not like me and my Suzie. But she died a few years back now, I miss her a lot, you know. And now Howard, too . . ." She sighs.

"He might be alive." I've said it so many times, I almost believe it myself. "Don't give up hope. I'll try to find him."

"You're a dear. Such a nice young man. I wouldn't expect it from your profession, but maybe that's wrong of me to think. Read too many stories about those hard detectives, cold and mean, maybe. But you're not like the stories."

"Only when it's raining," I tell her. The joke doesn't land. "Did you notice an odd smell in here, when you got back?" I ask. "Like fish? Did Howard eat lunch in here?"

She blinks, then shakes her head. "No. I didn't notice that."

"I'll come back when I find out more or if I have more questions."

"That's kind," she says, looking back out at the shop. "It's really very kind, but in my heart . . . I don't have a good feeling." She tilts her head toward me and I see her face shake, so she looks away again, trying to hide it. She's sad. Scared, too. The kind of fear she's trying to tell herself she shouldn't have, I think, trying to will it away. "Be careful."

The bell over the door chimes and a young woman with two small children comes in. DeeDee goes to greet them, leaving me alone.

TEN

I could leave via the main door, but I know Rose is waiting for me out there. I walk out the back instead.

And there's Rose, waiting for me across the alley, with a big smile on her face.

"What'd you learn?" she asks.

"Ms. Rainmeyer," I say, nodding at her, then walking quickly out of the alley. She follows. I'm not sure where to go, exactly; I can't head anywhere else related to the case, or back to the Ruby, without losing her first.

"Now, now, Mr. Mills, you won't get away that easily."

I sigh, but don't stop walking. "Ms. Rainmeyer, how can I help you?"

"Well, I have questions—who's your client, what's the case, where's . . ." She takes out her notebook and checks it. "Howard Salzberger, the other owner of the store?"

"Ms. Rainmeyer, I respect your job, but I'm a private eye. Private."

She nods slightly, acknowledging that, but keeps walking next to me. "Do you know what makes a good newspaper article, Mr. Mills?"

"I assumed it was determined afterward by how many copies the paper sold."

She laughs. "Maybe to some. But not me. For me, it's two things: the truth, and a good story. Now, you can have one without the other—you see that all the time. The truth without a good story is printed in papers daily; the stock market went up, then down. A train derailed in Oregon, injuring four, and killing two chickens. And a story without the truth—well, those are printed regularly, too, they're just press releases reporters repeat: the president vows to strengthen our manufacturing, Margo Lamontaine says her new formulation of their lily-scented soap was inspired by the smell of her newborn daughter's hair."

I almost laugh aloud at that one. Definitely not the truth, knowing Margo. "How do you know that's not true?" I ask.

"Because I'm very good at my job. Most people don't believe that, of course; they see a girl reporter, they assume I'm going to keep my head down and write what they tell me about perfume or clothes. And I do, sometimes, to pay the bills. But you know I'm good at my job, otherwise you wouldn't have gone out the back door."

I smirk. She's right about that.

"So," she continues, "trust me when I say I can sense a good story here. Call it women's intuition, if you'd like. But something is happening here—maybe it's you, leaving the police. Was it for this case? Cases like this? Or maybe it's just something about the romance of a bookshop, safe and unassuming but maybe . . . criminal? Preyed upon?" She ticks off her theories faster and faster, my heart knocking the inside of my chest with each one, like someone counting down to my electrocution. "There's a story here, and there's truth, and so far, you've told me neither."

"Again, Ms. Rainmeyer, private. They're not my truth or story to tell."

"I can help, Mr. Mills. Privacy is . . . an old-fashioned idea. The truth belongs to everyone. And my job isn't so dissimilar from yours. I can find out things, you know. Like that Mr. Salzberger frequented an illegal casino run by the mob."

I stop walking and she stops, smiling at me. "You knew that one," she says.

"I did," I say, raising an eyebrow.

"I did, too." Her smile tilts up at the edges with a flash of pride and maybe mischief. "See? Good at my job. But I don't know why you were checking up on the owners at the DA's office. Maybe something to do with the mob? Did he fall into debt and they let him pay it back by using the bookshop as a front for drugs? Hollowed-out books filled with white powder? Or maybe they weren't that creative—the Mafia controls all sorts of things, including dirty magazines. Did they sell those through the bookstore?"

I step back and lean against a building, and take out my cigarette case and offer her one. She plucks one from the case and sticks it in her mouth, then leans forward so I can light it, then my own. I take a long drag, deciding what to do. She's not going to let up, that much is clear. And if I try to stonewall her, she'll just go digging on her own, like she did to find this place, to find out about Howard. She could find out more—about the book service, that would be a story that would ruin people. She could even find out about me. Maybe she's right—it's about a good story, and the truth. The key will be telling her versions of both that won't hurt anyone. Well, aside from me, if the chief finds out.

"If that was their business," I say finally. "If they sold dirty magazines for the mob, then they'd also have to sell some through the mail. But the post office has been cracking down on that kind of thing."

"Oh, so you think the post office caught them!" She lights up, excited. "But they don't know about the Mafia connection. So they just think they have a pornography distributor . . . if they have him."

"I couldn't find that part out," I concede. She's already leaping to conclusions that are closer to the truth than I'd like. I want to just walk away, but she'd clearly give chase. I take a long drag on my cigarette. It tastes too sweet. I need to give her something, keep her busy. And if she can help me while doing it . . . "So . . .

are you really helpful?" I ask. "Can you find out if the post office and the feds have a case against Howard Salzberger, and arrested him?"

"I might know someone at the post office," she says, trying to be demure, and failing. She's thrilled. "But if you want to talk to him, I should get to know what you're working on."

I shake my head. "I don't want you ambushing my client, peppering them with your questions. It'll ruin my business."

She stares at me, holding the cigarette, smiling slightly. She waits.

"You can be there when I talk to your contact," I say finally. "And no stories better show up in the *Examiner* before the case is over."

She sticks the cigarette in her mouth and then extends her hand. I shouldn't, but I shake it. I can almost feel a chasm opening in my stomach, everything in me falling down into it. But when all the options are bad, not choosing is worse.

She takes the cigarette out and grinds it under her heel. "Hate those things," she says, grinning. "But I'm so glad we're finally on the same page."

I don't say anything to that, but she starts walking.

"Come on." She motions me to follow, and I do. "His name is Tim, and he usually takes lunch around twelve thirty." She glances at a watch on her wrist. "We have plenty of time."

We get on a trolley heading to the post office again. Close to the police station. And this time, I'm with the very woman the chief told me to avoid. If he were to spot us together . . . I hold on to a strap as the trolley rolls downhill, and lower the brim of my hat.

When we get off, she doesn't lead me back to the building with the DA's office and post office—instead we go down the block from there, where there's a diner called Hansen's. It's not the usual greasy spoon—the bar is wood, the booths have dry leather stretched over the seats. I only came here a few times when I was on the force. Always seemed too fancy.

"We stopping for lunch?" I ask.

"Yes," she says. "And he'll be in here soon. He always is."

"How do you know that?"

She glances at her watch. "We probably have time for some drinks, though. We should get to know each other."

"So now you're not answering my questions?" I ask.

"You're not answering mine," she says with a smile, sliding into a booth.

I don't have anything to say to that, so sit silently as she flags down a waiter.

"A gin martini for me, extra olive, and a highball for our guest who hasn't arrived, and . . ." She looks over at me.

"Whisky soda," I say.

She raises her eyebrows. "Of course." The waiter nods and walks off and she turns back to me. "Look at us, working together. That's nice, isn't it? I know this will be a great relationship."

I flinch when she says it. She sees it, but doesn't look surprised.

"I'll wear you down, you'll see," she says. "Maybe you just don't know enough about me yet." She starts taking her gloves off. "Let's see, I started out working for Annie Laurie, but the sob sister thing wasn't quite where I wanted to go. I learned a lot from her, of course, about how people respond to other people, their stories, but honestly what interests me most is crime." She lays her gloves on the table. Her nails are painted red. "When men report on crime, it's always shoot-outs and arrests and grisly details." She fakes a shudder. "But crime is about people, too. The criminals, and their victims. And talking to people about crime, hearing their perspectives . . . that's the best kind of story. So many reporters forget that. Sometimes they forget about the victims altogether. And so many of those victims are women. Crime reporting needs a woman's perspective. So I've worked hard to become that."

"Yeah?" I ask. "Is it working?"

The waiter puts our drinks down in front of us and she sips her martini, then closes her eyes in pleasure. "Perfect." She opens her eyes to look at me. "And yes, it's working . . . somewhat. They still mostly give me the puff pieces, and I have to fight for stories, scrounge them up myself, like I'm doing here with you, or like I was doing waiting in the DA's office. The paper would never assign me anything from the crime desk. You know, that first story we met on, the mob murder, they weren't going to do anything about it, a paragraph on page six. I took the initiative, marched into the police station when people were interviewing you, and just asked questions along with the others."

"I remember," I say, sipping my drink, but only a little. Rose is clearly the kind of woman to stay clearheaded around. "You had good questions. Smarter than most of the men."

"Thank you," she says with a slight nod. "I had more, too, that's why I asked your chief if I could interview you, and he was wary—he said it wasn't the sort of story a lady should be reporting on, but I just reminded him I'd been covering Mafia stories for over a decade. First published piece, I actually talked to some of them. Mobsters, I mean. Turns out they don't mind talking to the papers if you smile and bat your eyelashes and don't write anything libelous in print."

"You talked up mobsters?" I ask, impressed.

"Sure. They have stories, too, after all."

I nod, but don't tell her it could be a mobster's story I need to go looking for next if her post office lead doesn't pan out.

"So what kind of stories did the mobsters tell you?"

She smiles, but different than her usual showy grins. This is a small, private thing, a memory. "Oh, they started complaining about girlfriends, they like that. But then they complained about the job—all in code, of course. The shipments were late, and it wasn't their fault but someone was going to blame them anyway. They had someone working for them who was always late. Stuff like that. If you treat them like normal people with normal jobs, they're just like anybody else."

"And you were never scared, never threatened?"

She laughs and sips her martini. "Oh, I was scared. I was scared all the time. I'm scared right now. But that's fine, that's normal, and I pride myself on being able to push through the fear. It's exciting. In fact, I think it's what makes me a good reporter—my instincts. I can sense fear, because I'm so used to it myself. My father . . . he used to knock around my mother and me growing up."

"I'm sorry," I say.

She waves me off, sipping her martini again. "It's the past, and I don't like pity. But we were so scared of him, my mother especially. Because it wasn't like he was a drunk or anything—he just would suddenly get very angry if something wasn't to his liking. So we lived in fear. It wasn't until I moved out, took myself to college by working three jobs, that I realized I was different—to me, fear is like air. I breathe it all the time, so it's just part of me. But other people . . . well, they don't. So when they're afraid, I can pick up on it. Soothe them, or follow them to the source of their fear to get the story." She lifts her martini but doesn't drink from it, just stares over it, considering me. "I think that's why I'm so interested in you, Mr. Mills. You seem afraid. A big strong man like you, a cop who's gone up against the mob, former navy minesweeper—now that's a scary job. I remember it from research for my first article about you. So what could scare you now? That's where the story is."

Rose sips her martini, tilting her head back, and I stare at her neck. She's what scares me.

"That's quite a gift," I say.

She shrugs. "Surely you must have some skills of your own, to have done so well as an inspector."

I feel the corner of my mouth go up a little, the old pride. She sees it and cocks an eyebrow.

"I'm good at secrets," I say. "Spotting them."

"Why's that?"

Because I spent so much time hiding my own. But I'm not going to tell her that, so I just shrug. "Just born with it, I guess." I sip my drink now, to cover the lie.

"Well, I'd love that one. I love secrets." She smiles, holding her glass to her lips with both hands.

"You do?" I ask, surprised.

"Well, I love exposing them."

I swallow, not saying anything. The door to the kitchen swings open as a waiter brings something out, and for a moment there's the sound of clanging pots, sizzling food.

"Secrets are lies in a nice suit," Rose says, taking the stirrer out of her martini. "They're the parts of society we have to hide because they mean society is failing someone, and we're ashamed of it. Bring secrets into the light, tell the truth, and everyone is better for it."

"Not the people whose secret it was."

She tilts her head. "Maybe not in the short term, but in the long run . . ." She straightens her back out. She's been gradually leaning forward as we talk, vulturelike, but now her shoulders are down, her chin high. She pops the olive from the stirrer into her mouth, and then puts the stirrer back in the martini, one olive left. "I sent my father to prison. When I was twenty, I went home, and I saw him punch my mother, and I was ready this time. I'd bought a Simplex camera, one of those handheld ones, and I'd gotten good at it. Took the photo just as he slugged her. Went to the police. Even Mother couldn't deny it now, and it all came out. He went to prison and she divorced him. Married a lovely man, a Jew, if you believe it, and moved to St. Louis. He's very sweet, and I love seeing them on Christmas. Her life is good now, because a secret was exposed."

I nod, sip my drink. "Not every secret is like that. What about the husband who buys his wife an expensive fur to surprise her with?"

She laughs, long and loud. "Mr. Mills . . . Andy, may I call you Andy?" I nod. "And you should call me Rose. But, first of all, I'm not sure those men exist outside of romance novels. But if they did, I would say that that's no secret. That's just a truth waiting to be told. Not the same."

"How do you tell the difference?"

She rolls her eyes, genuinely annoyed with me but trying to make it look playful, and sips her drink. "You just do." She puts down her drink and dives into her purse for a moment before taking out a ruby-studded card case and opening it. She hands me one of her business cards: ROSE RAINMEYER, REPORTER. There's the address of the *Examiner,* and a phone number. "That's the general line, but they'll forward calls to my desk. Not really my desk, but *a* desk, anyway. If you have a hot tip on this case." She snaps her card case shut and then looks at me, expectantly. "Do you not have a card? I might want to reach you with a hot tip."

I pause. The number is unlisted, but she's plucky enough she might be able to trace the address anyway. But if I say no, she'll just get suspicious, and I know she'll see right through a lie about not having cards at all. So I take out one of the plain ones, just my name, and hand it to her. I wonder if this is how Howard felt, inviting Merle back to his place. Like he was playing with a loaded pistol.

"Just your name," Rose says, holding it in both hands and examining it. "Very chic, very in-the-know and hush-hush."

"That's the job," I say.

She considers that for a moment, still staring at the card, before putting it in her purse.

"Oh, here he is," she says, spotting a man who just walked in the door. She waves at him with just her fingers. He spots her and sighs.

"Let me talk," I tell her. "We want to keep my client out of this."

"Right," she says, still watching him. He doesn't look happy to see her, but walks over and sits down opposite, where the high-ball is waiting. He drinks half of it before even saying hello.

"Rose," he says finally.

"Hi, Tim," she says. "This is Andy Mills. Mr. Mills, this is my ex-husband, Tim Rainmeyer. I kept the name because it rolls off the tongue so nicely, don't you think? He's assistant to John Fixa, the postmaster general for San Francisco. Tim, Andy's a friend. We're working on a story together."

I turn to stare at her. Ex-husband? So much for not wanting secrets. Although maybe this is like a surprise fur—she always intended to tell me.

He looks over at me, his eyes up and down before he sighs. "Didn't tell you I was the ex, did she?"

"No," I say, looking at her again. She smiles. "She didn't."

He downs the rest of his drink in one sip, then motions for a waiter.

"Let's make this fast. What do you want?"

I nod, appreciating that. But I wish I had a little more time to think. The key here is that I can't mention any names; I don't want the bookstore to be something he thinks he should look into. I stay silent as he orders eggs, coffee, bacon, and another highball.

"I'm curious about any criminal cases the post office is pursuing in the city," I say when the waiter is gone.

He shakes his head. "There are more than you'd think. Mail fraud is more common these days. Scam artists, mostly. A few cases of people mailing things they shouldn't. We usually settle those, sometimes people don't know any better. Sometimes we have to sue . . . this a general piece on law and the mail?"

I nod. "So nothing recent and noteworthy?"

"I thought you said you were working on a story, not fishing for one," he says. He looks around for a waiter.

"Well—" I start.

"There's a particular bookstore," Rose interrupts. "Walt's, you know it? We're wondering if there's a case against it."

My body goes cold the moment she names the bookstore, like lead in the freezer. I knew a guy who hid bullets there. And that's how I feel, like a frozen bullet, about to be loaded and pointed right at her. I'm so angry. At her, and at myself for trusting her at all. I keep my face still, though, looking around the restaurant—the seatbacks between the booths are high, the tables spaced far away. No one seems to have heard. I turn back to Tim, studying him for a reaction.

He shakes his head. "Never heard of it. We should be looking into them?"

"No," I say quickly, and trying to think quicker. "They were just being . . . blackmailed." It sounds plausible. But I'm not sure where I'm going with it. The waiter comes back and sets down the highball and the coffee. The smell of the coffee is strong.

"Yes," Rose says. "There's . . . a rival store owner, you see . . ." She looks at me, eyes wide.

"He was threatening to tell you that this store was sending dirty magazines through the mail if they didn't let him buy them out," I say, the story coming together. "We were wondering if he'd followed through, and if so, what you do in cases like that— how you keep yourselves from being a blackmail tool, if, say, someone wants to put a place out of business?"

I watch him, but I can feel sweat forming on the back of my neck as I go back over what she just said. It sounds believable. It's definitely a lie, though, which I didn't think Rose would be so comfortable with. Maybe she realized she screwed up and was trying to make up for it.

He tilts his head, thinking, then straightens himself out, and looking directly at Rose, rattles off the kind of statement I used to hear the chief give to reporters. "The San Francisco Post Office investigates all claims of wrongdoing perpetuated through the mail. These investigations are not a burden on the investigated, and only turn into legal cases when warranted. We never go beyond the scope of our job, and we would never intimidate a business."

It's vague, clears them of wrongdoing, and means very little. Just like the chief's statements.

"So you'd never go after a business that wasn't doing anything wrong?" Rose asks.

"No. And we'd never go after one without an official complaint, which means filling out a form, or talking to someone and giving evidence of why you think wrongdoing is happening."

"And you'd never open the mail of someone without asking?" she asks. "Just to check on a complaint?"

He smirks. "If we did, and we didn't find anything, then the complaint would have been unwarranted to begin with, and no one gets in trouble."

"So you do read people's mail," she says, wagging a finger at him. "Naughty."

"Rose," he says, immediately tired.

"Well, thanks," she says, scooting out of the booth. "Always a pleasure to see you, Tim. Give my love to Janice."

"Absolutely not," he says, turning to me. "And I don't know you. But be careful with her." He jams his thumb in Rose's direction. "I used to work for the FBI. Brought home a case file. Next day it was on the front page. I had to divorce her just to get a job at the post office."

I stare at Rose, who's lifted her chin slightly. "The truth should be public."

"Not all of it, Rose." He doesn't even look up at her. She rolls her eyes and walks out, her heels clicking on the floor louder than usual.

"Thanks for the advice," I tell Tim, putting my hat back on. He doesn't say anything, just nods, weary, and I follow Rose outside, where she's waiting for me, her foot tapping.

"Rose—" I start.

"I'm sorry!" she says immediately. "It just slipped out." She bats her eyelashes.

"No, it didn't."

She tries a sheepish grin. "But it worked, didn't it?"

"Rose," I say with a sigh, and I realize I sound just like her ex-husband.

"I went along with your lie, didn't I? I knew I'd made a mistake, and I fixed it." She steps closer. "I am sorry, Andy. It really did just slip out. I'm not all as bad as Tim says—that file he brought home? The FBI was wiretapping private citizens without a warrant. He might have lost his job, but it stopped the wiretapping." She stares at me without blinking for a moment, then looks away. I notice she didn't say she lost her marriage. She looks back up, and shrugs. "Besides, now we know—the post office isn't investigating them."

"But they might, now."

She laughs. "No, they won't. Tim will forget all about this, look—" She glances in the window of the restaurant and I follow her gaze. His food has arrived, and his highball has been refilled. "He always does this after we talk. Has a few too many to try to erase the horrors of my company."

"I'm thinking I might need another, for the same reason," I say, though I believe her that DeeDee and Howard are probably safe from the feds. Tim didn't seem like he wanted to spend another minute thinking about this.

"So then, is the case closed?" she asks. "Is it really blackmail?"

I turn back to her. She is looking up at me, eager. She reminds me of a seagull, somehow, standing at your feet, pretending to beg for food, but really demanding it.

"I need to go see my client," I say, turning away from her and walking, not really caring about the direction.

"Oh, so may I—"

"No."

"Andy, please, I just helped you out."

"I will ask my client if they want to talk to you," I say, still not turning around. "Best I can do."

I hear her sigh and stop walking. "Fine," she says, disappointed. Then, more hopeful: "See you soon."

I wonder if she can sense how much fear those three words plant in me as they land in my back.

ELEVEN

Rose may be trouble, but she's right that unless her ex-husband was lying—and he didn't seem like the type who would bother—that it's not the post office who took Howard and the books, and without the post office, I doubt any other government agencies would know about them. Which means right now, the only other option is the mob. I'm tempted to go right to the casino, but Bridges would just put on his mask and tell me nothing again. I need more information on the book, and its author. Joe, the missing mobster, seems the most obvious candidate, but I'm not sure, and neither was DeeDee, which means Howard was keeping it secret. Even from her.

I wonder if that was at Joe's request. Or just Howard trying to protect her. A gay mob memoir means angry mobsters. I wonder if Joe might be having second thoughts himself, and decided to cancel publication—which Howard objected to. Writing it in the first place seems like suicide . . . though the way DeeDee talks about Howard, getting caught up in ideas, schemes . . . if he heard a bunch of stories from Joe, maybe he wrote them up himself. That would be suicide, too.

And I know a thing or two about suicide, the games I've been playing with the loaded gun that is Rose Rainmeyer. I'll need to investigate Joe and Howard more, but I want to check her out before she turns up around another corner. I head over to the library, the periodicals section. It doesn't take much digging to find Rose Rainmeyer's published pieces. There's the one she did on Jan Westman, where she interviewed me, and then going back about fifteen years there's more—some puff pieces or profiles of important women in the city, and then some of the crime writing she prefers to do—profiles of victims, mostly. Her work is sporadic, and credit is often shared with a man, even the one about the wiretapping that got her ex fired. There's even a few by R. Rainmeyer, like they didn't want anyone to see her name and know she was a woman. But the stories are always good. I take the time to read all the crime pieces; several on the mob, with surprisingly candid quotes from "unnamed sources" who are clearly high up in the Mafia. Or maybe just the one source, who she makes sound like a bunch of different guys. He's chatty, too, revealing a lot more than Bridges ever has to me.

There are also lots of interviews with victims of muggings, robbery. She has an ability to coax them, or maybe just an intuition for where the story really is, but she focuses on their experiences. She tells their stories compellingly, and paints them as fully realized people, complex, and undeserving of what's been done to them. And that makes the crimes seem that much worse.

It would all be swell, I suppose, except for those stories that clearly prioritize the truth, and her complex writing, over people's safety. A piece where she talks to Black dockworkers and quotes one by name saying they should be paid more—I'll bet that got him fired, or worse. An interview with a man in Chinatown who claimed his landlord refused to repair anything, and the police wouldn't help. He and his store are named. I wonder where his store is now, if he even has one. Even in the Jan Westman case, she spoke to a friend of Jan's, Amelia Carson, and then revealed that she had also been involved in the pornography Jan was forced into. That would probably ruin her life. The story takes priority over the people. Which is just what Rose has been telling me this whole time.

I can't find anything by her before 1936, but she might have been writing under her maiden name then, or maybe that's when she started—though she said it was when she was much younger. It doesn't matter—I know what I came to find out for sure; that under all the charm, she's just as dangerous as I thought she was. She might have been helpful, with her mob contacts, and under different circumstances, I might even like her. But I can't let Rose Rainmeyer keep digging into this story. I need to find Howard to find the list, or it's going to be much worse than that list getting out—it'll be me on the front page, and all my clients in danger.

Leaving the library, I half expect her to be there, waiting with a smile on her face and wiggling her fingers in a smile. But it's just the city, chilly and gray. I'm not better prepared for her, I realize. I just know even more what kind of threat she is. I need to focus on the case, the list, and that means I need to know more about the missing book, and there's one place I haven't looked yet.

I feel in my pocket for the key DeeDee gave me, and hop the streetcar back up to the bookstore, but walk past it, to where she said Howard's apartment was. It's afternoon now, and the neighborhood still smells like smoke and sweat, and the vague smell of drugs. I see a few kids in black reading a book together on a stoop, passing a cigarette between them. They look up when I walk past, and laugh. A few buildings down from them is Howard's building—star on the door, like DeeDee had said.

His apartment is on the ground floor, in the back. It's small and crowded, which makes it feel smaller. I call out Howard's name, but there's no reply. There's a little kitchenette, but the table and counters are all covered in books and papers, so I can't imagine he cooks much. The living room has a worn floral sofa with a dent on one side, and a coffee table in front of it. Both of those are also covered in books, letters, papers. On the table, there's an empty teacup with a picture of a knight on it, and next to that, a typewriter on the table, no paper in it, the ribbon worn and loose, faint imprints of all the words shared still on it. There's

a radio, but no TV, and the brown carpet underfoot smells like
dust. I open the door to the bedroom: an unmade bed, shelves of
books, some lying on the bed itself, some on the ground. The one
on the bed is *Tales of King Arthur and the Round Table*. The bathroom is the only place without any papers in it, but there's two
books piled on the back of the toilet. The windows look out on a
little garden behind the building. The shades are all drawn, and
without the lights on, the place is dark. He probably turned on
every lamp as soon as he got home, and then wandered around,
reading his books, his letters. And he clearly hasn't packed up,
running from the mob, or away with a lover. Wherever he is, he
wasn't expecting to be there this long.

I poke in the drawers and cabinets, looking for the list—a little
brown address book, DeeDee had said—but I don't find one. No
address books at all—which, when I look at all the letters around
the place, means he either had it on him, or he really is as good at
remembering addresses as everyone's said. Neither are comforting thoughts. I try looking for signs to his whereabouts outside
the letters, hoping for matchboxes, ticket stubs, receipts from his
favorite spots, but it soon becomes clear that if I want to figure
out what was going on in his life, how he spent his time aside
from reading, I need to go through his mail. I don't love the feeling, it's somehow a more intimate invasion than rifling in his underwear drawer; it's exactly what Rose Rainmeyer's ex-husband
talked about doing, what I thought could have started all this.
But if Howard's alive, and I find him through these letters, and
keep him from turning over addresses—like Pat's—then it'll be
worth it.

I start on the sofa, just trying to get a sense of what all the
letters are. Many of them seem to be from subscribers to the book
service: letters about books they loved, people thanking him for
recommendations, their feelings on what they've read, how they

loved it, or hated it, how they cried or threw the book across the room. Several thank him for introducing them to other pen pals—other people Howard was writing. They're friends now, too, through the letters, through Howard. Some are even more than friends. The letters also talk about books, about being gay, about how reading makes them feel, about movies, TV, theater, art, family. It's like a tapestry of readers—one Howard wove himself. A whole community, across California and a few other states, too. Joined by being gay, and stories about being gay. It's like the Ruby, but in writing. It's beautiful. I know I'm just a voyeur here, but reading them all, I feel like I'm part of something, a new family I didn't know about. I feel the sagging sofa grow more comfortable as I settle in, reading, becoming part of something, even just on the outside.

Some of the letters are romantic, or at least flirtatious. "Your mind is beautiful, Howard, I wish we could meet in person so I could see if your face matches." "Oh, Howie, I dream about us meeting in person someday, and drinking cocoa while talking books at a café, or maybe at my place?" I snort a laugh at that one, flipping through them. I wonder why he left these out if he was bringing Merle over. Maybe he trusted that Merle couldn't read them . . . but he could have been wrong. Merle seems fragile, but I've seen fragile people kill.

I keep looking through the letters, hoping for evidence of . . . what? A sign of where Howard could be? Something that would make Bridges tell me if he had him? Joe, maybe? There are a lot of letters from Joes.

It takes me about an hour just to go through every letter, looking at the names at the bottom of them. I divide all the Joes and Josephs in their own pile and read those first. Most of them are just thank-you notes, for books or recommendations. A few are flirty. None mention publishing a memoir, or being in the mob. Though I'd be surprised if they wrote that down.

I put the flirty ones aside, then go through all the rest of the letters. One letter, signed only *M*, says that he'd love to see more stories about criminal men—"we're all criminals, anyway"—and talks about organized crime. One talks about having fun at a casino with Howard, but it's from someone named Arthur, not Joe. A few letters talk about memoirs, though, and one of those is signed *J*.

DEAR HOWARD,

```
I agree with you that more gay memoirs need to be
published. I've often thought of writing one myself.
My life is very interesting, you understand. And the
men I've been with--the things I've done. I'd show you,
if you wanted. But how does one go about writing a
memoir? Do I just buy an electromatic typewriter and
start clacking away? There must be more to it than
that, right? Some art? Do you know the secret? I'd
love to discuss this in person. Stop by the milliner
sometime!
```

I'm not sure what a milliner is, but I'm pretty sure it's not where a mobster would be hanging out. Still, I make a note of it, and all the others. Only a few have addresses on their stationery, and only a few of those are even in the city, but visiting them feels like a waste. What I've found here isn't clues, it's a community. My community, I guess, if I read more. And this almost makes me want to. The people talk about books and the way they see themselves in these stories when they can't see themselves anywhere else. It reminds me of the first time I went to a gay bar, back in LA. I was nineteen, terrified. I had walked by the place a few times and it wasn't until the week before that I'd sensed something different about it. The men going in felt familiar in a way I couldn't place, like the guys I sometimes locked eyes with in regular bars, in the locker room in school, that electricity. I'd been afraid and drawn to it all at once, and told myself it was just a bar, there was no harm. Inside I realized exactly what kind of a place it was, though. The men let their fingertips brush each other, they laughed in high voices and let their wrists slope beautifully, terrifyingly, down to the ground.

I knew what a faggot was, of course. And I knew I might be one. But I never knew that we could get together in groups and laugh. I'd stood in the door for what felt like an hour before one man with a pencil mustache came over and laid his hand on my arm and said, "Don't be shy. You're new?"

I'd looked at him, and he looked at me, and I knew he saw me the way I saw him. I turned around and left. I heard him sigh as I did.

I wonder if I would have been braver if I'd seen myself not in a bar first, but in a book. With a book, I would have seen myself without feeling like someone else could see me. Safer. I envy these people, this group of gay book lovers. Maybe I will read more. When the case is over.

But if Howard knew all these people, and he had a real memory for addresses, then all the more reason to find him, and soon. It's not just Pat and baby Rina at stake. It's everyone writing these letters. Enough people to fill the Ruby twice over.

It's fragile, too. It may not have a central meeting spot like the Ruby, where the cops could find everyone, but if the police were to come in here, read these letters, see these names . . . a lot of people could be in trouble. All it would take is one of them mentioning the letters, the book club, and all these people . . . all of them would be in danger. But I don't think any of them would have done it. Not with the way they write Howard, with so much affection and appreciation. There are no threats, nothing angry, not even in the trash bin.

There are really only three suspects left; Bridges is the most obvious choice, or at least some mobster, who got wind of the book and decided to cancel its publication, or found out about the affair with Merle and decided to protect the family. This is the most frightening option, too, because they could easily already have dozens of names for blackmail, if they thought to ask. It could be Joe himself, having second thoughts about the memoir and deciding to go back on the deal. He could have taken Howard and the books and run, in which case Howard is probably already dead. This one I'm not sure about, because Joe is a big question mark in my mind. What kind of man would be a gay mobster? Violent? Or more like I was as a cop—arrogant, so proud of his hiding? Until I know more about Joe, I can't be sure. And then, it could have been Merle, in an act of jealousy. Did he know about the memoir? Did he know Joe? There was something so unsteady in his eyes, his wispy body. Howard was his only lifeline to the world outside the mob. He was everything to him. If Merle felt Howard had betrayed him in some way . . . well, all it would take would be one moment—Howard wasn't young, and Merle might be weak, but he's strong enough to hold a gun, and there are guns aplenty in his world.

But all roads lead me back to the Shore Club. I don't know how I'll get anything else out of Bridges, but I need to try. Maybe something else about Joe. If I knew more about him, I might know what's in the book that makes it worth taking all the copies of it. I pack up my notes and stare at the pile of letters. When they're stacked up, they look small. Paper is thin. But I can't just leave them here. If people are after Howard, just leaving them in plain sight isn't safe. Someone could come in and suddenly have so many names. Even though most of the addresses are gone, there are details in the letters. Enough to paint pictures. And they talk so openly. Too openly. One ripped envelope, and too much blood would pour out. I roll them up and stuff them in my inside pocket. They bulge a little.

The sun went down as I read the letters, and it's cool out and starting to rain, just a sad drizzle, but the kind that clings to your skin and gets inside and chills you. I wrap my coat tight against my body as I run down the street to Walt's.

I walk in the back door, not wanting to be too conspicuous, hoping to just leave the letters on the desk there. But DeeDee is back here, sitting at the desk, and turns with a gasp as I come in.

"Oh," she says, taking me in, her hand at her chest. "I thought you were . . . I thought . . ."

"Sorry," I say. "I didn't want to draw too much attention. You thought I was Howard coming back?"

She laughs at that, but softly. "No, no . . . I thought you were a mob hitman, come to take care of me." She shakes her head. "Don't know why I thought that . . . Howard . . . he would have come right in the front door. Whistling, probably, as though nothing had ever been wrong."

I smile a little at that thought, and then hold back a sigh as I take out the letters. "I went by Howard's place. He's not there. But I found these, and thought they might be safer with you . . ."

I hand her the letters. She takes them, pressing the soft pile in the middle, the ends opening like wings. She looks at them a moment before realizing what they are, then glances up at the desk, where a similar pile, but unopened, sits.

"All these people . . ." she says.

"Maybe he still will come in whistling," I say.

She laughs, sadly. "He always did. Even the time he forgot to lock up and we were robbed—cleaned out the till, some of the books, front door wide open. It rained that night, too. Ruined a rug by the door . . . He strode right in, wet rug, shelves a mess, whistling all the way to the register in the back where I was. Then he saw my face and looked around and said, 'What's wrong?'" She laughs again, and shakes her head.

"That doesn't seem like it should be a happy memory."

"It's . . . a Howard memory," she says with a shrug. "So many of them are like that. We had a different location, you know, our first year? Thought it made sense to rent from someone in the community. Young man who'd inherited the building. He liked us. Howard especially. And Howard liked him . . . and then he didn't. That's why we moved. I was furious when I found out why we were being kicked out. But Howard found us this place, bigger, lower rent, more customers, and . . . I could never stay mad at him too long. He was my friend. So many people's friend . . ." She sighs and puts the letters on the desk in a pile, next to the unopened ones, and pats them down, like the head of a child. "I don't know how I'll . . . This is what he was good at, you know." She taps the stack of letters again. "Talking to people about books, getting people to buy them. The one thing he always wanted to do, and has always stayed true to—selling books."

"How about you?" I ask. "You always sell books?"

"Oh, no. I mean, always worked with them. Howard got a job right after college at a bookstore and worked at a dozen more over the years. Not me, I loved books but I tried my hand at other sides of it. After secretarial school, I worked for a publisher for twenty years, but the company closed down, so that's when I tried being a librarian. Only started at a bookstore about fifteen years ago, and five years into that, Howard told me he wanted us to open a store together."

"So you stayed friends through all those years, those different jobs?" I ask.

She laughs, leaning back in her chair, her feet leaving the floor for a moment. "Of course we did, of course. He was the first person I told . . . and I was the first person he told. A thing like that . . . we didn't even meet other gay people for a decade after. We just had us, and our books, to feel less alone. We were a little book group, just the two of us, met every Sunday, like it was church. Read a gay book, talked about it. Every week. More than that, of course, we met for coffee most afternoons, and lunch when we could, and we just talked about our lives, movies, books . . . Howard's problems. He always had problems. Got fired so often, and then I had to get him a new job through a friend or something."

"What did he get fired for?"

She pats the edge of the desk, inviting me to sit, and scoots back in her chair as I do so. "Lateness, mostly. He decided to go for a walk through the park, or stayed up all night reading, and then he was late. Once he decided to repaint the store's sign without the owner's permission. He's always been impulsive. Always follows his heart."

"And you always cleaned up after him?"

She shrugs. "Like a big sister. That's what we are, I think, after all these years. Big sister, little brother. Even if we're the same age. And we've kept that book group going for decades. Even after we met other gay people, even after I met my Suzie." She takes her purse off the desk and fishes out her wallet and from there takes out a small photo that she holds up for me. A white woman of forty or so, smiling at the camera, with a narrow face, pointed nose, and short frizzy bob. DeeDee turns the photo back to her and smiles at it, hugs it, before putting it back. "She came along, too, of course; she loved to read—she was a poet. It was a few years back when . . . she got sick. That's when I decided to start trying to publish our own books, too . . ." She looks up at the shelves of books in the store and then, with a sad smile, walks toward one of them.

"So, it was your idea to publish your own books?" I ask, surprised.

"Well, yes, but Howard loved it. I ran it at first, mostly because I knew how it worked. Printers, typesetters, binders . . ." She stands suddenly and leads me out into the main shop as she talks. It's empty, no customers, the windows dark with the rain, drops tapping on the glass. "She was so good. Used to spend time with Gertrude Stein, in Paris. Stein said she had talent!" She stops at a shelf where five or six identical books are laid. She pulls one down and hands it to me. *The Last Time, Poems* by Suzanne Ward. "But no one would publish her work, and so, when she got sick, I thought that if I did . . . maybe she'd get better." She shakes her head.

"I'm sorry she didn't," I say.

"It was a foolish notion," DeeDee says, throwing her hands up in the air, and walking to the register. I follow her, still holding the poetry book. "Silly . . . fantasy. But once we did one book, I thought there are so many good books out there that never get published. So I did another. Howard helped, of course, helped me find writers, but I chose the books, did the editing. I read them to Suzie, even as she . . . She was so proud of me." She smiles, then plucks the book from my hands. "But then, after she passed . . . I decided to take some time off. Left it all to Howard. So he chose the next book . . ." She glances at the back room. "And look how that's gone."

"So the missing book was Howard's first book?" I ask.

She takes Suzie's book and looks at it a moment. "Well, he helped on all the others, like I said, but that was the first one he picked out, edited . . ." She pulls out brown paper from under the register and starts to wrap the poems. "When I finally felt up to coming back he was so excited, but wanted to keep it a surprise for a little while. Said it was going to knock my socks off. Didn't tell me until . . . just before. I was tired so I let him keep his secret until then. Wanted to ease back into it, and he'd already decided to completely reorganize the books in the store, so I had to learn all that." She chuckles, taping the paper around the book and finishing it with a ribbon. Her hands move with an ease from years of practice. "That's Howard, though." She hands the wrapped book to me. "A gift. For helping."

It seems rude to refuse, so I take it. "Thank you." It's a small book, fits in my inside pocket. I almost want to ask her more—more about Suzie, about Howard, about their years together—but the bell rattles as a man comes in, newspaper held over his head because of the rain.

"You looking for something, or just seeking shelter?" DeeDee asks him, her eyes crinkling at the corners as she smiles.

"I'm looking for something for my son," he says. "He's nine now. Something we can read together at bedtime. He loves fairy tales and knights and all that."

She smiles and comes out from behind the corner and goes to a shelf, pulling down a book with a shiny green-and-yellow dustjacket. *The Merry Adventures of Robin Hood.* "I think I have just the thing."

I leave as she walks toward him, arm outstretched with the book. Outside the rain is soft, hitting the pavement like the murmuring of people in a theater. I ride the trolley back to Fisherman's Wharf. The rain hasn't kept everyone inside, at least not here. Neon signs in the shape of fish are reflected in the water, distorted by the rain rippling its surface. It becomes a mess of colors and the occasional recognizable part of a sign—an eye, a fin—and makes it so when I look away, and back at the street, the real signs are too bright. People huddle under awnings, or rush between them into restaurants, sometimes laughing at the chill of the rain.

I turn down the alley and walk to the Shore Club. No awnings down here to keep me dry, and the pavement gets slick under my feet. Inside, the doorman smiles at me again.

"Getting wet out there, huh?" he asks as I shake my hat off.

"Nah, that's just me," I tell him. "Got my own personal rain cloud."

He laughs as he opens the door. Inside, the band is playing on stage, but Merle isn't up there singing. It's more crowded than last time, swarms of people around the tables, shouting at their wins and losses. I spot one man in the corner openly sobbing into his hands. Cigarette smoke trails through the air in the shape of handwriting, cursive, old—or maybe that's just how my eyes see things after reading all those letters. I weave my way through the crowds to the bar, and Bridges, who sits on the same stool as before, both stools on either side of him empty, even as others crowd the bar farther down. He's smoking a cigar that veils half his face in smoke as I approach, but the other half smiles at me.

"Hello again, Andy. You think about my offer any?"

"Still working on this case," I say. "Need to do things one at a time."

He nods, not offended. "I understand that. I always tell the boys, one thing at a time. Do it well, then move on to the next. I thought yours might not be finished yet. Someone else was in here looking for Howard last night."

"Oh?" I ask, trying not to look too curious.

"Some broad, just said she wanted to know if his debts were

still open. I said he owed a few bucks, and she paid. I thought maybe she was the widow or something."

I shake my head. "She paid? Was she a reporter, maybe? Rose Rainmeyer? Forties?"

He grins. "You know Rose? She's great, but it wasn't her. No, no, she was older, maybe sixty, short curly gray hair."

DeeDee. She didn't mention having come here. Made it sound like she went straight to the bookstore. I wonder why.

"Well, I guess a lot of people are missing him," I say carefully. "Any chance he's hiding out with Joe, wherever he is?"

Bridges smirks and turns away, reaching for his drink. "Could be."

"And you don't know where that could be?"

He shrugs theatrically. I'm really not getting any more out of him.

"Tell me this, then. Was Joe a reader?"

That seems to crack his mask for a moment, as he looks confused. "A reader? Like of obituaries?"

"No, just books."

"I really wouldn't know. Joe, he was a good coworker, but we weren't pals, you know? Always did his job excellently, but we weren't in a book club together, if that's what you're asking."

"I'm asking if he read, maybe wrote."

He scoffs. "I don't think he harbored any literary aspirations, no. Not many in our business do. We like telling stories, don't get me wrong, but there are the ones we tell each other, and the ones we tell other people. The ones we tell other people are usually pretty boring. And the ones we tell each other aren't fit for publication." He sips his drink. "Why do you ask?"

"There are some missing books, that's all," I say. "Missing Howard, and missing books. You don't know anything about any of that?"

He smiles, the mask fully back on. "Not a thing, Detective. What would books have to do with the man?"

I can't tell if he's goading me with his lies or genuinely doesn't know.

"What kind of a man was Joe, anyway?" I ask.

He considers the question, debating if he can answer it. "Like I said, he was a good coworker. Diligent. He made the headlines a while back. You can find that yourself, so there's no harm in telling you. Someone had managed to infiltrate a piece of our organization, and Joe sniffed him out, and took care of it, made a show. Not that anyone could prove anything, of course. Had to leave town for a little while. Came back a hero. People liked him. He was a planner—always saw steps ahead. Smart, that way. We all miss him."

"Sure," I say, nodding. "Sounds like a good guy to have around."

"Oh, for sure. Between his charm, his foresight, his instincts . . . the boss misses him something terrible."

"Then I'm surprised he hasn't tracked him down," I say.

He takes a drag on his cigar, looking at the stage, but doesn't say anything more. I follow his glance and see Merle walking out onto the stage. He looks worse than before, his bow tie undone, his face pale and sweaty. He smiles and a few people clap for him. His eyes look all around the audience, and then looks all over again, searching, but his eyes passing over everyone, including me. Eventually he stops, forcing a smile, his eyes wide with something—fear, grief, maybe both. He turns to the band, and they start playing "It Had to Be You," skipping the prelude. Merle starts to sing, his voice as beautiful as last time, even if he doesn't look as well.

"It had to be you," he sings, clutching the microphone in front of him a little too hard. "It had to be you. I wandered around, and I finally found, the somebody who . . ." His other hand reaches up to grab the microphone, steadying himself on it. He's wobbling. I stand up, and next to me, so does Bridges. "Could make me be true, and could make me be blue. And even be glad"—his voice is turning breathier—"just to be sad. Thinking of—" The note dies out as he collapses backward onto the stage. The band stops playing in a clamor, all of them surrounding Merle on stage. Bridges is running for him, and I follow.

"Give him some air, give him some air," Bridges says to the band, who immediately back off. Merle is lying on the stage, his knees bent, one arm out to his side, the other curved so his hand rests over his heart. "Merle?" Bridges says, kneeling down and turning his face up. His eyes are closed. "Merle." He lightly smacks Merle's face, and Merle's eyelids flutter gently, eyes opening, but not seeing yet. Bridges looks around, but the other Mafia guys are still at their posts, so it's only me and the band. "Andy, could you give me a hand bringing him back to his dressing room?"

"Of course," I say, kneeling to lift Merle's shoulders. Bridges takes his legs and we walk him offstage.

"Play, just play anything," Bridges says to the band, who scramble back to their instruments. An uncomfortable jazz starts to play as they try to find a melody, and I follow Bridges's lead, carrying Merle to the back of the room and through a door marked STAFF.

Behind it is a hallway, dimly lit, and we go down to another door, with a star, Merle's name carved into it. Bridges carefully twists the knob open, still holding Merle's feet, and then leads me into a plush blue dressing room. There's a black sofa we put Merle down on, and then Bridges rushes out without saying anything. I stare down at Merle, who looks up at me, his eyes starting to come into focus.

"You all right?" I ask, kneeling next to him.

He closes his eyes and murmurs something I can't make out.

"What?" I lean in closer.

"'s dead," Merle whispers into my ear. "I saw his ghost. Howard is dead."

TWELVE

"What do you mean, you saw his ghost?" I ask, wondering if Merle spotted Howard somewhere, if Bridges is holding him somewhere.

"In the audience," Merle whispers. "His chair was empty. Like a ghost. He's dead. I just know he's dead." He starts to sob, but quietly, someone who's had to hide crying his whole life. I take out a handkerchief and give it to him, but he doesn't even move his hand to take it. "He was supposed to be my Galahaut. He was supposed to save me."

"We don't know he's dead yet," I say quietly. We're alone, I realize. This could be my only chance to ask him anything before Bridges comes back. "I'm still trying to find him. I need to save him."

"No, no," he says quickly. "Galahaut doesn't need saving. Only Lancelot. He saves him."

"Well, maybe he's more like Arthur, then," I try.

"No, Arthur never needed saving." His voice drifts off, and he looks at the floor. "Who will rescue me now?"

"I'm still trying to find him," I say, reassuring as I can. "He might still rescue you. Did you know Joe? Howard's friend, the other mobster. Do you know where he is?"

Merle stares at me, but it's like he's looking through me. I'm not even sure he's heard me until he shakes his head. "Never really knew him. Howard said he was nice, but we didn't talk about him much."

"You don't think they were lovers?" I ask carefully.

His eyes focus immediately, bullets fired right at me. "No," he hisses. "Howard would never."

The door opens and Merle's whole body shudders. Bridges walks in and looks between the two of us, confused. He's holding a glass of ice water, which he brings to Merle.

"You all right?" he asks.

Merle is demure, his eyes fluttering closed again, then open. They're not on fire anymore. His face is practically slack.

"I don't know what happened," he says to his uncle. "I didn't feel well, and then I got dizzy, and . . ."

Bridges nods. "You've been working too hard. You sing all night, you practice all day. You gotta rest, kid." He looks genuinely worried. His mask is gone, and he's softer without it, older. He seems to remember I'm in the room and turns back to me, the mask slowly falling back into place, but uncomfortable now. He doesn't like me seeing him like this. He doesn't want me here. "Thanks, Andy," he says, and nods.

I nod back. "Feel better, Merle," I say, and turn to the door. There's a dressing gown hanging on a hook there, and as I open it, I slip one of my cards into the pocket. The one with the address, but no name. Hopefully, he'll know it was me—it doesn't look like anyone else comes in here. It's a risk, but this way at least he'll know he can reach out. I have to help this kid—either to get out, or to get help somewhere far away from where he could hurt people, if that hardness I just saw drove him to kill. I've seen that kind of hardness. I think I was close to having it myself, back when I was a cop. So paranoid and scared that I would have done anything to protect whatever made me happy—if I'd had anything that did. Merle had his fairy tale with Howard. Without it, he's collapsing inward, a tree hollowed out from the inside, eaten away by rot.

Outside in the casino, everything has gone back to normal. The band is playing over the clatter of dice and roulette, people are murmuring, shouting, pleading with Lady Luck to change just one thing. Just like Merle must be doing—just one thing. I wonder if the one thing is bringing Howard back from wherever he is, or making himself no longer interested in men. Bridges, too, if he knows, asking for just one thing—for his nephew not to be a fairy. Everyone is hoping for something. I push my way out amongst the gamblers, out into the street, where the rain has turned earnest, falling in fat drops on the brim of my hat, then sliding off in thin strands like a spiderweb.

At the Ruby, the rain hasn't kept people away. Coming here after the Shore Club is like sitting down by the fire after a day in the snow. It's warm and crowded, the place already smelling like gin, perfume, and that lipstick smell again. Lee is on stage, singing "Till I Waltz Again With You" as couples slow dance across the floor.

Both the Ruby and the Shore Club are illegal, for different reasons. People go to both these clubs because they're desperate, though—all that changes is what they're desperate for, and how the place gives it to them. The Shore Club doles out luck and winnings on whim, if ever, making people come back, but the Ruby is generous with what people need. Here, we're all in it together. Lee is at the mic in a blue dress, looking out over the crowd like she's their mother. She's making them feel safe. Making them feel loved. And she loves doing it.

If Merle could sing at a place like this, I wonder if he'd be more like that. Or at least not so scared. He's got a great voice, he'd be good here. I'm not sure he could ever break away, though. It would be too dangerous—if any mobster ever saw him again, and reported back to Bridges . . . like me and the cops. When I was working for the police, I broke myself in two, became two shadows instead of a person. Merle seems to have done the opposite, and gathered himself up like too much fabric, trying to wrap it around himself over and over, getting lost in it, feeling so much he faints.

I breathe it in as I sit at the bar. Gene isn't here. Instead, Pat is behind the bar. He's got a towel over one shoulder, and is wearing his butler's outfit—black vest, white shirt—running around making drinks. He's smiling, flirting a little, too. He's always been good-looking, even though he's close to sixty, with a lot of his dark hair streaked with silver, but it's his smile that always made Pat most attractive. It's welcoming, reassuring. It feels like the smile of an old friend, even when you first meet.

I take a seat by the bar, and wait for him to come over. He finishes a few other orders first, then sidles up with a smile. "What'll it be, stranger?" he asks.

"The feds don't have the list," I tell him.

His face, already smiling, starts to melt, the slow melt of candle wax, from his professional smile to relief so intense he might cry. He puts his elbows up on the bar to cradle his face for a moment and I sling my hand around the crook of his arm.

"It's okay," I say. "It's okay."

He looks up, his eyes red. "So Rina is safe? I can go home?"

I take a deep breath. "Rina is safe. Yes. But . . . the mob may still have the list—or have Howard. They could reach out to blackmail you."

He snorts a laugh. "How?"

"By threatening to tell your employers about you . . . and if your employers don't seem to care . . ."

"So I'd have to pay, to protect them."

"Yes. Which is why I think it makes sense for you to stay here, just a little longer, until I finish this up."

He nods. "All right. Yes. That makes sense. We have to tell

them, though. Elsie . . . she's not back yet. Pearl found a book we missed cleaning up, one of her Sappho translations, and she called in a panic, so Elsie drove up there to take it. She should be back soon. We can tell her, and then we can tell the family."

"Okay," I say. "That sounds like a good plan." I look around the bar, the red wallpaper like a warm fireplace. "You know where Gene is?"

"Elsie sent him home early, said he looked tired."

"Oh." I try not to sound too disappointed. He must have looked really tired for her to send him home. Maybe I should call him. I hate not telling him about my day, not hearing about his, and he seemed pretty upset about the delivery guy this morning. But if he was tired, and he's sleeping now, I don't want to wake him, either. "There was this delivery guy this morning . . . he seemed upset. Say anything about that to you?"

Pat shakes his head. "He was working most of the day. He had to show me the ropes, and then he was calling up liquor places . . . I didn't understand why, to be honest. But he was also so helpful in getting a list together of places I can stay instead of Elsie's— friendly YMCAs and the like. He knew a dozen of them. He's clever, your boyfriend."

"Yeah." I realize I'm smiling. "So you got along?"

"He's great," Pat says. "Good boss, too. Wasn't hovering or anything. And funny. He's very funny. But he was also tired, I could tell. Especially after all those calls he was making."

I hold my smile, but feel a little sad for a moment, knowing Pat got so much time with him, and I didn't. It's a silly thought, though, and I try to brush it away.

Lee finishes her song to a long round of applause, curtseys, and then walks offstage, over to me, where Pat sets a drink down in front of her.

"Thank you, sweetie," Lee says to Pat. "I hope you stay for a while. Gene makes a great martini, but your gin fizz beats his."

"The secret is extra gin," Pat says. Someone down the bar calls out to him, and he dashes off to make another drink.

Lee turns to me and looks me up and down. "You live upstairs, you could go dry off before sitting down."

"I didn't want to miss a note," I say.

She sips her drink, smiling. "Save some of that for Gene."

"He went home. Apparently Elsie thought he looked tired."

"He did," Lee says.

"There was this delivery guy he was arguing with earlier," I say. "I tried to help but . . . maybe it wasn't enough."

"Maybe." She shrugs, her emerald earrings catching the light. "I know it's been rough for him, taking over. People don't take him seriously."

I nod. "Because he's not white. That was this asshole."

"Exactly."

"I just wish I could help more. I want to . . . I hated the way that guy was talking to him."

"He can handle it. That's part of the job for him, and he knows it. Same as for all of us."

"I'm just even more upset he's not here for me to try cheering him up."

She tilts her head back and laughs loudly. "You can cheer him up, can you? Because you're such a cheerful guy?"

I snicker. "I can be cheerful. When I'm with Gene, anyway."

She rolls her eyes, but she's grinning. "That's almost adorable. But he should sleep. Cheer him up tomorrow. For now, tell me how the case is going."

Part of my deal with Lee is that I tell her all about the cases I'm working on. She loves crime stories, and issues of *Inside*

Detective aren't nearly as exciting as knowing a real live PI. So, in soft whispers that others at the bar can't hear, I tell her—about Merle, and the look in his eyes; Joe, the missing and possibly gay mobster; DeeDee, and her lying about where she'd been; and Bridges, who admired Joe, but doesn't want to talk about him. And then I tell her about Howard, and his letters—his friends, readers, the family he built with just ink on paper. We drink as I tell her, and she asks questions, and around us the club dances, the red wallpaper barely visible from the people.

"Yeah, Howard loves to talk books," Lee says, staring at her drink, now mostly empty.

"Reading all those letters, I sort of feel like I should read more."

"You should." She waves at Pat, who brings over a fresh drink. "Why don't you?"

I shrug. "I was never the type, I guess."

"Types change. You prove that more than most."

I stare out at the room. Two women dance by, nearly right in front of us, both in long dresses, one throwing her head back in a laugh. In their clasped hands is a lit cigarette, I don't know whose.

"Pat lent me this book, months ago, *The Homosexual in America*."

"You still haven't returned it," Pat says. "But you can keep it. I bought another."

Lee laughs. "Pat, you seem like a very nice man, and you are an excellent bartender, but look at him." She points at me, still dripping wet. "Look at this man. Does this seem like a man who wants to read a harrowing autobiography about the injustices people like us face every day?"

"It's an important book," Pat says. "And when I gave it to him he . . . needed perspective."

Lee tilts her head. "That may be. But he doesn't read."

"I didn't know that."

"We need to find him a more introductory book. Something compelling without being dense."

"Something fun." Pat nods in agreement. He turns to me, at least one of them remembering I'm right next to them. "Try *The City and the Pillar*, by Gore Vidal. It's about a young man just sleeping his way around the country."

I laugh. "You think that's the sort of book I should start on?"

"Yes," Lee says simply. "Perfect choice." She smiles at Pat, then turns back to me. Pat spots another customer and goes to make another drink.

"I don't know if that's the right book . . ."

"What, you want a fairy tale, like Merle?" Lee asks. "You won't buy in to those. Though it sounds like Merle does. Like he's having a hard time separating truth from fiction, waiting to be rescued by his knight."

"Yeah." I shake my head and light a cigarette. "Sounds like Howard never read him this memoir." The smoke from my cigarette tastes soft, grassy, and smells like a fireplace.

"Joe's memoir," Lee says. "I think you're right about that. I'd love to read it. Sure, Bridges told you about Joe, but you never got an ending."

I nod and tap my cigarette into the bar ashtray. "Yeah, I'm hoping I can figure out Howard's story, too."

"DeeDee told you plenty of those, right? She talks so much there's too many stories, but she told you about who Howard was, about growing up with him."

"We all tell stories," I say, watching the dancing couple again. The cigarette was both of theirs, apparently. One woman takes a drag and then places it in the mouth of the other, both of them still dancing as she does so. "Tell them to ourselves, mostly. Those are always the easiest lies to pick out, the ones people keep telling themselves."

Lee shrugs, slow, elegant, her shoulders like slow waves, and lays one hand flat on the bar. "I don't think lies are the same thing. These are stories of who they want to be." One finger of her hand on the bar curls up. "How they want people to see them." Then another. "You write them all the time for our matchmaking clients." Another finger curls. "And when you call your mother." She arches an eyebrow and lifts the hand to her drink. Lee has heard me on the phone when my mother has called. She sips, watching me.

"Isn't that just a fancy way of saying a lie?" I ask. The Ruby is packed with liars now, their energy steady, joyful. Because they're not liars here. Here they tell the truth, or something closer. They laugh and dance and drink and tell the truth. I look out at all of them and think of the letters and the truths in those, too.

Lee shrugs again and sips her drink. "What's the truth, then? What's a true story?"

I think about what Rose had said before. "There's a reporter," I say, turning back to Lee. "She's bumped into me at city hall and has been hounding me during this case—useful, because her ex-husband works at the post office, so she got me a little information, but . . ."

"A reporter?" She narrows her eyes. "That's dangerous, Andy."

"I know. I'm . . . handling it best I can. But I couldn't shake her, so . . ."

"So you're telling her a story."

I nod. "One that protects everyone. Hopefully one too boring to print."

"That's quite a gamble."

"I didn't feel like I had any other choice. She was going to look into the bookshop even more if I didn't help her." I shake my head. "It's like she was waiting for me in the DA's office."

"Reporters sniff out stories—and like I said, there are a bunch going around. Including yours."

I laugh. "Mine?"

"I'd read that book," Lee says, raising her glass in a toast.

"It would be pretty short and boring. And if my name were on it . . ." I sigh.

"Yeah. That's why she's dangerous. But she's right to think there's a story in you. You just have to make sure she never finds it out."

"I think by working with her, I've got her under control. I'm going to tell her the case is cracked, I was just investigating a shakedown, and with her help, we know the threat was toothless, so I just . . ." I shrug. "I dunno, I told the blackmailer off."

"Say you punched him, that'll make it even more boring." She nods at the idea.

"It will?"

"Former cop turned dirty detective?" She raises her hand like she's printing out a headline in the air. "That's an old story. No one cares about that."

I frown, thinking of people seeing me that way. "I've been working hard not to be that guy . . ."

"I know. But it's the safer thing to tell her. Be a dime-a-dozen PI and she'll think there's nothing there. Don't let your pride get in the way. You know who you really are. And so does everyone who matters to you, right?"

"I hope so." Especially Gene. I swallow, thinking of him seeing me as the kind of PI who beats people up and takes the kind of dirty photos that ruined his life. I wish he were here to weigh in on this. I sip my drink. "Right," I say. "People who matter will know the real me." I hope.

"They will. It's the smart play. A boring story."

I nod and take my notebook out of my pocket and flip to the page with the notes on Howard's letters. "So, you know any of these names? They were the ones I noticed in the letters. Joes, and *J*s, and Arthur who mentioned a casino."

Lee looks over the list, frowning.

"And do you know what a milliner is?"

She throws her head back and laughs. "Hats, Andy. Ladies' hats. And if it's a gay *J* milliner, it's probably Joshua Cantor, he has a place on Eddy Street. Does a decent business, though he's no Mr. John."

"Okay . . . so not Joe."

"No." She laughs, looking over the rest of the list. "I know a lot of Arthurs, but none who I've heard of frequenting casinos, and these other Joes . . . you only have two last names."

"A lot of the letters were on plain stationery, nothing personal, and the envelopes were all mixed up, I don't even know if they're all connected."

She nods. "Well, of these two, I don't know Joe Pucci. Maybe he's not in San Francisco, or just doesn't leave the house much. I do know Joseph Woolfrey, though—he's definitely not a mobster."

"What is he?"

"A bore."

I laugh. "Sure that's not just a front?"

"He works as a personal aide for an old woman just outside the city. Holds her purse when she goes shopping, cleans the house, that kind of thing. He talks about nothing else. If it's a cover story for his secret mob life, it's very convincing."

"All right, I'll put him low on the suspects-who-could-be-Joe list."

"If he's still alive," Lee says.

"Yeah, if that."

"I'll ask around—if anyone dated a mobster, I'm sure people would be talking about it, even in whispers."

"Thanks, Lee. If you can find him, that would be a big help."

Lee grins. "What kind of girl Friday would I be if I weren't a big help?"

"Still the best I got. But be careful, okay? There's a chance Joe changed his mind about the book getting out there, and he would be upset to find out people are asking about it."

Her face flickers for a moment, serious, and she nods. Then a fan comes up to Lee, and she smiles, and he asks to buy her a drink, which she allows, chatting with him for a little bit. I watch and try not to think about how the day has gone—the chief, Rose. I look across the bar and hope Gene will be there, reaching out for my hand with his cold fingers. But he's sleeping, and he needs it. And I need to focus on what to do next for the case. Maybe DeeDee can help me find Joe—she must have known something about him, about the book, even if she doesn't know it. I'll try her again tomorrow, and see why she lied about when she got into town, too.

"You look almost as tired as your boyfriend," says a voice behind me. I turn around, and it's Elsie. She's understated tonight, in a black suit, and if anyone looks tired around here, it's her.

"It's been a long day," I say. "How is the family?"

"Worried. Any progress?"

"Yes." I look back to the bar, and motion Pat over so he can be there when I say it to Elsie. "The feds don't have the list. The only way Mrs. Purley gets it is if the Mafia sells it to her, and I'm pretty sure Mrs. Purley wouldn't deign to do business with the mob. If they even have it."

Elsie breaks out in a smile of relief that makes me feel lighter. "Oh, that's good." She turns to Pat, and reaches across the bar to hug him. "That's really good."

"Yeah, but the mob hasn't been ruled out yet. And Howard is still missing. Which means they might try to blackmail Pat . . ."

"So I'm going to stay here a little while longer, if it's okay with you," Pat says to Elsie.

"Of course it is," she says, smiling. "Pat, you're family, too.

I know it's Pearl who says that all the time, tells you you're family, and you, too, Andy. But . . . we all feel it. You working for us . . . that's just so we can take care of you like you take care of us."

I smile, and meet eyes with Pat. I know he's thinking the same thing—that Elsie believes what she's saying, even if she doesn't quite understand that it's not the same.

"Still," I say, "I wish I had better news. Howard back safe and sound, the list in his pocket."

"I wish you had that, too, but this will be good enough news that when I tell Margo and the rest of them they'll feel relieved. In fact, let's go call them together."

"Isn't it late?" I ask.

"Didn't you hear me? None of them are sleeping. This will help." She motions for me and Pat to follow.

Pat looks around. "Gene is off, so I'm the only . . ."

"Oh, right," Elsie says. "Damn."

"Go tell them without me," Pat says. "Tell them . . . I'm sorry. I'm glad it's better now, though. And . . . I'll be home soon, if they'll still have me."

"Of course they will," Elsie says. "Though honestly, you're a great bartender. How much do they pay you? Think I can beat it?"

Pat laughs, waving us off. "Go tell them."

Elsie gives the bar a quick survey before walking out, and I follow her upstairs to my office, where she calls the house. Margo picks up and Elsie puts her cheek next to mine, the phone on both our ears as she talks.

"Who is calling this late?" Margo asks, her voice iron. "It's incredibly inappropriate and—"

"It's me, baby."

"Oh." Margo's tone immediately turns softer.

"I have Andy, he says it's not the post office."

There's a long breath through the receiver, so soft I think it could just be static at first.

"Really?" Margo asks, finally.

"Really," I say. "We haven't ruled out the mob yet—I'm working on if they even know the list exists or something else is going on—but I talked to a guy at the post office. They don't know anything about the book service."

"Okay," Margo says.

"That's great, right?" Elsie asks.

"It is . . . let me . . . everyone is still wandering the house . . . I'm in the living room, smelling flowers—oh, here's Pearl. It's Andy and Elsie. They say the feds don't have the list."

"Oh, gracias a Dios," I hear Pearl's voice say in the background, and I can picture her face, the way she takes a deep breath of relief, bending over slightly. "I'll go let everyone know."

"Maybe we'll actually get some sleep tonight," Margo says. "Thanks, Andy. Now get your ear off the phone so I can say something private to Elsie."

I step away and watch Elsie smile silently, listening for a moment.

"You too," she says, before hanging up, and turning to me. "See? They needed that. I think she was falling asleep as she hung up."

"I doubt that, based on your smile."

She shrugs. "I'm going to sleep, too. And so should you."

"I will. But one other thing first: the number for my office—the one on my cards—that's unlisted, right? No one can find this place from it?"

"The phone company, maybe. Why? You give your card to someone you shouldn't have?"

"Yep."

She looks me up and down. "Well, I'm sure you had your reasons."

"I did. But maybe, if you can, call the company up and see exactly what someone could find out if they wanted."

She crosses her arms. "What kind of someone?"

"Ah . . . a reporter. And my old police chief."

Her arms drop and she closes her eyes. "Andy."

"The chief got it off someone he picked up, found it in his pocket. We knew that was possible."

"That's why we have the ones without your name."

"I know, but some people get the ones with the name, some without. He says he won't trace it as long as I don't talk to the reporter."

Her arms drop with her jaw. "The one you gave your card to?" Her voice is loud. She's not wrong. I'm taking too many chances.

"Better she thinks we're working together and I have nothing to hide. But you might want to call the phone company and find out what kind of privacy they have."

She sighs, glaring at me for a while, but finally nods. "Fine. I'll do it in the morning. But Andy—"

"I know. I don't like it either. But it was the best of a lot of bad options. And everyone knows what kind of club this is—if she reports on it, it'll be about me. Ex-cop, gay PI. And if that happens, I'll leave. Go to LA or something."

She sighs, suddenly looking very sad. "We'll figure it out, if it comes to that."

"Yeah."

She sighs and turns around, leaving my office, but waiting in the hall. I follow, and lock up.

"Weren't you going to bed?" I put the key in the lock of my own door.

"Just . . . phone company aside, good work today," she says, wrapping her arms around me, tightly. "Thanks."

I hug her back. "Just doing my job."

She laughs, walking away, and calls over her shoulder, "No one is paying you."

I smile, opening my door. Inside, I wash up and strip, then lie down in bed, and wish Gene were here again. Wish I could have at least talked to him. But then my eyes close and I'm asleep.

I'm woken by the phone ringing again. When I open my eyes I think I must have dreamed it—some nightmare about the chief again. I turn on the light and look at the clock—5:30 A.M., even earlier than yesterday.

I run across the hall half-naked again, and pick up the phone.

"Mills," I say, my voice hoarse from lack of sleep.

"Is that how you sound when you wake up?" Rose Rainmeyer asks, sounding perky as ever—far too perky for how early it is. "You should smoke less."

"Rose, why are you calling so early?"

"Early bird gets the worm, Andy. Or in this case, the corpse."

"Corpse?"

"Got a call from a contact at the coroner's—they just fished Howard Salzberger out of the bay."

THIRTEEN

"How do they know the corpse is Howard?" I ask her.

"The wallet in his pocket," she says. "But the body is in bad shape, apparently. Looks like it's been in the water a while. I'm doing my hair now. Meet me outside the ME's office?"

"Give me half an hour," I say.

"Oh, you're going to be a mess." Her voice is on the verge of laughter. "I can't wait."

I hang up. I do my best to wake myself up with a fast shower, and think about shaving, just to prove her wrong, but there's no time. Luckily the coroner's office isn't too far, inside the Hall of Justice next to Chinatown. The sun is barely peeking over the horizon, and fog is rolling between the buildings in heavy waves, but I still spot Rose easily, like a lighthouse, dressed in a yellow jacket and skirt far too bright for how much sleep I've gotten. The hat, at least, is black. She leans against the wall next to the door to the coroner's.

"See? I told you I'm trying to help. Unless you also have a friend at the coroner's?" she says, looking me over. "Did you not shave?"

"No time," I say. "And you seem to have friends everywhere."

"That's my job." She turns from the wall and heads to the door of the Hall of Justice.

My teeth pin my tongue to the roof of my mouth before I get them loose enough to say "Wait."

She turns, raising an eyebrow.

"I can't go in there," I say. "I really don't have a PI license. They won't talk to me." And I really shouldn't be seen with her by anyone who could report to the chief.

"Why not?" she asks.

"Hasn't come in the mail yet. I'm just starting."

She looks me up and down, clearly not sure if she believes me. "Well, I have a press pass. That'll get me in, at least. Why don't you wait here, and when I'm done, you can buy me breakfast and we can trade information?"

I don't like the idea of trading with her, but I nod. "Find out what he was killed with, and if anything else was on him."

"This isn't my first murder," she says, hand on her hip.

"And how long he's been in the water."

She rolls her eyes and turns away, going into the building. I go across the street and light a cigarette. It feels like forever waiting for her, and every inch of it, I think about turning and running just so I don't have to work with her anymore, get any closer to her, or let her any closer to me, or this case. But I need to find out who killed Howard. And she can get her hands on information I can't. She's useful, like she said. I can't fault her for it. But I need a new story—punching some guy out won't be boring enough now, not with a dead body in the mix.

I'm halfway through my second cigarette when she comes back out. She walks across the street to me, smiling, then shrugs. "Breakfast?" She turns, walking down the street, and I almost stumble to follow, tossing my cigarette in the gutter.

"What did you find out?" I ask, catching up to her.

"There's a diner right around here." She looks around, walking. "Jimmy's? Jaime's?"

"Jane's. What did you find out?"

She turns to look at me, the sun high enough now her skin is turned gold. "Let's get some coffee in us, Andy, it's early for talking murder. Ah, there it is," she says, turning a corner and spotting Jane's. "So you know the area? Lots of meals after seeing corpses from your time on the force?"

"Sometimes a newbie would vomit, and we'd take him here after, get something back in his system."

"Charming," she says, opening the door to the diner. It's nearly empty this early, but a few guys are at the bar, eating eggs, drinking coffee, their days starting with sunrise. We take a booth in the corner. This isn't a fancy diner, it's got Formica tables and cheap blue vinyl seats that match the dingy blue walls, but Rose doesn't seem to mind. A waitress gives us menus and Rose orders us both coffee, which she brings quickly. I drink mine fast, still scalding hot.

"Slow down there," Rose says.

"I haven't gotten much sleep lately."

"The case?"

I shake my head quickly, but don't think of a good lie in time. "Insomnia," I say finally.

"You do look tired," she says, teasing.

"What did you find out, Rose?"

She sips her coffee, then shakes her head. "Trade information, that was the deal. You first."

"What do you want to know?" This is exactly what I was worried about. I wonder if I could go back, get into the examining room myself. I still know some guys at the coroner's—but they've probably heard about me by now.

"What's the case? Who hired you?"

I shake my head. "That's private. But the case was looking for Howard. So now I guess the case is finding out why he was in the bay. Where did they fish him out, anyway?"

"Fisherman's Wharf," she says. "Apparently his face bobbed to the surface as some drunk tourists were getting ready to . . ." She smirks. "Unload a night of drinking into the water. Gave them quite the shock."

"I'll bet."

"My turn. What do you think could have gotten Howard killed? Were you telling the truth about dirty magazines?"

I pick up my half-empty coffee cup and cover my mouth with it, thinking. I can tell her a lot of the story, as long as I don't mention anything too close to the truth. Lee said to make it boring, though.

"They were publishing a book someone didn't want published," I say. True enough. "An autobiography. It was going out through their book service. I thought someone might try to use the post office to shut them down, but I guess they just decided to kill Howard instead."

She smiles, her expression victorious, like she's made headway. "An autobiography is worthy of murder? What was in it?"

I shake my head. "My turn. How was he killed?"

"Stabbed through the chest and bled out before he was put in the water. The killer used a short knife, tapered edge, no hilt marks, thin blade. They're not really sure what it could be—not a common knife, in any case. Maybe something custom—a professional killer."

I nod, thinking of the mob. "That it?"

"What's in the book that makes it murder-worthy?"

I shrug, trying to make a murder seem dull. "I don't know. Howard was the only one who really knew, apparently, and all the copies are gone."

"DeeDee doesn't know?"

"If she does, she's too scared to speak."

Rose smiles and sips her coffee. "Well, I think that was a very profitable discussion on both sides, don't you?"

"You didn't get anything else from the coroner?"

She shakes her head. "Body had been in the water more than

a few days, but less than a month—it's hard to tell, apparently. He guessed maybe a week, based on how much of his eyelids had been eaten by fish." She shrugs. "So nothing definitive."

"Fits with the timeline."

"But nothing new."

"Anything on him?" I ask, trying to make it casual. An address book doesn't fit in a pocket, but it's still the most important thing I need to find to protect everyone.

She looks confused. "Just his wallet, keys . . ." She shakes her head. "Why?"

I shrug. "You never know what a lead will be."

We drink our coffee quietly. More light is starting to come in through the windows, the city opening its eyes, the fog clearing out. The coffee isn't very good. Burnt. I think of what Lee said—make the story boring.

"Are you really still interested in this case?" I ask her. "About books?"

"About murder, now."

"Still. It seems beneath you. A cheap little story—a tell-all that gets someone killed. It's a tabloid story, not real news."

She tilts her head, considering. "When you say it like that, it does sound a little . . . small."

I try not to smile, hoping this is working. "I mean, I have to keep working it, it's my job, and you've been helpful, but it doesn't feel like front-page stuff to me."

She shrugs. "Like I said, it's all in how you tell it. And I think it'll depend a lot on what was in the book. If that's juicy . . ." She smiles. "That's a real story."

I shake my head. "I don't think it was. The author was just a friend of Howard's, some other old guy who Howard thought led an interesting life."

She laughs. "Really trying to convince me it's a boring story. But it probably was an interesting life, if someone's died over it."

"That could just be some small vendetta—the book claimed the guy was a gambler or something."

She sips her coffee, amused, eyes locked on mine. "Is that what it claimed?"

"I'm just guessing. That's the kind of stuff they sold."

She doesn't say anything, just keeps looking amused. The silence stretches until she puts the coffee back down. "Well, I'll keep that in mind. And you'll tell me if you find a copy?"

I nod, an easy lie.

"Good. But I'm still curious about you, Andy. Why did you leave the police?"

"I told you—"

"The hours, right. You do look a bit of a mess. Clearly not an early riser. Insomnia, right?"

"Yeah."

"I hear alcohol helps."

"I try it every night."

She laughs. "You seem like the type."

I smile at that. Good—just a drunk, tired PI. Boring. I take out my wallet and put down money for the coffee.

"You don't want to eat with me?" She frowns a little, but a play-frown, not really offended.

"I want to go back to bed." I stand up, stretching a little. "Howard is dead. I'll check if my client wants to know who killed him."

"Who is your client, really? Is it DeeDee? I can't imagine it's anyone else."

I shake my head. "We're done with this game. Have a good day, Rose."

I start walking away, putting my hat on.

"See you later, Andy," she calls out behind me, just as I reach the door.

I try to get some shut-eye, but I keep going over the case as I lie in bed. The timeline means anyone could have done it; Bridges, Joe, even Merle. A knife is an odd weapon—with the mob, I'd expect a gun, but a custom knife could be some signature of one of the made men that Bridges asked to carry out the hit. Or it could just be some other kind of knife the coroner couldn't place. It's an amateur's weapon, too—anyone can pick up a knife and stab someone, especially if they're not expecting it; Merle, even DeeDee, if I'm looking at everyone. Could even have just been some random mugger. If that's the case, at least the list is probably safe—thrown into the river with his body, ink already run beyond reading. I should have asked if there was any money in his wallet . . . but if he still had it at all, he probably wasn't mugged. No, this was something intimate. Someone with a reason to want him dead—Merle, in a fit of jealousy, Bridges, for sleeping with Merle, or to stop the book. Joe for the same reason. But would they really have done it like this then—killed Howard, but not DeeDee? That points to Merle, or Bridges killing him over the affair. But then there's the taken books, which imply the murder was to stop the publication, something Merle didn't even know about.

And none of that answers the most important question: Where's the list?

After I get tired of pretending to sleep, I get up again, and shave this time, then go across the hall to my office. I want to try to find out more on Joe, and what was in his book. I think that'll lead me to who wanted the book to disappear. But Lee and I have an appointment with that new couple we're putting together: Oscar Santos, an administrator at the Public Health Service Hospital hired us to find him a girlfriend, and I think Elena Moleno fits the bill. We're introducing them today, and I already told Lee not to postpone. I fish their file out of my cabinet, and flip through it again, the backstory I've created for them, the timeline of their relationship. She's younger, and works at her family's flower shop; her family has started to notice she only goes out with girlfriends. A boyfriend for a while should throw them off the scent. I have some background on them, a proposed "how they met" scenario, and a list of what they'd be agreeing to do for one another. Most of these work out, though sometimes they take an instant dislike to each other, and we go back to the drawing board. Lee shows up as I'm going through the pages.

"Morning," he says. "You look tired."

"I got a call early, had to go . . ." I sigh. "Howard is dead."

"Oh." He sits down, his face falling. "That's really a shame. He was a good man. Good for the community. You tell Pat yet?"

I shake my head. "I haven't seen him yet this morning—maybe still up at Elsie's, or down in the bar, but . . ."

"You don't want to tell him."

I shake my head. "The list is still missing, and whoever killed Howard could have gotten addresses out of him first, so . . . I want something good when I tell him. Something."

"You can't hide this from him, though."

"I know. I'm just . . . going to take until later, I think. The cops are probably talking to DeeDee by now. She should know first anyway."

Lee nods. "Well, it's a real shame, and I hope you find his killer."

"I hope I find the list," I say. "Gene is on it. He said not to worry, but . . ."

"I think he's downstairs, if you want to go see him."

I almost stand up immediately, but then Oscar walks in, a nervous smile on his face.

"I guess I'm here to meet my girlfriend?" he says, taking his hat off.

"Yes, you are," Lee says, his face immediately shifting to the one he uses with clients—the same as the one he uses on stage, just with less makeup—warm and welcoming. "We think you're going to like her."

Elena comes in a moment later, looking just as nervous. We introduce them and they awkwardly shake hands before we go over the match. The new couple will officially "meet" later today, after she's been back at work. He'll go into the shop and order some flowers for his mother, and ask for her number. She'll smile and give it. He'll call that night. That'll be the setup, and the story they can tell his colleagues at work. She'll go to a few company parties, he'll pick her up on Saturdays for a few months, and do one dinner with her family. Then, after three months, they'll break up. He'll say she was pushing him to get married and he wanted to focus on work, she'll say he broke her heart and she thought he was cheating on her with someone from work, so she'll never trust a man again. All in all, they should be good for a little while before anyone pressures them about dating again. Oscar and Elena ask a few questions, and we have them talk for a bit, to make sure they don't hate each other.

They get along smoothly—the matches usually do; Lee has an eye for this, once I tell him what kind of cover they need.

After we've gone through it all, everyone shakes hands, and Oscar kisses Elena on the cheek, as practice for how they'll act at parties. They work well together, they'd make a cute couple.

"My girlfriend is going to think this is so funny," Elena says, putting her jacket back on.

"My boyfriend, too," Oscar says with a smile.

"Maybe we should set them up next," Lee says. Everyone laughs, and Oscar pays me, in cash. After they leave, I give Lee his cut and put on my jacket.

"Thank you," he says. "I think that went well."

"Very."

"And Ralph is open to meeting Virginia. I set it up for Monday, but we can postpone it if . . ."

I shake my head. "Let's keep it for now. You find out if they both play chess or anything?"

"Not chess, but they both like jigsaw puzzles. That's something, right?"

"Really?"

"She says it helps her think, he says it helps him relax. Can you work with it?"

I turn it around in my mind, trying to work it into the cover. "Yeah, sure. They could meet at . . . a store that sells puzzles. Maybe one of the department stores. There's only one puzzle left—something feminine, flowers, maybe."

"Won't that make him look too girly?"

"No, not if it's about it being a hard puzzle for him. For her . . . we let her say it was flowers, and him say it was . . . what's a lot of pieces for a jigsaw puzzle?"

Lee shrugs. "A thousand?"

"Sure. So they tell the story of them both spotting this puzzle, and she says it was beautiful flowers, and he says it was a thousand pieces—he looks like he wants it for the difficulty, she looks like she likes flowers. Good cover for both of them. I'll write it up before Monday—they can go pick out the puzzle together."

Lee nods. "That all makes sense. I'll tell them Monday then. Afternoon, maybe one, so it's on their lunch break."

"Perfect."

He stands up. "I should get to the music store. See you later tonight?"

"You know I never miss your singing if I can help it."

He smiles as he leaves. "Say hi to Gene for me."

Downstairs, in the bar, Gene is mopping the floors. When I come in, he looks up at me, and smiles, but not too broadly.

"I'm sorry I missed you last night," I say, walking toward him.

He leans slightly on his mop. "Yeah, I needed some alone time."

"Because of the delivery guy?"

"Partially," he says, going back to mopping.

"You want to talk about it?" I ask, bringing the bucket a little closer so he can get to it easier.

"You don't have to do that," he says.

"Do what?" I ask.

"I mean . . . I can mop the floor alone, Andy."

"I know . . . I was just helping."

He stops and sighs, then leans the mop against the wall and goes to the bar, where he pours a whisky.

"Kind of early," I say.

"It's for you." He pushes it toward me. "Sit down."

"Okay . . ." I say, doing as he says, suddenly nervous. Is he breaking up with me?

"I really care about you," he says carefully.

I wrap my hands around the glass.

"And what you did, taking that punch from the cop . . . that was very heroic. And very sexy." He grins, and I feel a little relieved. "And I appreciate you stepping in with some patrons when I give you the sign, like you did last week. But I don't always need rescuing."

"Oh . . ." I say, confused. "So . . . you want to fight the cops?"

He laughs. "No. I don't want to fight. But yesterday, the delivery guy . . . I asked you to stay out of it."

"He was being an asshole," I say. "The things he was saying to you—"

"Are things I have heard my whole life. I can deal with them. I know you don't like that I have to, and I know that that was probably the first time you saw anyone calling me that, so you felt . . . bad, right? That you couldn't stop it?"

I nod.

"And I appreciate that. But it wasn't about you. It was about me. About my job. If he thinks there's always going to be someone else around, a white man, then . . ."

"Then he's never going to take you seriously until I show up," I say, understanding. "I'm sorry, I didn't realize I was . . ." I take a sip of the drink. "I just wanted to help."

"I know. Which is why I'm talking to you instead of fighting with you in my head, like I did last night."

"You were fighting with me in your head?" I ask. "I don't like that."

"Neither do I," he says, leaning across the bar, and kissing me on the lips. "But it was fine. I looked over the books, called a different liquor supplier, talked their prices down, and pitched it all to Elsie, who signed off—we're switching suppliers to one I know hires plenty of Black, Chinese, Japanese, Mexican, and Filipino drivers. We're going to lose one brand of vodka, but gain two brands of tequila."

"You . . . took care of it all yourself." I'm proud, I think. But not in the way a dad would be proud of a kid. More like in the way a kid would be proud of his dad. And then a little ashamed, too, because I had acted like I didn't think he knew how to do this himself. I never would have thought of this. I would have just punched the guy, caused more problems. Gene actually fixed it. "I'm real sorry. I should have known you could."

"Of course I took care of it myself." He shakes his head, his eyes elsewhere for a moment. "It wasn't just dangerous for me; imagine if he'd seen Lee coming in to rehearse one day, or figured out what kind of bar this is. Having that guy as our delivery man was dangerous. Elsie always dealt with him before and all he did with her was flirt, which she could handle. But with me it became clear we needed to make a change. So I did."

"You did the saving." I squeeze his hand, feeling that pride and shame again. I'm an idiot, but I'm a lucky idiot.

"We all have to save each other, Andy." He strokes my palm with his thumb. "And this was my job."

"I'm sorry," I say again.

"You can stop apologizing. Just remember, I'm the hero in my story. Not just . . . someone who needs rescuing in yours. So next time I say I can handle something, let me handle it, okay? It's my job."

I nod, feeling grateful. "Okay. But if you do need help, you'll ask, right? And you'll ask me?"

"You want to help me go over the books?" He raises an eyebrow. "I made it work, but the shifting-over period means some tight margins."

"Well, maybe not with that."

He laughs. "I promise to ask for your help when I need it or want it." He lays his hand on the bar and I put mine over it.

"And I'll try not to be all heroic every time I see you."

"I mean, I don't mind you being a little heroic," he says. "But only when I'm asking for it. Or when my life is in danger. You can help with that. Really it's just the work stuff I don't need you being heroic about."

"So what other kinds of heroic can I be?" I grin. "A list would be very useful. You know I like to be helpful in any way I can."

"You do like to lend a hand," he says, grinning.

"If I were to mop up the place for you, for example, maybe I could then show you some of my heroism upstairs."

He grins, then glances at his watch. "I do have time . . . but no, I have to do the mopping myself. That's a work thing. My job."

"Ah," I say, disappointed.

"But it can wait if you want to go upstairs right now."

Naked in bed, I lay my head on Gene's chest and listen to his heart beating.

"Very heroic," he says, his breath still catching up to him.

I laugh. "You too. I am sorry I didn't listen with the delivery guy."

"I know," he says.

"I hate that that's how it looked to him, and that I didn't realize."

He strokes my hair. "That's how it's going to look to a lot of people."

"Is that why you don't like keeping too many clothes here?" I ask, realizing it suddenly. "You don't want to look like . . ."

"Like the heroic white detective's kept Filipino boy?" he finishes, almost laughing as he says it.

"I wasn't going to say it like that," I say, propping myself up to look into his eyes. They're dark brown, but warm, and he smells like he always does, like that perfect moment in summer when the sun heats up the bricks.

"I know you weren't, but yeah, I worry about that. I'm new at this job, at manager. I don't want people to think I got it because I'm sleeping with the guy upstairs, friend of the owner."

"No one will think that," I say quickly. "You worked here before I did."

"If I were white, maybe not, but . . ."

"Well, I hate that," I say. "I'd prefer you have at least a few nights' stuff here. Not even for me, but just so you can stay over when you're tired."

"Not even a little for you?" His fingers dance on my spine.

"Maybe a little," I concede, laying my head back on his chest. "Is there anything I can be doing—to make it clear that . . . you're your own man? The boss?"

He laughs. "Boss. That's a funny thing to call me."

"It's what you are. Including of me, in that I'm security. You outrank me."

His hands comb through my hair for a moment again. "I guess I do." He almost sounds surprised. "But no, there's not much you can do, I think. I don't want to hide our relationship, I never want to hide a relationship again. So . . . I'll have to figure it out, I guess. That's about me." His hand stops stroking my hair and I look up at him again. "But I tell you what. I'll bring two nights of clothes over tomorrow."

"Yeah?" I ask.

"Sure. And if people are snippy about it . . . I'll deal with it."

"And I'll help," I say. Then add quickly: "If you ask."

He laughs. "Good answer." He leans forward and kisses me.

"I'm learning. Not everyone needs saving."

The words rattle something loose in my brain as I say them.

"What's that look?" he asks.

"Just . . ." I sit up. Galahaut saved Lancelot. Merle is Lancelot, Howard was Galahaut, but there was one more in the story— Arthur. Arthur didn't need saving. Arthur was Galahaut's friend. "I just figured something out," I say, getting out of bed. I look down at him, naked, confused, and don't want to leave. "Sorry," I say, bending down to kiss him again.

"That's all right. Some people do need saving, I guess."

"It's the case," I say, finding my jacket on the floor, and getting the notebook out. "I think you just helped me figure something out."

"Yeah?" He sits up in bed. "What?"

"A code name." I flip through my notes—the letter from Arthur mentioned the casino. If Joe were to write to Howard, especially if he were to talk about being gay, or reading a gay book, he would use a fake name. And he could still be using it—hiding under it. If Howard told his Round Table story to Merle, he could have told it to Joe, too. Arthur from the casino—it's got to be Joe. If any of the letters are. But there was no address on the letterhead. I could go back to Howard's apartment, but the cops might be there by now. I sigh, not sure what to do with this. Maybe DeeDee will know an Arthur, even if she doesn't know Joe.

I sit down on the bed, and lean over to kiss him long and deep. "Thank you."

"I didn't do anything."

"You did," I say. "And I wish I could thank you some more . . . and just . . . tell you about yesterday. It's been . . . a lot. I saw my old boss."

His eyes bolt open at that. "What? Are you okay?"

"Yeah, I'm all right, just . . . It's been a long couple of days. You're working tonight, right?"

"Yes."

"And you won't go home without saying goodnight again?" I ask.

He smiles, and reaches out to stroke my chin. "I'll come up here if you're not back by the time I'm off. Then you can wake me and tell me all about it."

"I love you," I say. It tumbles out involuntarily, almost hurried. I barely realize what I've said until I've said it, and then I quickly stand, turning away, looking for my underwear.

"Andy," he says softly, and I turn around. He's smiling, his eyes soft. "I love you, too."

I feel something like sunlight inside me and kiss him again. "I really wish I could stay," I say.

"I need to finish mopping anyway. But I'll see you tonight. Go solve your case."

I get dressed quickly, and he stands up, buttoning my shirt for me as I put my belt on, then tying my tie as I tuck my shirt in. When I'm dressed, and he's still standing in front of me, naked, I pull him close around the waist, and kiss him again.

"See you later," I tell him, and look at him a moment longer, feeling the sun inside me, before I go.

FOURTEEN

DeeDee is behind the register, ringing up a customer, when I get there. She spots me, but takes her time wrapping the books in paper and tying them up with a string before handing them back to the customer and turning to me.

"Hello again," she says. Her eyes are red, like she's been crying. When she sees me noticing, she looks away. "I already know about Howard, the police dropped by, they were very nice about it, didn't ask about the books at all, just wanted to know who his friends were, and I told them I didn't really know, aside from me. Thank you for bringing me those letters from his house—otherwise they wouldn't believe me." She laughs, a little sadly. "Those were his friends, though, even if they didn't meet much . . . Someone should tell them . . ." She sighs. "It's all so . . ." She shakes her head and sniffles a little, then takes a handkerchief out of her pocket and blows her nose. She looks up at me, suddenly, like she's remembered something. "Oh, but I've got good news."

"Oh?" I say.

She nods, leading me through to the back room, where she lifts from the desk a brown leather address book and hands it to me. "The list."

I feel a lightning bolt of relief through me as I take it from her. "Where did you find it?" I ask, flipping through the pages to see if it's real.

"It was just in the back of the drawer," she says. "He must have left it here. He's always shoving things around in here, messing them up, losing track."

I keep my smile still as I nod. I went through that drawer

very carefully, and this wasn't there. Did someone return it, because they knew I was looking for it? Or is she confused or lying? DeeDee has no motive—getting rid of those books has practically destroyed her business, and she cares about it. She definitely wasn't lying about that.

"Well, good thing," I say, as neutrally as I can.

"Yes, imagine if he'd had it on him when whoever it was . . ." She looks away, at the other side of the room. There are boxes there, filled with books. Then she turns back to the desk, covered in unopened letters.

"Those for the next mailing?" I ask.

She nods. "*The Night Air*, by Harrison Dowd. It's not my favorite, but it'll do. After that . . ." She sighs. "I'm not sure what to do without Howard. I ran the place all yesterday and I felt like I was missing an arm. There's so much to do, and I'm just no good at it alone."

"Can Pat help?" I ask.

"When he has the time, sure, sure, he said he would, and I know he will, but I'm just one old woman. Maybe . . ." She sighs. "My sister, her place in Vegas has an extra room. They need bookstores there. I could open one."

I nod. It's not really about the store, I think. It's about Howard. Especially being murdered. "If you're scared," I tell her, "just know I'm going to find who did this to Howard. And I don't think they're after you."

She stiffens a little, and looks at the door to the main shop, then back to me. "Going to take down the whole Mafia yourself?"

"Maybe."

"Tough guy." She shakes her head. "Like Howard. Afraid of nothing. And look where it got him."

I watch her, weighing which of my two questions to ask her

first. "Did you know anyone named Arthur?" I ask. "Friend of Howard's."

She thinks for a moment, then shrugs. "Not that I ever met, but he could have been one of his pen pals." She pats the stack of letters. "Why?"

"Just a hunch," I say. "May I?" I reach for the letters, and flip through them. No Arthur on the return addresses. "You going to open these?"

She looks away. "Eventually, I suppose. To tell them he's . . . Not sure how to write that. Maybe I'll ask Pat for help. He's better with writing. I just like reading. That's another reason I can't keep this up without him . . . who's going to reply to all the letters?"

"I'm sure Pat will help you," I say, wishing I were more reassuring. Next I flip through the address book, the list of subscribers—and there, at the very end, I find Arthur Pendred. An address in Palo Alto. I write it down.

"Find anything?" she asks.

"Maybe a lead on your mystery author."

"Oh . . . I really don't think you should pursue this. The list is safe. Howard is dead. What harm is there anymore? Everyone is safe. Don't put yourself in more danger—I couldn't stand it if . . ." She brings her hand to her chest for a moment.

"But what if Howard gave up addresses he had memorized before he was killed?" I ask, hoping that didn't happen, and selfishly, if he did, hoping none of the addresses he remembered were my friends. "And don't you want to know who killed him? Don't you want justice?"

"It was the mob," she says simply. "And there's no justice coming."

She looks at me for a moment, and I expect her to say something more, to ramble on like she does, but instead, she just turns to leave.

"One question," I say, when she's at the door. "Why did you lie to me about when you got back into town?"

She turns slowly. "Lie? That's quite an accusation, Mr. Detective. I know it's in your job, but accusing me of—"

"Someone saw you at the Shore Club, the night before you said you were back. You paid off Howard's debts."

She frowns, and folds her arms, her demeanor changing. Less batty old lady now, more haughty, like when someone points a knitting needle at you and you see how sharp it is. "Yes. I did. I got in the night before and I saw this place had been ransacked, so I went looking for Howard. He wasn't at home, so I went to that casino he always hangs out at. No one there had seen him, so I paid his debts and left. I thought if I paid them off maybe he . . ." She sighs. "I don't know. I did it out of habit. I'm always cleaning up his messes, you know. Ever since . . . Well, that tree house? He didn't put it up right. Started to come down one night while we were in it, floors slipping away—it was raining, too, which made it worse. He was afraid to just jump through the hole in the wall, the rope was gone, so it was me that jumped down, in my skirts and Mary Janes, which were ruined in the mud. My mother boxed my ears for that. But I jumped down and then I leaned one of the fallen planks back up there so he could slide down it. And he did. Landed light as a feather on the moss, and was only a little muddy when we got home. That's what it's been ever since. So I paid his debts. It wasn't much, and I knew then, if they had killed him, which they did, that they wouldn't come after me."

"Why didn't you tell me all this before?" I ask.

"Didn't I?" She looks confused for a moment, then shakes her head. "I thought . . . but what does it matter? You're done, aren't you? What does it matter he gambled? What does it matter I paid his debts, even after he was dead? Why tell you all that, when I knew he was already gone? Knew it the moment I came back and opened the door and saw the boxes, the dead fish."

"Dead fish?"

"The mob left one for us," she says. "That's their sign that they're annoyed. There was one wrapped up when I got back. Message clear as day—don't try to publish the book, or you'll end up like Howard did."

"It was here?" I ask. After I had already searched the place—left by the mob, maybe with the address book. Why? And it had already smelled of fish when I searched the place. "After you got back? You said you didn't smell anything."

She stares at me a moment, and I can see her thinking, then she shakes her head. "When else could it have been? I . . . threw it out. I didn't notice if the smell lingered. I never did smell things very well. My Suzie, she used to buy me perfume—wasted on me, I thought, never wore it, until she said it was for her."

I don't say anything. But I searched this place high and low and there was no fish, no address book. Something isn't adding up. Is it just her memory, or am I wrong about her not having a motive? Maybe she just *is* confused.

"Just leave it alone, Mr. Detective," she says. "Tell Pat we're done. I can't do this anymore. Not alone."

She sighs, and then turns around and walks back out the door. I know she's right, the case is closed. I could just walk away, and hope Howard didn't give up any names to whoever put him in the water. But there's something wrong here. A lot of things, really. And when I walk out into the bookstore, I spot one more.

"Hi, Andy. I see you shaved." She's still in yellow, standing in front of a shelf with an open book, thumbing through it. She holds it up: *The Front Page*, by Ben Hecht and Charles Mac-Arthur, with a yellow-and-brown cover that matches her outfit. "First edition. It's rare to find a play in a bookshop, but this . . ."

She closes it and holds it to her chest. "A treasure." She walks toward the register, where DeeDee frowns at both of us, but rings her up.

"What are you doing here, Rose?"

"Background," she says. "No need to wrap it," she tells DeeDee, paying, then putting the book in her purse, and walking for the door. I follow. Outside, the sun is high and cold, the light it casts like a spotlight in an interrogation room.

"Background?" I ask.

"Well, there's a murder now. At the very least that's a story, even if you keep trying to tell me there's not. So I wanted to really get a feel for the bookstore, so I can describe it. I was barely here last time, DeeDee wouldn't talk to me. But maybe she'd be more willing now, if you think . . ."

"I don't. She's real upset about Howard, she doesn't want to talk right now."

"So she is the client?"

I stay silent, following her.

"Oh, it is a beautiful day, isn't it? Sun's out, but not too hot, and it's somehow not raining, though I'm sure that'll change in a few minutes." She stops at the corner and turns on me. "I've been wondering, since this morning, though. You say they were publishing an autobiography, something someone didn't want published, a naughty tell-all."

"Something like that," I say, taking out my cigarette case.

"And there are no copies left?"

"Nope." I don't offer her one, just light mine.

"And you don't know what it was about because DeeDee is too scared to tell you?"

"That's right."

"Then she's not the client," she says, with a triumphant smile.

"She'd tell you who it was if she were. Unless . . ." She studies me. "Did she just fire you?"

I smirk. "Rose, I'm not talking about my client."

She frowns at that. "Well, now I'm not sure which it is. But if she's not the client, then who is? Did Howard have a sweetheart? I couldn't find a marriage license, and the landlord said he lives alone. Maybe family? But then they would have shown up now. Whoever it is, I'd love to talk to them for the story."

I shake my head, and start to walk away.

"I'm going to write it," she calls. "At least as a sad murder piece, about a nice bookshop owner . . . Even if you're off the case, I'll figure out who killed him."

I frown at that, turning so she can't see me. I don't know if she'll solve it, but she'll definitely keep poking around, and if she does that, then she could figure out what was going on, the kind of case it was, the kind of clients I might have . . . I turn around and smile. "I can ask my client again if they're willing to speak with you. Even recommend it. But they might want approval of the story."

She takes a step forward. "I won't do that, but I'll let them approve their quotes."

"All right, let me ask them. Give them a few days to think it over, though, they're very private."

She raises her eyebrows at that, excited. "I'll give you until tomorrow night. But then I'm going to start writing up what I know, with or without them."

"And am I going to feature in this?" I ask, trying not to sound nervous.

She thinks about it. "You don't want to?"

"Kind of makes me seem like a less-than-private private eye. Bad for business."

She nods. "All right. I'll leave you out of it . . . unless I can figure out why you're on the case in the first place." She takes another step closer. "There's still something you're not telling me."

"Well, maybe my client will let me tell you before tomorrow night."

"I'm off to get more background. Tick-tock." She winks before turning away.

I watch her walk back to the bookstore, a line of warning-sign yellow. She doesn't turn back, and I take a deep drag of my cigarette, clenching and unclenching my hands. I have until tomorrow night to figure out enough of a story for her that she won't print mine.

She's just across the street, about to enter the bookshop, when there's a sudden squeal of a siren. I tilt my hat down, instinctively hiding my face from my old colleagues, but I see her pause, watching as a police car turns a corner and stops in front of the building the kids in black were always sitting in front of. Suddenly, the door of the building flies open, and those kids come running out. The cops hop out of their car, chasing them. Another cop car pulls up with a squeal, police everywhere, chasing the kids.

I watch Rose, hoping this could be enough to drag her into a new story. She keeps looking, the cops dragging the kids in black back to their cars in cuffs. And then she waves, not at me, but behind me. I turn, slowly.

The chief. Out doing one of his favorite things—overseeing rookies on small-time stings. He's staring at Rose, and then his eyes rotate—to me.

My body goes numb. He recognizes me. He sees Rose, the one he told me to avoid, half a block away from me. He looks at me for what feels like forever, and I keep staring at him, unable to break away, to run, like I know I should. I half expect him to pull out his service weapon and shoot me right there. But instead he nods at me, then at Rose. I watch Rose smile, and then go back into the bookstore. When I turn around again, the chief is gone. All that's left are the rookies, throwing the kids in black into their cars.

I couldn't move at all before, but now I can't not move. I start to run, quickly, just away from the cops, the bookstore, Rose. I'm not sure where I'm going, but I feel my body break out into a heavy sweat, the kind that pools in every crevice of my body.

I don't know how long I run, but I can see the water by the time I stop. The sun is reflected in it, nearly white. I slump against a building. Somehow I'm still holding my cigarette, but it's gone out, barely a stub. I drop it, and think about pulling out another, but decide I don't want it. I let myself slide to the ground, sitting on the pavement. A few people stare at me. I don't really care.

He didn't kill me right then. That's something. I'm not sure where to go. If he knows where I live, then . . . I swallow. Then the Ruby is in danger, too. Everyone there—Lee, Elsie, Gene. I stand up, and listen for a moment. No sirens. No cops around me, no one following me.

I make my way back to the Ruby fast, but carefully, making sure no one has followed me. It's just after noon when I get there. The bar is empty, aside from Gene, still mopping. He looks up at me, his eyes narrowing.

"You all right?"

I shake my head, then nod. "You've got to get out of here."

He almost laughs, then sees how serious I am. "Why?"

"I . . ." I don't want to tell him. "I made a mistake. The police . . . they could be coming here."

"Okay." He nods, coming closer. "We've dealt with raids be-fore. That's part of the job." He's close enough now he takes my hands, but I pull them back quickly. I'm poison now, I want to tell him. Touch me, be seen touching me, and they'll come for you, too. "Andy," he says, a little angry. "What's going on?"

"The chief," I say finally. "He saw me. With Rose. Who he told me to stay away from. He's going to come for me, Gene, I know it. And I can't have anyone get hurt because of that. You have to go. Elsie, too, if she's here. Close up for the night. Just keep everyone away. That way it'll just be me."

"Look, I understand you're scared. You should stay at Elsie's tonight. Or maybe even a hotel. But we can't close up, the cost of one night of business is—"

"The cost could be your life." It comes out almost angry. He flinches, and I hate myself.

"And I'm telling you, I can handle a raid." His voice is stony.

I swallow. "But this is different," I plead. "This is the police, we—"

"Deal with them every night. And if they come for you, you know to wait in Elsie's place."

"They won't care about that this time. Please, Gene, please, I just . . ." I feel weak suddenly, like I'm going to faint, like Merle. Too many emotions, wrapping around me like a blanket so I can't breathe.

Gene sees it and steps forward, taking my arms under the elbow, holding me up as my knees start to buckle. He leads me to a chair, sits me down. Then he goes over and gets a glass of something, and brings it back.

"Drink," he orders.

I swallow it down. It burns, but it's cold. The sweat pooling on my body starts to evaporate.

He sits down in the chair opposite mine, across a small circular table.

"You're scared," he says. "More than usual. Why?"

I shake my head. I don't know why he doesn't understand. "The chief told me to avoid the reporter, Rose. And he just saw

me with her. He has my card, he can backtrack the number, find this address . . . come for me."

Gene nods. "And yet you ran back here to tell me to leave. To tell all of us to leave?"

"Yes, I need to . . . I don't want you getting hurt because of me."

"We just talked about this, Andy. You promised. I don't need you to rescue me. The cops come every week."

"But it's different—"

"For you. We need to figure out a way to keep you safe. But you can't keep . . ." He stands up. "I love you. I meant it. But I can't be a damsel in distress you put over yourself. Go up to Elsie's. Wait there. I'll call her. Let us rescue you for once."

I shake my head. "No, that's not . . ." I stand up. "I'm sorry. You're right. I was doing it again. I was scared. I am scared. For you. Everyone here. But I guess this is just . . . about me." I'm the bomb going off. I shouldn't have come here.

"So what are you going to do?" He stands and comes close enough I can reach out and take his hands, hold on to them, but I don't. I know he doesn't want me to, but he needs to be saved. They all do. And I'm the danger he needs to be saved from. He just doesn't understand.

"I'm going to fix it," I say. I know how. It's dangerous. But if I'm a bomb going off, I'm going to make sure it's not near him. Not near anyone I care about.

"I bet if you just hide out for a couple days at Elsie's. Or maybe at Lavender House?"

I shake my head. "I think I have another way." I pull him tight to me and kiss him, I hope not for the last time. "I'm sorry I did it again after I said I wouldn't."

"Okay. But it can't keep happening. And what do you mean, fix it?"

"I . . . have to go talk to someone." I pull away from him, and walk toward the door.

"Andy, be careful," he calls behind me. "You said you loved me. And that means it's not just you, you know. You have to look out for yourself. For me. That's what it means."

"I know," I say. It's a lie. I have to look out for him, even if it means doing something really dangerous and stupid. "I'll be back soon." I hope that's not another lie.

FIFTEEN

Rose knew where her husband had lunch every day, and I know where the chief does: a small diner on Bryant called Bayview. A lot of the guys went there, but usually earlier. Chief went later, I think to avoid eating with us. Sometimes he'd invite someone along, but only as a special treat. Usually, he ate alone.

He's eating alone now. It's a quiet sort of restaurant, white walls, black tables. He always sits in the back. I walk to his table and sit down opposite without an invitation. He's having the soup of the day, something creamy with oyster crackers. He looks up at me, and his eyebrows rise.

"This is stupid, Mills," he says, by way of greeting.

"I know you saw me with Rose," I say, not wanting to get caught up in whether or not me coming here was a good idea—we both know it wasn't. "I wanted you to know I'm handling it."

He chuckles, low, almost a whisper. "Are you now?"

"She's hard to shake, so I'm feeding her another story. She doesn't know about me, and I'm not going to let her find out. We want the same thing."

"You're not going to let her find out?" he asks. "How?"

"I told you, by giving her another story."

"About what?"

"A dead bookstore owner."

He considers this, takes another spoonful of soup.

"I'm a good detective, sir," I say, surprising myself. I thought I came here to beg, but watching him slurp his soup, I'm angrier than I thought. Angry that he has me so scared, angry that he thinks I'm bad enough at my job to end up in the headlines. "I was a good cop, too. If this world were a better place, I'd still be one. I'd have been promoted by now."

He takes another spoonful.

"And you know all that. That's how you know I'm a good detective, too, license or no. I am handling the situation. You need to trust me."

He shakes his head. "I trusted you to be a regular guy, and look where that got us."

"It didn't get *us* anywhere. It got me out of a job. But I never let you down because of who I am. I was always professional, always good at . . ." I take a deep breath. "You let me down, sir. Not the other way around."

He puts his spoon down softly on the table. His bowl is empty. He looks up at me. His eyes are hard, dark.

I'm going to die, I realize. Everything I've just said. He's going to kill me.

A waitress materializes next to us, apparently oblivious to the bullets he's shooting at me from his eyes.

"Can I get you anything else, Chief?" she asks.

"Coffee, please," he says, eyes still on mine. "Andy, would you like anything?"

"Same," I say, without really knowing why.

"Sure thing," the waitress says, then walks away for a moment and comes back with a pot of coffee and a mug for me. She refills the chief's and pours me one, then leaves us.

The chief brings his mug to his lips and sips, slowly. "I come here because the coffee is good."

"I remember. You brought me here twice. After each promotion. You said the same thing both times."

A corner of his mouth twitches up.

I lift my own mug to my lips and sip. It's strong coffee, too, bitter enough to wipe the remnants of Gene's drink from my mouth, and the lingering tipsiness of it. I didn't realize how hard it had hit me. Hard enough to come here. To do this. I sip again, because if I'm going to die, I may as well enjoy the coffee first.

"If I see your name in the papers," he says finally, "I will find you, Andy, and I will make sure you cannot damage the department's name again. I will respond to any allegations with a full accounting of why you were fired, and how you were found in the men's room of the Black Cat, pants around your ankles, on your knees." He almost spits the last part. "And when that newspaper article is published, I will buy a copy, and send it to your mother." He takes a long sip. "You will not only be hunted by every boy in blue in this city, but probably by a lot more people I don't know, who will want to do a lot worse to you. You won't be able to be hired anywhere. Your clients, as you call them, will all be suspects of crimes. If you leave San Francisco, I will make sure your reputation follows you wherever you go. Any embarrassment you inflict on my guys, on me, on us, I will inflict on you tenfold, and violently." He says it all softly, in an even tone. "Do I make myself clear?"

"You do."

"Good. Then take care of this reporter situation."

He says it like it's the end of the conversation, and I feel a shock go through me. The courage I had, from the liquor, from already being bold enough to talk to him, seems to exit me in a flood, and my arms and legs feel deflated. My hand shakes as I take a final sip of coffee.

"Leave through the back way," the chief says. "Some of the boys like to hang out in front when I'm done, to ask favors."

I nod, put my cup down, and leave through the back. It exits out into a small alley filled with trash and the smell of rotting food, but to me, it's the freshest air I've breathed in days. I lean against the wall, and run over everything in my head again. I'm safe—Gene, the others, they're safe, too. Unless I show up in the papers. Which means I have to make sure Rose doesn't write this story.

My car is parked under the Ruby, and the most sensible next step is to grab it and drive to Palo Alto to see if my hunch about Arthur being Joe is right. If anyone knows if his book was worth killing over, it'll be him—especially if he's the one doing the killing. But it's only just after two, and my gut tells me to go somewhere else first—the library again, back to the old periodicals section. Bridges had said Joe was in the papers a while back, so I start in 1930, just looking at mob stories. I find him in '34. An FBI agent murdered. The agent was embedded in with the Mafia, undercover, until he was found out, and then was found dead, his body laid out in front of the DA's office, with a dead rat in his mouth. No one saw who put him there, but a car belonging to Joseph Aldermann, an associate of the mob, was seen a few blocks away an hour or so beforehand. Joe is wanted for questioning. The first story to break it is in the *Examiner*, a headline by James Morgan and R. Goodwin. It details how impressive it was that the agent had embedded himself. But it suggests he had participated in illegal activities to prove himself, and questions the ethics of that. Then all the other papers picked it up, either defending the undercover agent or questioning the whole plot. There are a few more stories as the weeks after it go by— Joe still wanted for questioning, but no one has found him, the DA trying to claim the agent never committed any crimes, while other witnesses saw him break a union boss's fingers. It's not a pretty story. The last one is in '35—Joe is back in town, and finally questioned, then released. The DA says they don't have enough evidence. And that's it.

He sounds dangerous. If he could ferret out a fed, he's smart, too. And the body with the rat is gruesome. Theatrical. The theatrical ones are always the most eager to make a scene—with words or bullets.

It's past four by the time I get back to the Ruby. It should be less than an hour drive to Palo Alto, but I'm also going to see someone I suspect is a mobster—on the run and hiding out. So I go up to my office first. I have a small gun I took off a guy a few months back during a case. But instead of a gun, I find Merle, slumped in the chair opposite my desk, asleep maybe. I hope asleep. He's bent funny, his eyes closed, like a trampled stalk of wheat.

"Merle?" I ask, closing the door softly. He shakes and looks up at me. He's wearing a black hat, but too far back on his head, brim up, like a farmer.

"I found your card in my pocket," he says. "No one else had been in there but my uncle, and I don't think he knows what amethyst is—it's not an expensive stone. Do you know something? Where's Howard?"

I sigh, realizing no one else would have told him the news. I take out a bottle of rye I keep in my desk drawer, and two glasses, and pour us both a shot.

"Did anyone follow you?" I ask as I pour. "Or see my card?"

"No. No one pays attention to me except when I'm on stage, and I still have the . . ." He reaches out and drops my card on the table. It's crumpled. He's been clutching it since he found it.

I put a drink in front of him, but he shakes his head, pushes it away. "I don't drink."

"Okay," I say, and swallow mine and his, then look back at him. His eyes are huge, almost bulging, and the shadows under them deep. There's no way to soften the blow I'm about to deal him.

"I'm sorry, Merle, Howard is dead."

He looks at me like he didn't hear me at first, his expression confused. He even turns his ear at me, as if asking me to repeat it, louder, but as he does it, it's like the words catch up to his brain and he starts to melt, the turn of his head going too far, and slumping down, his shoulders falling, his body unable to support itself anymore, falling back into the chair. His hat falls to the ground like a dead bird.

I go around to him and put my hands on his arms and lift him up.

"I'm sorry," I say again. "I wish I had better news for you."

I realize he's making a soft whining noise, barely audible.

"You sure you don't want that drink?"

He nods, which I take as a change of heart, and I refill his glass and push it over to him. He slurps it down greedily, then looks at me, eyes dry, face paler than his white hair.

"I knew it," he says finally. "Death is the only reason he wouldn't save me."

"Yeah," I say, refilling his glass, though I don't know if it's true.

"Men like me, born into families like mine . . . I knew one of us would end up dead."

"He really loved you, though." I'm not sure if it's true, but it's what I think he needs to hear.

That seems to finally tip him over the edge and he starts to cry. Not cry, weep. He bends over his legs, and moans slightly as the tears fall. I take out a handkerchief and give it to him and wait. I've seen grief. I've had to deliver plenty of bad news. There's no way to help someone going through it, except to wait, and offer them handkerchiefs, drinks, food. They need to find their own way out—all you can do is let them know you're waiting for when they do. I don't know if anyone ever really finds their way out, but it's like getting to the windows of the house they're trapped in. They can see outside again.

Merle cries for twenty minutes, maybe more. He looks up eventually, his face red now, and wet, and he downs the rye in one swallow.

"Who did it?" he asks finally.

"I don't know yet," I say.

"You have to find out."

"I will."

"Good," he says calmly. "Then you tell me."

"Merle . . . it could have been your uncle. If he found out about you and Howard—"

"No," he says quickly. "He cares about me. He might think I'm weak, I'm . . . not right for the family business, but that's okay. He's right. He cares about me. He'd do anything for me."

"Like spare you but kill your lover to end your relationship?" I ask.

He shakes his head, looking down. "He didn't know, anyway. No one knew."

I nod, though I'm not sure I believe him. "How about Joe, the mobster who vanished? He and Howard were friends, right?"

Merle looks up, confused. "They talked a lot at the casino, but . . . why would Joe kill him?"

"Books," I say. "A book."

Merle just looks more confused.

"What do you know about Joe? When did he vanish? Did he seem angry or scared before he did?"

Merle shakes his head. "No . . . he was . . . nice. I didn't speak with him much. Oh. I once heard some people talking about him, either before or after he left. It wasn't a big deal when he left, so it didn't seem important . . . but my uncle was talking to someone. He said Joe was sick."

"Sick?"

Merle nods.

"Sick like a cold, or sick in the head, like . . ." I don't finish the sentence, but Merle knows.

"I don't know. Is he? Like us?"

"I think so. I have to talk to him." But if the Mafia knew he was queer, they probably would have killed him. The address I have could be a dead end. Or he could be hiding, waiting to shoot anyone who gets close. I frown, having no idea where that lead could take me.

"Howard and I fought. Maybe that's why he died." His voice is wavering and he looks through me as he says it. I try not to look too surprised at what sounds like the start of a confession.

"Oh?"

"I wanted to leave sooner. He said it would take longer to get the money. I cried, he told me to be brave, like Lancelot. I told him I was so tired of being scared. I cried for a while."

"That's a fight?" I ask.

He sniffs. "Isn't it?"

"Did you . . . hit him, or hurt him during the fight?" I ask carefully, wondering what he remembers.

"No, no, I wouldn't," he says, maybe too quickly. If he did it, he really doesn't remember, or he's a better actor than I've taken him to be before now. Downstairs, I hear the band start to play, practicing, and Merle looks up, surprised by the sound. "They play music here?"

"Yeah," I say. "We have singers, too."

"Ones like us?" he asks slowly.

I nod. "Want to go downstairs and see?"

He nods, silent. I take him downstairs in the elevator. The band has stopped for a moment so the saxophone player can adjust something on his instrument, and Gene is behind the bar. His expression when he sees me is half-worried, half-annoyed. I owe him an apology, I know, but there's not time for all that now. He looks at Merle, confused. I shake my head at him, and he goes back to unloading a crate of beer. I lead Merle over to the bar, and sit him down. He stares in awe at the band as they begin to play again.

"Are they all . . ."

"I don't know, actually," I say. "But they don't mind it if you are. You want another drink?"

Merle shakes his head.

"Okay, well, this is my boyfriend, Gene," I tell him, hoping it's still true. I look at Gene, who pauses a moment before nodding. "Gene, this is Merle. Merle, if you want a drink ask Gene for one, okay?"

"Okay," Merle says, still staring at the band. I walk to the other side of the room and beckon Gene over.

"Who's that?" Gene asks.

"Howard's boyfriend. I just told him Howard is dead . . . He's . . . unsettled."

Gene nods. "I've seen something like that before. Are you okay now? Did you . . . What did you do about the chief?"

"I . . . fixed it," I say.

He frowns. "Tell me what you did, Andy."

"I talked to him. And yes, I was doing it because I was trying to protect you—but I was protecting me, too. This was about me, Gene. You were right. And I'm sorry if not wanting to see you as collateral damage is being overprotective." I reach out and take his hand. He lets it be taken, but limply. "I meant exactly what I said. And you're right that saying it means I have to protect myself, too. And I did. I just . . . did it in a way that was very dangerous."

He sighs, and squeezes my hand. "Well, I knew that was how you operated."

"I am sorry that I came here, and tried to get you to leave. That was . . ."

"It made me really angry," he says. "It was everything I'd just asked you not to do."

"I know. I'm sorry. I was scared. And I wanted to protect you because I had just fucked up, and I thought it was going to hurt you. It's easier to care about you than it is about me, I think."

"Then care about you *for* me," he says. "Remember, I can save myself."

"I know. I'm sorry."

He licks his lips, considering, then nods. "So what about him?" Gene asks, tilting his head at Merle.

"Keep an eye on him for me? But be careful . . . he's . . . off a little."

"Okay," Gene says, then looks over at Merle, who's still staring at the band. "So you're not protecting me from him, then?"

"Is that wrong?" I ask. "I can find somewhere else—"

"No, no, if you think I can handle it . . ."

"I think he'll be fine."

"He seems . . . enraptured."

I look over. Merle's hair is like a white candle in the dark. "I think Howard was the only other queer person he ever knew, and now seeing queer people who play music . . . He's seeing a life for himself he didn't think existed, I think. He's imagining himself singing on this stage, surrounded by people like him, and . . ." I realize I'm still staring and look back at Gene. "At least, that's what I think. His life fell apart five minutes ago and now a whole new possibility for one has sprung up in front of him, like flowers on a corpse."

Gene smiles and kisses me. "See? You can create poetry when you want to."

I laugh. "I think I just relate to him, is all."

"I get that. Well, Stan called out sick for tonight. I was just going to have the band go instrumental, but maybe he can sing."

"I bet he'd like that," I say. "Make sure he calls his uncle and gives an excuse, though. Sore throat or something."

"Got it."

"And like I said, be careful."

"I will. Thank you for trusting me . . . But where are you going?"

"I need to tell Pat," I say. "And then . . . go see a gay mobster so I can make sure a reporter doesn't expose me, and probably a lot of my clients in the process."

Fog rolls in over his eyes. "You be careful, too, then."

"I will, I promise."

"Okay," he says, and kisses me again. "Pat was out buying some dry ingredients we were low on. He's in the storeroom. Tell him, then . . . go solve the murder."

I keep holding his hand, wanting to kiss him again, but I let go, everything suddenly chilly, and walk back to the storeroom.

I'm seldom in here. It's a brick small room with a large refrigerator in the corner, and a small freezer Elsie told me she got so they could serve ice-cream drinks, but the thing broke and she hasn't bothered getting it fixed yet. The walls are lined with shelves of alcohol and jars of olives, cherries. Pat is putting a crate of lemons in the fridge when I walk in. He turns to look at me and smiles as he closes the door.

"Hey, any progress?"

I nod. "Yeah . . . some good, some bad. The list is safe. But Howard is dead. Murdered."

He's quiet for a while, the only sound the buzzing from the fridge. "That's awful," he finally says, leaning against the wall. "And it's awful that I also feel relieved, isn't it?"

"It's normal," I tell him. "And you can feel them both. But just because the list is back doesn't mean you're safe. Howard had some addresses memorized, and he may have given them to whomever killed him." I swallow. "And there's a reporter sniffing around his murder. She's good. I'm worried about what she'll dig up."

"Do you know who killed him?" He wipes his eyes with the back of his hand. I take out a handkerchief and hand it to him, and he nods thanks, letting himself cry into it.

"No. I think it has to do with the mob, and this book they were publishing, the gay mobster biography. I think I'll know more after I talk to him."

"The gay mobster?"

"Yeah. I think I know where he's hiding out."

He looks up at me, his eyes going wide. "So you're going to go try to talk to a gay mobster in hiding who maybe killed Howard?"

"I am."

"Why? The list is safe. Howard is dead. Andy, I don't want you to . . ."

"DeeDee asked me that, too," I say. "And part of the answer is that everything I've learned about Howard makes me think there should be some kind of justice for his murder. And part of me also needs to get as much information as I can before the reporter so I can sell her a story she'll print that doesn't endanger any of us."

"I just don't think all of that is worth your life," he says, and I can hear the fear in his voice.

"I'll be okay," I say, thinking of what's in the safe in my desk. "I just want to talk to him."

"Does he know that?"

"Hopefully I'll be able to tell him."

"I don't like it . . . but I understand. Just, please be careful. I would never forgive myself if . . ."

"I'll be careful. Thanks, Pat. And sorry about your friend. He seemed like a good guy."

"He was. He loved books and talking to people . . . DeeDee is going to have her hands full, trying to run the store alone."

"Yeah . . . she said she wasn't going to. Said she was going to close it down. Move to Vegas, maybe open a shop there."

"What?" His face is filled with more terror than when I told him I was going to see a mobster. "Why? No one reads in Vegas!"

"Honestly, she seemed scared. Confused, too—she was telling me she found stuff in the shop after I'd searched it. A dead fish . . ."

"What?"

"Like a mob warning. But that doesn't make sense. Does she . . . get confused sometimes?"

"Confused?" He tilts his head, considering.

"Just . . . she's mentioned some things one way, and then another. She said she found the list in a drawer, but I'd searched it. She doesn't have any reason to murder Howard I can think of."

"No," Pat says quickly. "They're family."

"But she's acting suspicious. Or just . . . mixed up a little."

He takes a slow breath, nodding. "I think sometimes she talks so much it's hard to tell exactly where she is. With her stories? Like she lives in the past sometimes. Ever since Suzie died. Or maybe it was before, and we just didn't notice because Suzie covered for her. DeeDee rambles, but Suzie could always get her to focus. Then the cancer came, and it was pretty fast. DeeDee was different after that, sure, more . . . afraid, more scattered. But who wouldn't be?"

"Yeah." I'm not sure what else to say. There's an itch on my jaw, and I scratch at it. The confusion, or lies, or both, is bothering me.

"She just loses track of things sometimes. He was more organized. Great memory. When we sent out the books, he was just writing everyone's address by heart. She would always go over them and check with the book, of course, just in case. She'd tease him if he got one wrong. If your suspects are the mob or DeeDee, I'm going with the mob."

I laugh. "Yeah, you're probably right. I should go, though. Tell the family for me, would you?"

"Of course. Be safe, Andy."

"I'll do my best."

I hope that's enough.

SIXTEEN

The drive to Palo Alto isn't too long, but it's after five, and I get caught up in the rivers of cars heading home to the suburbs, the sun turning us all a warm liquid orange as it sets. Palo Alto is one of those places that's growing fast, sprouting up like an oasis of wealth, with the college in the center. I pass fancy modern homes carved in sharp shapes, white concrete and glass, roofs like low pyramids. Everything smells new, and like money. An odd place for a mobster to hide out. But maybe that's the point.

I find Arthur's address near the college, one of the new houses, but with a high white picket fence that reminds me of the gate at Lavender House. I park in front and open the gate slowly, my head low, in case he's waiting by the windows, ready to fire. But nothing comes. I step onto the property and can see more of the house—windows with curtains drawn, flowers planted along the wall. And I hear music, faintly. It's not at all what I was expecting. There's nothing menacing about it, none of the stale and quiet you expect from a hideout. Carefully, I walk to the front door and knock. I can hear the music louder now, and voices, I think. Laughter. I knock again and the door is opened by a handsome young guy, maybe twenty, with a great body, which is being shown off almost in full, aside from a small pair of yellow swim briefs.

He smiles at me, confused. The house smells of marijuana. "Hey."

"Hi," I say. "I'm looking for Arthur . . . or Joe?"

He smiles and nods. "Joe's by the pool with all of us."

He waves me into the house, and I follow. It's nice in here—warm tan walls and a pink carpet. Dean Martin sings "Zing-A Zing-A Zing Boom" from one of those new Columbia record players. It stands to the side of the white-tiled kitchen, which has glass sliding doors into a tinted solarium with a pool. About a dozen young men—all in swimsuits, except for the two who are nude—are running in and out of the kitchen, laughing. They look at me strangely, but with smiles. Several drape arms around each other's waists, a few are kissing, dancing. The one who greeted me at the door points at the pool, and I walk carefully out into the solarium area. If that's what it can be called. All the glass in the walls is tinted, dark enough the neighbors can't see in, I realize. Only the ceiling is clear. The place is warm, humid, and I feel vastly overdressed in my coat and hat.

I spot Joe easily, sitting at the edge of the pool. He's the only one over twenty-five, closer to sixty than fifty, with a full head of bushy white hair, and more of it on his chest. He's in white swim trunks, his heavy belly curving out over them as he looks around the pool, smiling at everything. He spots me, and the smile doesn't fade at all. He waves me over instead, and I go and stand next to him.

"Take off your shoes," he says. "Dip your feet in. It's heated."

"Thanks, but no," I say. "You're Joe?"

"I am. And who are you?"

"My name is Andy Mills."

He looks up at me again, squinting. "The cop? Really? Why are you out here?"

"I'm not a cop anymore," I say. "I'm a PI. A gay one."

"Well, clearly a gay one, the way you're looking at all the fellas. They're all students from Stanford. Pretty, aren't they?"

"Yeah," I say after a beat. He's not what I expected. There's none of the usual defensiveness from mobsters, no sense of secrets. He's relaxed in a way a man in hiding shouldn't be. And he doesn't seem to mind me here at all. Doesn't even seem surprised by it. I look around at the college boys. They don't seem afraid of him. "You let them use your pool?"

He laughs. "Sure. I like the company. They're all open-minded, about relationships, sex . . . age. You sure you don't want to get in?"

I laugh, and sit down next to him, taking off my shoes and socks, then rolling up my pant legs. "This is not what I was expecting."

"What were you expecting?" he asks.

I take out my cigarette case and offer him one, which he takes, then light us both up. "Honestly?" I blow out a stream of smoke. "A gunfight."

Joe laughs, a big belly laugh that fills the room and makes the guys turn to him. He smiles and waves and they go back to kissing, swimming. He waves his hand, the cigarette trailing a spiral of smoke. "I'm done with all that, Andy. If someone wants to shoot me, they're welcome to do it. Is that why you're here? Someone send you to kill me? It's a few months earlier than I expected. Just do me a favor and don't hurt the fellas, huh?"

I shake my head. "I'm not here to . . . You were expecting someone?"

"In a few months."

"I thought you were hiding from the mob. Because of your book."

"I am. Sort of."

"Sort of?"

He leans back on his hands and watches the guys, smiling. "Technically, I'm retired. Not really my choice, but . . . they don't know where I am. But when they find out about the book, they'll start looking. They'll find me, probably, but by then . . . two months. I think that'll be about right."

I stare at him. He's smiling slightly. Then I remember what Merle said—sick. It hits hard and quiet, the realization. They didn't mean gay.

"What have you got?" I ask.

"Cancer." He taps his head. "It's not so bad now. I get the shakes sometimes in my hands. But they say in two months, probably, it'll start getting real bad. So that's when I think it's a good time for someone like you to show up. I have it marked on my calendar, so I know when the fellas should stop coming over. I have it planned out. So . . . you being here. That's confusing. That's not part of the plan."

I kick the water slightly. He turns to look at me.

"Why are you here?" he asks.

"I want to understand the plan first," I say. "Wasn't Howard going to get hurt, too?"

He waves the question off. "Howard is leaving for Mexico with Merle in a few weeks. I told him, I said, if he sent that book out, put it on shelves, to give it a week to get to people, but then he needed to be gone, before the reviews, people talking about it—'cause that's when my old buddies would know. He'd been talking about running away with Merle for months. The book was going to give him the money to do it."

One of the guys splashes another at the far side of the pool, and another splashes back, all of them laughing. The sound of the water and laughter echoes in the space. Joe watches them, grinning.

I take a drag on my cigarette. "Why write it, though?"

"Oh, that was Howard's idea, been after me for years to write my stories down. He loved them, loved knowing this queer guy was in the Mafia doing . . . well, a lot. And doing a lot more with men, without the Mafia knowing. He said it was great stuff. I think he was right." He puffs up his chest, proud for a moment.

"But I never would have . . . until . . ." He looks down at his left hand. "When the doctors told me, they said there were new treatments. Experimental, but a lot of them working. Expensive, though. Now, technically, I was employed by Verdi Importers— vice president. We import olive oil, mostly." He winks. Drugs, he means. "And that job came with benefits—health insurance. But they weren't going to cover these treatments. So I went to my boss. I said, I've been loyal, I've been good for business, and now I need your help. He said no. He said nice knowing you." His face starts to get hard as he remembers it. His hands are tight on the edge of the pool, one of them shaking. The air is hot and humid. "After all those years. It wasn't so much money, not to them. They said I had my own money, but that wasn't the point. I wasn't going to spend my nest egg, give up my golden years . . ." He sighs. "They just wanted me to keep working. But I'm not in the family, I'm not a made man. Doesn't matter what I did."

He leans back again, and looks at me. "So I started thinking. Planned it out. I knew when the disease would get bad. I knew how long it would take to print the book. So I retired, bought this place cheap with a few suggestions of violence when I spoke to the seller." He shrugs, not really apologetic, and kicks the water. A drop hits me on the nose. "I wrote the book. And then I laid everything out for Howard—when to print, when to sell. It was mapped out. I get months of . . ." He looks up, sweat and a big smile on his face. "Paradise. And then I get an exit before it gets bad. Not to mention a big ol' fuck-you to my old employers. Imagine how embarrassing it'll be when they start writing about my book, about me. And Howard gets rich enough to run away with Merle. Happy endings for all of us."

I take a drag of my cigarette. "What about DeeDee?"

"Who?" He looks at me, confused, and wipes some of the sweat off his forehead.

"Howard's partner."

He turns away and shrugs. "I don't know. I never met her. Howard was the one I wrote the book with. We've been friends for years, you know? Practically since I moved to San Francisco. Well, when I moved back." He kicks the water again.

"After your public art with the rat?" I take a drag on the cigarette and watch him. At the other end of the pool, one of the guys jumps in, making a large, echoing splash.

He laughs, unbothered. "Yeah, that. I had some fame then, y'know, so I wasn't being watched all the time. Everyone knew I was loyal. And I wanted to . . . have something outside the job. I never really liked the job, if I'm being honest. I mean, I don't mind it. Maybe that doesn't sound good to someone from your line of work, but I'm big, and when I was young I was fit, strong, and I saw how people reacted to that, learned to think ahead. So it seemed like a good way to make money, and . . ." He gestures at the room, the young men in the pool. One of them climbs out, his bathing suit slung low on his hips. "It was. But I wanted something outside that, so I decided to become a reader. TV, radio, they make noise, can't have noise when you're hoping to lie low. But I like stories. So I pop into this bookstore. Not Walt's, that wasn't around yet, but some other place where Howard worked when he was younger. And he could sell a book to an illiterate, y'know? I walked out of there with a stack, and he told me to come back, tell him what I thought. So I did. It was years before we figured out the fact that we were both queer. I thought about maybe trying to take things further, but I wasn't Howard's type—he liked 'em thin, pretty. I was an ogre. Still am."

I sigh. "He's dead, Joe."

He turns to look at me suddenly, his face going from relaxed to sharp, menacing. I can see why people were afraid of him. "What?"

"Murdered. All the copies of the book are gone. I thought maybe you were having second thoughts. Or knew who wouldn't want it out there."

"He's dead?" His face falls, and he looks down at the water between his knees. He's quiet for a moment, and I look away, giving him privacy. The guys at the far end of the pool don't seem to notice. They're splashing and laughing. One does a headstand, his long legs swaying over the surface of the water. The smell of chlorine and sweat mingles in the steam. I can feel my shirt sticking to my back.

"I didn't think he would die," Joe says finally, voice soft. I look at him and he raises his head up again. His eyes are a little teary, but he runs his hands over his face and then he seems to relax. He looks at the guys again and waves, and one of them waves back, smiling. His hand shakes a little as he puts it back down, but he's back to how he was when I came in. Relaxed. "That wasn't supposed to happen," he says to me. "That's a real shame. You sure it was about the book? It wasn't Bridges catching him and Merle or anything? I told him that was trouble. All his knights in shining armor stuff . . . told me to go by Arthur in my letters. He always loved that shit, stories, secret names . . ." He shakes his head. "What a shame."

"It is," I say. "But I think it had to do with the books. They were gone. And Merle is still singing at the Shore Club."

"Well, Bridges would never let anyone hurt him. He'd do anything for that kid. But, if the books are gone . . . I guess somehow my old buddies could have found out about it earlier. When were the books taken?"

"Last week."

He nods. "I probably still have a week left, then." He looks at the young men, and smiles. "I'll make sure they stop coming around next week. To keep them safe."

"I don't know if it was the Mafia," I say. "DeeDee is still alive. She was part of this, too. And she walked right into the Shore Club the other day. Bridges didn't even know her."

Joe looks at me, confused. "Maybe they don't know her."

"She owns the bookstore with Howard." I kick the water again, wondering if Bridges has just been waiting for me to lay off before taking out DeeDee, too. Good thing she's leaving town. "Look, maybe it was the mob, but was there anyone else who wouldn't want the book out there? Anyone else who knew about it?"

"Hey Jimmy, be careful!" he calls to one of the guys, who's dunking the other underwater. "No drowning anyone."

"Sorry, Joey," Jimmy calls back, letting the other guy up for air. "Sorry," he says to the guy, and then kisses him softly on the mouth. Joe watches, smiling.

"So can you think of anyone else?" I ask.

He watches the guys. One of them is swimming closer, and they lock eyes. "I only told a few other people about the book," he says, watching the guy swim closer. "Folks who weren't in the mob, who I mentioned in it. I wrote them letters, in case they wanted to pick up a copy, y'know? Finally see all my stories. But that's . . ." He thinks.

"Okay." I nod, pressing my feet along the inside of the pool. Now we're getting somewhere. "Who were they?"

The young guy pops out of the pool. He's wearing small white swim briefs, the kind that would be considered indecent on any beach in America, and probably run-of-the-mill in Europe. He sits next to Joe and leans on him, without saying anything.

"Well, one was an ex-boyfriend," Joe says, letting his hand trail down the wet arm of the guy. "He never liked my work, we broke up over it. He moved to LA, but I don't know why he wouldn't have wanted the book published. I mean, he's mentioned in it, but it's very flattering."

"His whole name?"

Joe shakes his head. "Oh, no. Just first name. You'd have to have known me and him to figure it out, and even then, you'd have to have known about my job."

"Who else, then?"

"My sister, in Seattle. She knew all about me. But she's not in the book."

"Could she have wanted to protect you?"

He ponders, then shakes his head. "She loves me, even knowing everything, but she's not that type. She'd stay out of it."

"So who's the third?"

He smiles. "An old friend I hadn't seen in a while. I thought she could make it famous. And she'd like reading it."

"You know someone who can make a book famous?" I ask.

"Hey, I know people! Funny thing is, she's one of my best stories, but I didn't put her in it. She'd get in too much trouble. But you remember the rat thing?"

I shiver, and my feet stir the water by my ankles enough it splashes. "Who? What did she do?"

"Everyone thinks I knocked off a fed, but truth is, I never killed a man in my life. Beat plenty up, sure, but mostly all you gotta do is talk to people, explain the situation, and they come around pretty easy. The fed was . . . I was helping her out, taking the blame." His hand is on the thigh of the guy in white trunks now. He doesn't seem to care what Joe is saying. He just smiles, leaning on his shoulder.

"Someone else killed the fed?" I ask. "Who?"

"This reporter. Like I said, I know people. I thought if she liked the book, she could make sure it got reviewed, reported on in the press, so it made some money for Howard."

My body goes cold, then too hot, and I loosen my tie. "A reporter?"

"Oh yeah, known her for ages," he continues, waving his cigarette in the air. "Way back, she was always hanging around, trying to get a story. I thought she was funny, so I chatted with her. Then one night, she comes to me, tells me she killed one of our guys—but he wasn't really one of our guys, he was a fed. Said he tried to force himself on her, and she got lucky, threw his head back into a sharp corner. Found his badge after. Well, I liked her, and though I never killed anyone, I helped get rid of a few bodies in my time, so I took care of it for her. She told me, as thanks, I should show the boss his badge, say I handled it, so I did, made a show of it—made me famous. Infamous for a little, too, but no one could ever prove anything. I hadn't been seen with the schmuck in days because he'd been hanging out with her. But from then on, I was trusted. Frank loved me, Tony, too." He smiles at the guy who's nestled into him. "It's fun to imagine them reading the book, finally knowing the real me. I'll be in in a second, I promise," he says to the guy, and kisses him on the mouth. The guy stands up and Joe slaps him on the ass, which he smiles at before diving back into the pool.

"I kept up as her source on stuff for years, too. But we hadn't spoken in a while. So I just wrote her. I never heard back, so I assume she didn't care."

She cared, I think. She cared a lot.

"What was her name?" I ask, just to be certain.

"Goodwin," he says. "But then she got married. Can never remember what that name was. R-something."

"Rainmeyer," I say.

"Yeah!" he says, pointing at me. "That's it. Rose Rainmeyer. You know her?"

SEVENTEEN

She had been waiting for me. Not me specifically, but anyone who stopped by asking about DeeDee and Howard, the bookstore. I wonder why she chose the DA's office—maybe because of the mob connection, or maybe she was rotating between there and the police station, and just got lucky. But she's been on me since the moment we met—asking questions I can look back on now, and see for what they were. Had I read the book? Who had? Who was in it? Why was it worth killing over? She could have answered that one best herself, except she hadn't read it. If only she had . . . but just Joe telling her about it was enough to terrify her. Because she thought he was like her. That his book was about the truth, at any cost. And for once, it was one she didn't want to pay.

I watch the college kids, standing in the pool, the water lapping at their chests, hair stuck to their faces as they pass around a joint. My feet feel too hot in the water, and the rolled hems of my pants are wet.

"You all right there, Andy?" Joe asks.

"Just realized I've been running in the wrong direction for a while."

He laughs and pats me on the back. "I know that feeling. But there's always time to get to where you want to go, y'know? What, you think Rose had something to do with this?"

"If she didn't want the story of her murdering a fed out there, yeah. It would ruin her career, her life maybe."

He shakes his head. "But that wasn't in there. She'd like the book. She always loved my stories. That's why I told her, so she could help me get word out about it."

"I should still talk to her." I don't mention all the lies she's told me.

"Well, tell her hi from me. You want to hang around a while? Sammy there has been making eyes at you."

I glance up at Sammy, who smiles, water catching on his eyelashes. I shake my head. "Thanks, but no thanks. I still have to finish this case up." I stand, and put my shoes back on without my socks. The socks I jam in my pocket with the gun. "Hey, you think you got room for Merle around here?"

"Merle?" Joe asks.

"I think he needs to get away from it all. No one knows where you live now, right?"

He laughs. "Nah. And sure, Merle can crash here for a while if he wants. Little thin, but I bet the boys would like him."

I wonder if Merle would like it—no singing, but people like him, all relaxing, enjoying life. Nothing to fear. It would be a good place to start a real life. Like the Ruby, but far away from his family. From here he could head down to LA, maybe strong enough not to faint during an audition.

"Thanks, Joe, you've been a real help. Sorry no one will ever read your book."

He shrugs and takes the joint from one of the guys. "So what? These fellas like my stories, right, boys?" The guys all cheer, and Joe laughs, pleased. "Anyway, it's better when I'm telling them to people, friends, strangers I meet in a bar. Maybe they weren't really meant to be written down."

"I think it's all kind of the same thing," I say. "Books just get to more people. When the post office lets them, anyway."

"Maybe." Joe nods, then passes the joint back to one of the guys. "That's probably true. But it wasn't a very good book, anyway.

Come back and hear some of my stories sometime, though, while relaxing naked in a pool. That's how they're meant to be enjoyed." He grins at me.

"I'll think about it." I start walking away.

Behind me I hear him say to the guys, "And speaking of naked!" before there's a big splash. Luckily I'm far enough away not to get wet. The record player is skipping so I set it back to the start as I'm leaving, Dean Martin crooning me out the door.

The drive back to San Francisco is faster. The sun is down now, the sky the deep navy it gets before turning black, the fog already starting to roll back out. I think of Joe, swimming naked with a bunch of college boys, who all seemed to enjoy his company, or at least his pool. He must have spent years hiding himself in the mob—not just as gay, but the lie that made him a legend. I wonder what he was like before, if he was really that gregarious, or if he was scared, broken, like I was, and it's only now, free and dying, that he's become so cheerful.

I'm not sure what to do about Rose. I know the secret she killed to prevent anyone else from knowing now. So much for not having secrets. There's no statute of limitations on murder, although if it was in self-defense, she could probably get off with only a slap on the wrist. Especially now. But her career would probably be over. No one wants to be interviewed by a murderess. And people would have opinions about her case, opinions about her honesty. Her quest for the truth wouldn't matter—people would believe whatever they wanted. And she's smart enough she knows all that. I can even picture her as a murderer easier than I can a lot of people. The smile, the cutthroat questions, the way she went after what she wanted with so little care for what it might do to people.

By the time I pull back into the garage under the Ruby, I feel like a fool for not having seen it before. I'm just not sure what to do with this information. Get her to confess? Blackmail her into laying off the case so that me and my clients stay safe? Maybe there's a way to do both. Or maybe she'll kill me next.

Upstairs in the Ruby, Lee is on stage singing—with Merle. Merle's lost his jacket, singing with her in just a tie and pale blue button-down. Lee is in a striking purple dress, her hair done up with white flowers, but somehow they match perfectly—not just their voices, crooning out "It's Only a Paper Moon," but their movements. Merle seems different than when he's on stage at the casino. Looser. He's not just standing and holding the mic, he's singing with the band, with Lee. And Lee is loving it, too.

This could be his life, I think. Well, not this specifically—if he wanted to get away from his family, he couldn't stay in San Francisco. But some sort of life like this. The rescue he's always wanted, but without the fairy-tale promises. Just a stage in a dark bar the police could raid, living the best he can.

"I'm glad you made it back," Gene says to me when I get to the bar. "I was worried."

"I told you I'd be fine. No violence at all."

"You get what you need?"

"Yes," I say, though I'm not sure. "I just don't know what to do with it." Was Rose planning to kill me if I figured it out? Do I just walk away—or is the story she's writing for real? A way to cover her tracks. I shake my head and try to focus on the room, on Lee and Merle. "Merle seems to be having fun."

"He had a few drinks and took Stan's slot when I asked. He was good, and then Lee asked him to do a duet. I was surprised by that, but I guess she knows all about him."

I nod. "I told her, part of the deal. I'm glad, too. He looks happy."

"He keeps looking around like this place is another world, and then crying, and then being amazed again. I'm a little worried about him. But I made him call out. He made his voice sound hoarse and said he was going to hole up at a hotel so he didn't get his mom sick. He lives with his mom?"

"I don't know if lives is the right word," I say, watching Merle. His white-blond hair has fallen into his face and stuck there with sweat, turning it a little darker. He sways as he sings, and his voice is strong, clear.

"Well, he asked if he could crash in your office, I said yes. Elsie is back, too." Gene nods to the crowd, where I see Elsie dancing with one of the female impersonators, smiling. "She said to make sure you found her."

"She'll find me," I say. I look over at him. He's leaning on the bar with both elbows, watching the stage. "You want to stay over tonight?"

"Sure," he says, without even looking at me, a faint smile on his lips. The casualness makes me happy, and I lay my hand on his forearm, and he places his other hand over mine there, and we watch Lee and Merle finish their song. They're met with a lot of applause and both bow before coming offstage, over to us.

"You both sounded great," I say.

"It was amazing," Merle says, his skin damp and pink, eyes wide. "I didn't know it could be like that."

"It's like that every night," Lee says. "When I'm on stage, any-way."

"I'm glad you're feeling better," I tell Merle.

He looks guilty for a moment, and I feel like I've said the wrong thing, but he shakes his head. "I wish he were here. Did you find out who killed him?"

I'm not sure what to say to that. "Maybe," I decide. Probably. But what's the good in telling him if we won't be able to get jus-tice, to prove it? It'll just make him more miserable.

"Tell me when you do," he says, his eyes suddenly hard. He seems to feel his expression change, and his eyes go wide for a moment, like he's been hit by something. He looks down, and starts to cry.

"Oh honey," Lee says, "have another drink. You're mourning, but that doesn't mean all anger and sadness. There were great things he gave you, you gotta remember those." She pauses, but Merle keeps crying. "Tell us your favorite things about Howard."

Gene produces another drink for Merle, who takes it, but doesn't drink it, staring instead at the stage, thinking and sniffling.

"My favorite?" Merle asks. "The stories. The way he'd read to me. He . . . I know it sounds silly, like I'm a child, but he did voices, he acted things out, always made me laugh . . . or cry if it was sad. I interrupted him with questions sometimes and he would answer. I don't know if he was making things up or . . . I think he just knew things." He smiles, remembering. "I loved just lying next to him as he read, feeling his voice through his chest with his heartbeat."

"Which was your favorite book that he read you?" Gene asks.

Merle thinks for a moment. "I loved the Round Table stories, but . . . my real favorite was *Maybe—Tomorrow* by Jay Little. It's a silly little book, I know, but there's this part in New Orleans, and he goes to a bar . . ." He looks around. "Like this one. And it ended happily. I always liked that." He looks down at his drink. "It made me think our story could . . ." His face turns stormy again, and Lee brings him close to her chest, holding him as he sobs.

"Sorry, sorry," she says, stroking his back. "I didn't mean to make it worse."

"Let's all drink to Howard," Gene suggests, pouring himself a shot of whisky and raising it. "To the good memories of him."

"Yes." Lee raises her glass, too. "To Howard."

I raise mine. "To Howard. I never knew him, but I've learned a lot about him on this case, and I know for sure that his loss is all of our losses. He wasn't just part of our community, he was a community himself."

Merle looks at me, tears still running down his face. "He cared so much about . . . everyone."

"He did," Gene says. "He always held the new Narnia books for me without me even asking."

"He ordered mysteries especially for me if he heard of ones I hadn't read," Lee adds.

"To Howard," I repeat, and finally Merle raises his own glass and we all drink.

After that, Lee coaxes Merle into dancing with her, and I sit at the bar with Gene, watching. "I think I found a way out for him," I say.

"Yeah?"

"It's a little weird, but it'll get him out of San Francisco, away from his family, and surrounded by other gay guys . . . from there, maybe, he can go anywhere, right?"

"Maybe. You sure that's what he wants?"

"How could he not?"

"Well, it means leaving his family . . ." Gene stares at Lee and Merle dancing. "That can be tough. Losing family . . ." He sighs.

I put my hand over his. "Sorry. I know. I haven't had to do that all the way yet." I think of my mother, the occasional phone calls between us, where she asks me about my life, I spin nothing into words for half an hour, like the way the cotton candy machines at the zoo turn sugar into clouds. Sweet air, not much else. But it's more than Gene has.

"To me," I say, "this is family, though. I think he gets that."

Gene shrugs. "He's had a strange day."

I watch Merle, his eyes wide looking at the club, but bright red from crying, too. Gene is right. Who knows what he wants right now? He's had more liquor than he can handle, and he's still drenched in grief. He can't make a decision. I can tell him tomorrow, and he can take his time figuring it out. There's no rush . . . unless his uncle already knows.

I drink quietly for a while, Gene tending bar and then going to the stockroom to direct some of the crates being moved and then handling it when a singer shows up late. He's fast and fluid, careful in how he approaches everything, made to do the job, better than Elsie, maybe.

Lee dances with Merle, and then coaxes me into a dance, too, before we can see Merle starting to fade, his pale, thin body almost waving like a white flag. I bring him up to my office, and lay him down on a roll-out mattress Elsie keeps in storage for when a performer has a little too much to drink and needs a lie-down before going on again—or going home.

He falls asleep almost immediately, still in his clothes, and his face doesn't take on the delicate quality I'm used to seeing in sleep—instead it turns raw, almost like a blister, his skin dry and red where it's not pale, his mouth moving slightly like he might scream.

I write a note for him, reminding him where he is, and telling him to knock on the door across the hall if he needs me. When I turn around, Elsie is standing in the door.

"You renting out your office?" she asks. "I should be able to take a cut of that."

I close the door, and lead her to my place across the hall. She sits on my bed, legs crossed, surveying the place. "You've made it pretty cozy," she decides, finally.

"I'd offer you a drink," I say, sitting in one of my two chairs, "but I keep it in the office."

"Who was that? I saw him on stage and thought it was a replacement act Gene had found last minute. I was going to talk to him about making sure they're approved acts, but if he's sleeping here, I'm guessing it's not all that."

"Merle. Poor kid. Howard's boyfriend. He's . . . a singer. Not in the mob, but his uncle is, so he sings at the Shore Club, that casino, you know it?"

"Never been, but I've heard of it. That's gotta be a rough life. Nice voice, though."

"He did take Stan's slot tonight, so he was a replacement."

"Stan was out again?" She sighs. "I'm glad Gene handles the schedule now. If I had to worry about that on top of . . ." She runs her hand through her hair.

"Hey, it's all fixed now, right?"

"Is it? You say the feds aren't coming for us, but what about the mob?"

I shake my head. "Not them, either. I don't think they know anything about the book club."

"So you figured it out?" She smiles. "We're safe?"

I nod.

She narrows her eyes. "I am. But you're not."

"I'm working on it."

She laughs. "You put your neck out for us, and now it might be on the chopping block."

"I didn't put my neck anywhere I wasn't willing to put it. And . . . I should be fine. Just have to . . . figure out how to handle this one. There's this reporter after me. She killed once, and she probably killed Howard. But if I can get her to confess . . ." I shake my head. "I can't make her march into the police station. And anything else and they'll tear the bookstore apart, maybe figure out the rest of it, the book service, and then—"

"Then we're back on the chopping block with you," Elsie sighs. "So what will you do?"

"Not that," I promise. "Maybe she gets off. But at least so will all of us. I can talk her into that, I think. Unless she decides to stab me, too."

"How are you going to stop that?"

I pause. I'm not sure. "Politely."

She laughs, and stands up. "Well, thank you. The family wants to thank you, too. And meet Gene. I figure if we go up for a lunch, we can both take a few hours off before we open."

"You thought of that during all this?" I ask. "You should have been playing pirates with Rina."

"I did." She grins. "She likes the hat, but not the eyepatch. I spent so much time with that little buccaneer . . . and now I get to spend more, because of you." She leans down and kisses me on the head. "Thanks, Andy. And really, bill me for the expenses."

"Lunch at Lavender House will be fine."

She goes to the door. "How about lunch whenever you want? As long as you want."

I laugh. "Sure," I say.

"Night, Andy."

"Night."

I get into bed and try to crack open one of the books Pat lent me, to wait up for Gene. But I can't focus on the words, and instead I think about Rose, the way she's been playing me this whole time, and how to confront her. I drift off, and dream briefly of her on a ladder, slitting the throats of giraffes. I wake up when Gene slips into bed with me, so I can wrap my arms around him. He says nothing, but kisses my hands, holding them in his own, and when I sleep again, it's warm and dreamless.

When I wake up, Gene is in the shower already. I think about joining him, but I know I need to focus on finishing this case, so I fish Rose's card out of my wallet and call the number.

"Hello, *San Francisco Examiner*," a young voice answers.

"Rose Rainmeyer, please."

"Whom shall I say is calling?"

"Andy."

"Andy . . . ?" She waits for a last name.

"Just Andy."

I hear a click and a moment later Rose picks up. "Andy." I can hear the smile in her voice. I know what that smile is now. It's her knowing she's a step ahead. But not anymore.

"Rose."

"Your client decide they want to talk?"

"Maybe. I found something interesting out. How about we meet?"

"Sure. Lunch?"

"How about the zoo?" I ask. She's still a killer, and if it kept me safe before, hopefully it'll keep me safe again.

She laughs. "Really? You want to avoid a meal with me that badly?"

"I'll buy you peanuts," I say. "You can feed the elephants."

She snorts. "Fine. The zoo. When?"

I glance at the clock—8:30 A.M.

"Ten," I say. "Meet me by the giraffes."

"I love the giraffes," she says. "You remind me a little of a giraffe, actually."

"How's that?"

"Far away, but close, all at once, like you're trying to keep a secret."

I swallow, then try to laugh, but it comes out like a cough. "See you soon."

"Bye, Andy." I can almost picture her little fingers waving. It's strange to imagine those same little fingers killing a man, even in self-defense.

After I hang up, I check on Merle, who's still asleep. Gene is almost out of the shower when I get into the bathroom, and I persuade him to stay under the water a little longer. After we get out and dress, I check on Merle again, and he's gone.

I look for a note, but there's nothing.

"Listen," Gene says.

Then I hear it—singing. Faint, ghostly from up here and without the backing of the band. We go downstairs and find Merle on the stage. The lights are all out aside from a spotlight on him. He's in just an undershirt and his pants, which seem too loose on him, the legs too wide. He doesn't seem to notice us, or even mind that there's no band, no working mic. He stands and sings "How Long Has This Been Going On?" with a delicate sort of tone I haven't heard from him before. As he sings, he sways a little. His arms curl up like vines, his wrists turning up like they're looking for sunlight. His hips sway back and forth. He sounds great. Different. Softer. The strong straight song of a crooner is gone, and there's a gentle swaying now, a flickering match. A hand passes over his chest, caresses his own neck, then stretches out, filled with longing.

"This is better than last night." I hear a whisper next to me. I turn to see Elsie. She looks well rested for the first time in days, wearing just a red men's shirt and black slacks, a long necklace of pearls over it. She looks normal again.

The song comes to the part where there'd be an instrumental break before ending, and Merle dances a little on stage to the music in his head before stopping, and bowing. The effect is haunting. He looks out and sees us and Elsie starts to applaud, so Gene and I join in.

"I've always wanted to sing that one," Merle says, stepping down off the stage. "But only women sing it, so . . . not at the casino. Here, though, I thought . . ." He shrugs, a sad smile on his face.

"You're good," Elsie says. "I'm Elsie Gold. This is my club." She holds out her hand, and Merle shakes it. "You want a job?"

Merle smiles, but shakes his head. "I can't. If my uncle found out . . . He'd probably burn this place down just to make sure I didn't sing here again."

Elsie nods. "Well, it's a shame. You're good."

"Thank you," Merle says.

I look at my watch and peck Gene on the cheek.

"I gotta go see a murderer," I say.

"You know what you're going to do?" Gene asks.

I nod. "Blackmail. I hate it, but she always wanted the story to go away. I'm the reason she kept prodding it—because I was investigating, she was. So I'll offer a truce—I won't tell what she did, and she doesn't tell about the story."

"What about Howard?" Merle asks, his brow creasing like an old piece of paper. "What about justice?"

I frown. "I need to protect the living. I'm sorry, Merle. But Howard would want you to go live a real life . . . and I might be able to help with that, if you still want to run away. Can you wait until I get back?"

Merle looks confused. "Who is she?" he asks.

"Can you wait?" I repeat.

He crosses his arms, but nods. "I'll call Mother and tell her I'm still sick. She won't get suspicious for another day, I don't think."

"Good," I say. "I'll be back soon, I hope."

"Be careful," Gene says. I smile at him, and then I'm gone.

The zoo is pretty much the same as it was two days ago. Children laughing as they run back and forth, the animals calmly eyeing them, unbothered, or at least more interested in the treats the kids are offering up than the noise they're making. I buy a bag of peanuts and wait by the giraffes. I'm not sure I see what Rose was saying about the resemblance, and I definitely don't think giraffes are much for secrets, but I like them. Being so high up, they can spot danger farther away, but danger can spot them, too.

"Those for me?" she asks, slipping her hand around my arm. I feel my body tense up, knowing she's killed a man before, an FBI agent, and I could be next, if I don't handle this right. I try to cover it by handing her the bag of nuts. She takes one and cracks the shell open with her teeth, then fishes the nut out before putting the shell back in the bag. An empty peanut mixed with all the others.

She's in red again today, same hat as when we first met. She starts walking, and my arm linked in hers, I walk, too.

"Do you think people think we're sweethearts?" she asks. "Seeing us like this? I know I'm a little older than you, but I think I pass for younger. I think people would believe it."

"Maybe," I say.

"Maybe because I look younger? Or maybe because"—she leans in and whispers—"you're a homosexual?"

The words don't scare me as much as I thought they would. I think I knew she would figure it out sooner or later, and it's almost a relief to finally hear it, and see her already bearing it like a weapon, or a prize. Maybe I'm just getting less scared of people knowing. That's probably a mistake. I keep walking.

She pauses, clearly expecting more of a reaction, but this time I drag her along, our arms linked. We walk by the monkeys in silence.

"I didn't figure it all out until you mentioned the book service," she says finally. "So I went back yesterday, searched until I found one of those flyers in their books, asking people to sign up. I didn't know the titles, I had to look them all up at the library, find out what they had in common, but . . . then a lot of it became clear. Why you left the force. The sorts of cases you take now." Her face softens. "It's a good story, you know. Gay cop becomes detective for the gay community. Are they criminal deviants, or just treated that way by society? I could interview you, maybe some clients, we can talk about what you've done, how you help people." She takes a step closer to me. "Really convince people that you're a good guy, trying to do right by your . . . people."

"It's a story that would get me killed, and you know it."

"It's a story that would do wonders for the homosexual people of San Francisco. I know there are a lot of you. We all do. I've even been to that bar, the one with the female impersonators, Shelly's. I had a lot of fun. It was amazing the way they looked."

I believe her. She's right about it, too. The way she handles a pen, she could write a story that might make some people see our lives for what they are—beautiful, fragile, terrifying. But they'd also put a mark on every one of us—every name she mentioned, every bar. People who hated us already would hate us even more now, because someone thought we weren't so bad. They'd come to every name on the list, and they'd try to destroy it.

"I've seen your work," I tell her. "You name names."

"I can't publish a story of just anonymous sources."

"You put people in danger. That Black dockworker, the Chinese store owner? What happens to them after you publish?"

She shrugs, and takes a peanut from the bag. "I don't care."

"Of course not."

"I don't mean I don't care as a person. But as a journalist . . . those dockworkers voted to go on strike, even though the unfair treatment was directed mostly at the Black members of the union. The building in Chinatown was going to fall down— maybe Mr. Liu was kicked out, maybe the police ran him out of town, maybe they killed him." She cracks the peanut open. "But if I hadn't written that story, the city wouldn't have finally investigated and ordered repairs on the building, and it would have collapsed, and killed him, his family, his customers . . ." She takes the peanut out, it's rotten, and she tosses it on the ground, then puts the shell back in the bag. "I tell the stories that need to be told. Maybe that hurts people. But it helps more than it hurts. Your story could help people."

"I don't want to tell it."

"What makes you think I'm giving you a choice?" Her smile is gone now. "I'm writing about you, Andy. The only question is if you want to help me make the story better."

I feel a thousand things in me when she says it. Hot anger, cold fear. They mingle in my blood, hissing as they turn to steam.

"I have a different story to tell," I tell her.

She cocks an eyebrow. "Oh?"

"About a young reporter who killed an FBI agent and let a mobster take the credit."

She freezes, her eyes darting to me for a moment, and the smile falling, turning angry, sharp, before reappearing, soft and charming.

"So Joe's alive," she says. "Or there were more copies of that damn book of his."

"You never read it," I say, trying to sound amused as she always does.

She looks down, kicks her toe into the ground as we walk. "No. I knew it was a good story. How could it not be? A Mafia tell-all? I thought that if I read it, I wouldn't be able to destroy it . . . everything in it . . . I guess more than I knew. He was a homosexual, too, right? What a story. Would have saved me some time if I had just read it. I would have known all about you right away. But then I don't think I would have been able to burn them all. And I needed to."

I let that linger as we pause in front of the elephants. They're far away from the edge of the cage, gathered around a little pond.

"I'm sorry about what happened to you," I tell her, hoping it'll make her like me, make it easier to get her to kill the story. Confess. Something.

She snorts a laugh. "Does he still believe that? That the big bad FBI agent wanted to have his way with me?"

I frown. "Not the real story, then?"

"He wanted to hurt me," she says, raising her nose, and staring at the elephants. "That part is true. It was self-defense. He found out I was a reporter, and he wouldn't let me publish—I was writing about him, an FBI agent, undercover, doing awful, illegal things. He said it would have killed him. I said he could always run back to the FBI first. We fought and he got my hands behind my back easily. He said he was going to lock me up. He even tried to handcuff me. Well, I wasn't going to jail—that would ruin my career before it started. And I wasn't going to not write the story. So I did what I had to, and I gave him my shoulder to his chin. He fell back, and then I kicked him into the table. I saw how sharp the corner was, but I did it—for the truth. And I don't regret it, Andy. That story was important. It had to come out. Like yours." She turns toward me, soft again. "It's also an important story," she tries, her eyes large and earnest, as if she hadn't just confessed to killing a man for the same thing.

What I need to know now is how she killed Howard—and if he gave her any addresses before she did. With her not knowing, probably not, but she wants a story now. She's figuring it out. Who knows what he thought was happening, what he was sputtering out to save his life.

"You killed Howard," I say. The best way is to be honest. She doesn't like secrets.

Her face snaps for a moment, eyebrows coming together, mouth pinching. "What?"

"You just told me you burned all his books. I just want to know what he told you."

"Oh, sure, I burned the books." She takes another peanut, cracks it open with her hands this time, and eats it, putting the empty shell back in the bag. "But I didn't kill him."

"Really? Joe writes a book that could ruin your career, your life, and you knew about it, burned the books, but didn't make sure he never tried to write it again?"

"I didn't know where he was." She takes another peanut, cracks it open. "If I did, maybe I would have talked to him, and then . . ." She sighs. The peanut shell is empty. She puts it back in the bag. "I didn't kill him. Or Howard. I just took the books and left them a little message. A story."

"A story?"

She shrugs, takes another peanut. "To make sure they wouldn't try to publish again."

"Why should I believe any of this?"

She sighs, cracks the nut and eats it. "You want a full confession, fine: I asked around the casino to find out about Joe, where he had gone. No one would tell me, but they did mention his friend, the bookshop owner, Howard." She keeps her eyes on the peanut bag as she talks, taking out more nuts, cracking them, and piling them in her hand, putting the empty ones back. "I checked all the bookstores in the city, only one owned by anyone named Howard. So then I broke in through the back door. I found the books, loaded them all in my car, and I left—" She laughs, suddenly, a sound too loud and easy. "—I left a dead fish. You know, like the Mafia does. I thought that would scare them off."

I think of the fishy smell in the room. The broken back window. It lines up.

"Then who killed Howard?" I ask, only half believing her.

"I don't know," she says, and her voice is honest. "I waited in my car all night, watching, to make sure they got the message, and not some assistant. I didn't know what kind of operation they were. They came back in the morning. I saw them drive up and go inside. That was good enough for me. I left."

"When?" I ask.

"Wednesday—well, Thursday morning."

I flinch. "And you saw both of them—Howard and DeeDee?"

"Yes . . . why? Did you figure it out just now? Am I getting to see you in action?" She smiles.

DeeDee had known about the fish. She found it with Howard. She had lied about the days she was gone—if she was gone at all. If Rose is telling the truth, DeeDee makes sense as the killer—except for the why. Why would she murder her oldest friend, ruin her business?

"I wouldn't even know how to move a body, Andy," Rose says in a low voice. "Joe did it last time."

"Putting it in the water isn't hard to figure out," I say.

She shakes her head. "I had nothing against Howard. I just wanted to scare them."

I almost believe her. She hands me back the bag of peanuts, all empty shells now, the last peanut still in her hand, unbroken. "I still want to tell your story."

"No," I say.

"It could change the way people think of homosexuals," she says. "You're not some flouncing fairy. You're a strong ex-cop. Masculine. You save people. Think of what that could do for perception."

"No," I repeat, thinking of my old chief's perception, my old buddies on the force. I think of them coming to the bar, going for me, maybe finding Gene and going for him, too, just because he's there. Lee, Elsie . . . all of them. This story would destroy us all.

"I'll write it anyway," she says, lifting her chin a little. She spins the peanut between her fingers. "If you're part of it, you can control it, you can say what you want and—"

"If you do that, I'll tell the feds you killed one of their men."

She goes pale, the peanut goes still. "You wouldn't."

"There's no statute of limitations on murder in the state of California." I keep my tone level, unconcerned, like she is.

"Well, they wouldn't believe you. You're—"

"A story?" I say. "Publish it and I'll be famous, won't I? Imagine everyone who will want to talk to me—other reporters, right? And I can tell them your story. Think they'd look into it? Think that would make the feds believe it? Do you know how Joe hid the evidence you left behind? I do. He was happy to tell me."

It's a bluff, but it seems to work. For the first time since I've met her, she seems uncertain. She looks almost seasick with it.

"The truth . . ." she pleads. "It can help people."

"It's not your truth to tell. Just like yours isn't mine to tell. But you can write an article. About Howard, his awful murder—not because he was gay, but because of a mugging. Crime up in the area, the loss of a good man, a pillar of the community. That's a good story. But nothing about the book service in it, no implications about the kind of man he was, or who his customers are. And no me. As long as we agree on that, I think we'll be fine."

She looks away, at the elephants. They've wandered closer to the fence now, and seem to be smiling, their mouths curling up under their trunks, which sway like tired men. She turns back to me, her face normal again, almost triumphant, and I worry I've miscalculated somehow. I can feel my heart pounding in my chest and I worry she can, too, that she knows she can win this.

"Deal," she says, after too long a beat. She takes the last peanut she's been holding, cracks it. "But Andy, you are a good story. And you'll want to tell it eventually—maybe you'll even have to. Promise me that you'll think of me when you do?"

I look at her, the bright eyes, the smile, the little red hat. She pops the peanut in her mouth, drops the shell in the bag I'm still holding. The thing about Rose—the thing that makes her so dangerous—is that I like her.

"If you really didn't kill Howard . . . then sure. If I ever tell my story, it'll be to you."

Her smile turns wider. "Good. Because you're good at your job. I know you'll figure out the truth. I . . . made some mistakes. I won't deny that. But I didn't kill Howard. And honestly . . ." She wraps her hand around my arm. "I'm glad I made them— because it brought me to you. I think we'll meet again, Andy. I think you have good stories, and some will be worth telling, and you'll want to tell them. So I look forward to working with you." She stands on the tips of her toes, leaning toward me, and I back away, defensive. But she just falls forward a little, kissing me on the cheek.

"You know," I say, "Joe never mentioned what you did in his book. I only know because he told me. But he said he would never have put that in writing. It would have hurt you. And you're his friend. That's what he said."

For a moment, all her cheerfulness fades, and for the first time since I've known her, she looks something like ashamed. A breeze catches a few stray hairs and blows them across her face, and she stares down, and then away, at the elephants. Then she looks up, smiles, and reaches out to squeeze my hand.

"See you soon," she says. She knows it's a threat. It wavers a little as she says it, like maybe she regrets it. But then she shrugs at me, and we lock eyes. Some people don't change. They can't. They get so wrapped up in the ribbon of words they use to describe themselves that it ends up being the thing that holds them together. Like a typewriter ribbon, filled with ghosts of letters. Snip that ribbon, and everything about them unravels: who they could have been, who they should be. Change is just another word for death to people like that.

I'm lucky I survived my own snip, even if I have to live with everything I was and try to make up for it. That's a gift, I think.

When I blink, she's already gone, fading into the crowd around me, leaving me with just a bag of empty shells.

EIGHTEEN

I need to talk to DeeDee. The fish, the timeline, the confusion . . . it makes sense but it doesn't, either. Why would she kill Howard? But why would Rose make up such an elaborate lie?

Clouds start gathering by the time I hop the streetcar, and when we come out from the tunnel under Twin Peaks, it's pouring in thick glossy sheets, like magazine covers have been torn down to slivers and shaken down on us. When I get off, I pull my coat tight, but I'm still soaked by the time I get to the doors of Walt's—and they're locked. The curtains are drawn, and it's dark inside. I go around the back, where the lights are on, and pull the door open.

DeeDee is packing a box and looks up in shock, her hand fluttering to her chest, before she recognizes me. "Oh, it's only you, you scared me, I didn't think anyone was coming around today." She turns back to her boxes, and the books stacked on the desk. She picks one up and turns it in her hand. "I like this one. But I don't know."

"Packing?" I ask.

"Oh yes, I want to take some of it with me to Vegas." She looks down at the books, her eyes shining, wet. "My favorite books. I own plenty already, but some I gave away or lent and I don't remember to who, so some of these I'm going to take with me. The rest I'll leave for the landlord to sort out, but I deserve something after . . ." She sighs, and gestures at the floor. "All this."

"Howard's death, you mean?"

"His death, the bookstore going under, the mob coming after

us, everything, you know, everything. It's worse than that tree house."

"What happened that night?" I ask her.

She turns away. "What night?"

"The night you came back, and found the fish on the desk, the books gone?"

"I . . . what?"

"You told me yourself, you found the fish. Except I know who left the fish, and that wasn't until Wednesday. You should have been in Vegas by then."

She turns slowly, her eyes too wide. "I don't know what you mean. I don't remember that. I remember it smelled like fish, though. When I got back. You can still smell it, can't you? I'm just an old woman. I get confused. Always have, ever since I was little. My mother used to get so upset when I would misplace a dolly. And my Suzie, too, she told me I'd lose my head if it weren't attached. She—" She stops, suddenly, and swallows. "I get confused."

I take a step toward her, but put my hands in my pockets, try to look less intimidating. "DeeDee . . . what happened? You and Howard came in here, the books were gone, there was a fish . . ."

She sighs and goes and sits down. "Nothing."

"DeeDee, please. There are so many people who cared about Howard, they deserve to know—"

"And you think I don't? He was my best friend, my oldest . . . since we were kids . . . he . . ." She's taking deep breaths, her sentences falling apart as they spill from her mouth. She almost heaves in the air. I wonder if she's choking for a moment, before she starts to cry. I take out my handkerchief and give it to her. She stares at it a moment, confused, or maybe surprised, before taking it, and blowing her nose.

"Thank you," she says.

"Just tell me," I say.

She takes a deep breath and looks at me. I can see her deciding what to do, and then deflating, slowly, the air let out of a tire. She looks tired. She looks relieved.

"We fought," she says softly. "He had never told me what the book was."

"But you told me it was Mafia," I say.

"Well, I know that now," she says, glaring through her wet eyes. "Did you not know? But you said it was a memoir, so I thought you knew . . . If I had kept my mouth shut then you wouldn't . . ." She shakes her head.

"And if you'd just told me you'd had the list, instead of lying about finding it."

She shrugs. "I always had the list. He didn't need it. I don't know why I lied. Pat hired you and I thought if I just said it was misplaced, and I found it, you'd go away . . ." She sighs. A long, empty sound. "It doesn't matter. I didn't know then. He said it was going to make us rich, that it was a memoir of a friend with an unbelievable life. I figured someone he wrote letters with, one of those guys. They tell him stories. I wasn't here when the books came in, I'd gone home early—I had a date, if you can believe it. Howard set it up for me, some woman who wrote to him. It wasn't a very good date, but it was nice to . . ." She sighs, blows her nose again. "The next morning, he came over, picked me up to walk to work together, that was normal, we did that a lot. But he was so excited that day. Bouncing up and down like when we were kids. He said the books were in, that he was so excited for me to read it. I was excited too!" She smiles. "I was so happy he was happy. I always got caught up in that, even when it ended badly . . . I loved that tree house . . . But then we got to the store, and they were gone, and there was this . . ." She gestures at the desk. "Fish!" She laughs. "I thought it was a joke at first. I looked at him and asked if it was a prank. But he had gone white as a sheet. 'The books are gone,' he said finally. That's when I got worried. We put a lot of money into them, you know. So I look at the fish, and I'm thinking about what it could mean, and he takes me by both arms and bends down to look me in the eye and he's crying. He says he's so sorry."

She shakes her head. "That's when he told me what the book was. The mob. A memoir by a gay mobster. Of all the stupid ideas he had . . ." She looks at the door to the main store. "This was the one that was going to get us both killed. I said to him, I said, 'How did you think this would go?' I was screaming, I think, actually. 'How did you think it would go, Howard?'" she says loudly at the door, at the empty space where he used to be. She seems to realize she's talking to a ghost and turns back to me. "He said the money we got from it . . . we were going to run away. Him and me. Mexico or Cuba, maybe. There was enough money in the accounts to get us out of town—two weeks, he said. We needed to leave in two weeks. Then once the book became a sensation he was going to sell the publishing rights to a real publisher—we'd have enough to open a new bookstore, he said. Somewhere people didn't speak English, I thought. He had this whole idea of what our lives were going to be, and he never told me. Not once. Just assumed I'd go along with it . . . And then he said something about a boy. Marty."

"Merle?"

She nods. "Merle. A boyfriend he'd had who I hadn't even met, who needed to run away. So I had to run away, too. Because he'd fallen for some new . . . Howard and men were always trouble. And now my life was ruined because of some romantic adventure Howard had conjured up for himself. It was the tree house all over again. He was so focused on his vision. He never thought about what would happen to anyone else. You know, after

I jumped out of that tree house and ruined my Mary Janes, you know what happened? My mother spanked me so hard I couldn't sit for weeks. They were expensive shoes. I tried to tell her—I was just saving Howard, I was just helping . . . it didn't matter. No one cares if you're trying to help someone. You should know that. All they care about is what you ruined."

I nod. "I know the feeling."

"Well," she says, her hands wrapping into fists. "Howard ruined everything. He always did. And I was always there to clean it up, but this time . . . How can you clean up the Mafia?"

"So what happened then? When you knew everything, and knew the books were gone?"

She looks at me, her eyes so old, so tired. "You know."

I feel a sudden sadness well up in me, a drain spurting up black water that pools at the bottom of the tub. That's how I feel now. Like a stopped-up tub. "I don't."

She sits down at the desk, collapsing like a pile of clothes. "He . . . he said we could run. The printer must still have had the original manuscript. We were going to go to them, and take it, and run. He didn't even notice my knees were shaking so much I couldn't stand up. He had to get Merle, he said. He didn't know how. Had a plan where I would go into this . . . mob casino, because they wouldn't recognize me. Give a message to Merle. Never even stopped to check how I was, ask what I . . ."

I kneel by her and look up at her face. She's crying again. "What happened, DeeDee?"

"I was so angry. I never knew I could be so angry."

I wait. She turns to the desk, and looks at the pile of unopened letters. "There was a letter opener," she says softly. "But it was still in him when I dragged him to my car . . . used the dolly we use for books to . . ." The words fade. "I haven't been able to open a letter since."

I fall back, sitting on the floor now. She really did it. The noise of my falling makes her turn toward me. The tears are streaming now.

"I had to, you know. If I didn't, then . . . we'd both be dead. We both would. I even went into the casino after. I went right up to the one in charge. I could tell from how no one sat next to him at the bar. And I said, 'Does Howard owe you anything more?' and he looked me over. He knew what I meant. And he asked for a few dollars. I think it was symbolic, you know? I've never dealt with the Mafia. But we understood each other. And I was safe now. No book, no murder. I'm shocked it worked, but . . . it did."

I shake my head. "DeeDee . . . it wasn't the mob who took the books, left the fish."

Her mouth opens, but nothing comes out except a strangled gasp.

"It was . . . Someone else didn't want the book published. She made it look like the mob."

She looks back at the door to the shop, then to me, her hands at her own throat. "So I . . ."

I nod.

"He was my best friend." Her face collapses as she says it, like her skin has turned to a waterfall. The lines grow deeper, every-thing shakes, and she starts to pour tears and mucus. She wails. It's a long, hollow sound of pain. Then she covers her face with her hands, muffling it. I wait for her to stop, but she continues for a while. The rain outside hits the street harder, loud enough I can focus on it instead of her. It's calming. I think of each drop as a book, or at least a story. Someone's story that Howard knew or heard or told, all of them getting thrown down on us. There are so many. And a lot of them were good, sometimes. I think of Merle, lying on Howard's chest, listening to him read. I think of

Howard and DeeDee, crying in the tree house as they realized who they were. I think of Joe, smoking weed in his pool, surrounded by naked young men. I think of Elsie. I think of Lee. I think of Gene. Not all the stories are bad. But this one is.

"I can't go to the police," I tell her after a while. "They'll look into too much, figure out too much, put all your customers at risk. So there's not much I can do."

"I know," she sniffs. "That's why I'm leaving. I don't . . . deserve this place anymore."

"It's a shame," I say, standing up and going to the door to the main shop. "A lot of people love this place."

"Me too," she says from her chair. "But books . . . some books are too dangerous to read, or write, or sell. Some stories just shouldn't be told."

I turn around. She stands up and gathers the box of books she was packing, closing it with practiced fingers, overlapping the flaps to hold them in place. Then she opens the door. The sound of the rain gets louder and she raises her voice to speak above it, but doesn't turn around. "I'll go live with my sister. No one will ever need to hear from me again. Tell people . . . whatever you want. Tell them I'm sorry."

She walks out. I watch her fade into a blur behind the rain almost immediately. A moment later, her car pulls out of the alley and drives away. I've never written a book. I don't know how endings are supposed to go. That's the difference between books and real life, though—a book can end whenever you want. A life keeps going, even when it only gets sadder.

I go out into the bookstore and look around the store, until I find a copy of *The City and the Pillar*, the one Lee told me to read. I leave some money by the register. In the back room, I collect all the unopened letters. I don't know why, but I know someone needs to answer them. Under them is the address book—the list.

I tuck them under my coat with the book and wait for the rain to lighten up a little. It takes a while.

I'm wet when I make it back to the Ruby, but the letters are still dry. It's only a little after noon, but Gene is pouring drinks already, and it seems like people are waiting for me: Elsie, Merle, Lee, and Pat are seated at the bar, quiet, all looking up in unison when I walk in.

Merle spots me first, and stands from his seat at the bar. "Did you find out? Who killed Howard?"

Gene holds out a drink for me as I get there, and I take my wet jacket off. I hand the letters and address book to Pat, and put *The City and the Pillar* on the bar with my hat.

"You bought it," Pat says, smiling.

"Gene's going to read it to me," I say.

Lee smirks. "We don't need to know the details of your personal lives."

"So?" Merle asks.

"Yeah," I say, looking at him, wondering if I should tell him. Merle looks different than yesterday, though. Less lost. He's found himself here, I think. Without Howard. He can handle it. And he deserves to know.

I tell them everything. I start at the beginning, Joe's book, the gay mobster autobiography, how Howard got him to write it for his book service, how Howard thought it would make them all rich. But then Joe told Rose and Rose took the books, made it look like a mob warning, which scared DeeDee. Scared her too much, made her fear for her own life. She killed him, and now she's going to her sister's in Vegas, horrified at what she's done. There's nothing else I can do.

"She hates herself for it," I say, looking over them. "It was a moment of fear. Because of other people." I look at Merle. "I'm sorry. But so is she."

Merle nods, quiet. He's hunched over at a table near the bar, alone, but he doesn't look unhinged or angry. Just sad. Same as the rest of us.

"Damn shame," Lee says.

"Terrible," Elsie says.

"I can't imagine how she must feel," Gene says.

Pat shakes his dead. "Poor DeeDee. I . . . don't want to see her again but . . . she must be . . ."

Merle stands up. "I need to go home," he says.

"Merle," I say. "Joe says you can go stay with him, if you want. To get away from your family. To start somewhere new where you don't have to be looking over your shoulder all the time. You could have a real life."

"You're so talented," Lee adds.

"Thank you," Merle says to me, his voice soft. "But I need to go home first. I'll . . . think about it."

He goes to the elevator, and we all wait in silence as he gets in. He smiles as me as the doors close, and I think of him in the spotlight this morning, singing without music. I hope he comes back, takes my offer, goes to Joe. I want that for him—to be saved, the way I was saved, too.

"This is a bad one," Elsie says. "I mean . . . I'm glad we're all safe, Andy. I am. Thank you. But this is . . ."

"Yeah," I say.

"Anything we can do?" Lee asks.

"Make sure people know about Rose, that she's dangerous. I have enough dirt on her I think she won't pursue anything, but just in case."

"What about the store?" Pat asks, looking at the letters and address book he's been holding the whole time. "The book service?"

I shake my head. "I guess it'll get replaced with something. I don't know. The landlord will probably find someone new. Whatever's left in there will be taken, I bet, to cover whatever rent DeeDee's going to stop paying. I don't know how she's closing the place down. I just know she's gone."

"That . . ." Pat frowns. "That's awful. That place is more than a bookshop, you know. It's a center for people to meet and talk. The letters we got . . ." He looks down and realizes he's holding them. "Is that why you saved them?"

"Yeah," I say. "I thought they should be answered. And you're . . . who's left."

He nods, and for a moment, I can see his eyes getting watery. "I'll do right by Howard. I'll write them all back."

"Maybe . . . you can do more than that," Elsie says. She turns to Gene. "Make us all a round. I think we should scheme."

It only takes a couple weeks for Elsie to put it together. Pat helps, of course, handling the address book, the letters—writing everyone Howard knew, to tell them about his passing, to invite them to the Ruby to remember him. And so many of them show up—people from all over the state, some from outside it. And they bring money, too—gifts, contributions, all to keep Walt's open and the book service running. Pearl wrote Pat a large check, so they were already halfway there, but only an hour after the doors of the Ruby opened, with Lee singing, and Elsie passing the hat around and giving out free drinks, we've made enough to keep the store going for another three months—with Pat running it.

"It's strange," he tells me, sitting at the bar. Lee is singing "I

Hear The Music Now" as people dance around us. "I'm going to miss Lavender House, but . . . I don't feel sad about it. They said I should come back and have dinner with them. Like you. Ex-employees, I guess."

"They find a replacement yet?" I ask him.

He shakes his head. "Elsie is handling that. Looking at the bartenders, talking to them. I think your boyfriend is helping her." He nods at Gene, who is counting donations by the register. "I can't believe she did this. Donated a whole night to Howard and to . . . me, I guess."

"You said it yourself. That place is special."

"She said she deserves a discount on her Narnia books, though."

I laugh. "Yeah." I look around the room, all the people, and think of the letters I read in Howard's apartment. The tapestry of queer readers. "Imagine if he could see this," I say, sipping some sweet drink Gene made for me. "All these people he touched, all together. I read the letters, you know, for the case. I saw how people wrote to him. How they all relied on him. He was a center of a community."

"It's big shoes to fill," Pat says. "I'm a little scared of it, honestly."

"Really?" I ask. "You're going to be perfect at it."

"Maybe," he shrugs, his smile dimming a little.

"Are you sad to be leaving?" I ask. "Lavender House?"

He looks down at his drink and nods a little, then back up at me. "Sure . . . sad. Yeah, I think sad. Other things, too. Like . . . excited? But then I feel guilty, because after everything I just put them through . . . I shouldn't be leaving, right? I should be staying, helping them rebuild. Or maybe it's for the best I leave, maybe they'd never look at me the same again, never trust me . . ."

"They trust you."

"I know. I went back, to tell them, to move the books back,

bring back the family portrait, and Pearl, she gave me a big hug, told me she was so glad I was home . . . and I remember looking around—looking up at Irene on the wall, and thinking it's not really my home. It's theirs. And I'm family, sure, but . . . like a cousin. It's not my home. I need . . . something more my own. I want to go back and visit, of course. I want them to come to the bookshop. But . . . I think I'm glad to be going. Is that wrong? I feel guilty, I think."

"You shouldn't," I say, rubbing his back.

He swallows his drink. "Things change, I guess. It's a . . ." He laughs. "New chapter for me."

I roll my eyes. "It'll be a good one."

"I hope so. Look at all these people." His hand fans out, sweeping over the crowded room. "I can't let them down."

I stare at everyone here, so many of them Howard and Dee-Dee's friends, all of them readers. "You know, one of the last things DeeDee said to me was that some books are too dangerous to be written, or read. But I don't know. Seeing all these people . . . I think books are the opposite."

Pat laughs. "No, no, Andy. Books *are* dangerous."

I turn to him, surprised. "What?"

"It's just about who they're dangerous to she was wrong about. She meant her, Howard maybe. If people are afraid of you reading a thing—a reporter, the mob, the government—that means they're afraid of reading it too. Afraid of knowing what's in the book, whether it be some personal secret, or just some story of love that could make someone feel less alone. Books are just as dangerous to the people who don't want us to read them as they are to us. Because they make us less alone. They make us see ourselves. They make us realize what we deserve. And sometimes they make people who aren't like us realize it, too. That's why

they're dangerous. And that's why we all have to live dangerously—
so we keep reading them."

I nod, not quite sure if I understand, especially not after four
of whatever these drinks Gene made are. "I think you're a lot
smarter than me, Pat," I say, slapping him on the back.

He laughs. "I'm not, Andy. We all have our gifts. What's important is sharing them. And look what you did . . . look what
you've shared with me . . ." He gestures at the crowd.

"That's not me, that's Howard."

We look around the room quietly for a moment before someone calls Pat's name and he goes over to them. I watch him,
and my eyes for a moment catch Virginia, the astronomer. She's
standing with a woman, but also with Ralph, who we introduced
her to two weeks back. They were very formal but seemed to
get along. He says something to her now, and she turns to the
woman next to her and rolls her eyes, but then laughs. I wonder
if she'll make it the thirteen months. That's the problem with
telling stories like those, the ones with real people. They're not
flights of fantasy like Howard dove into. No knights in shining
armor, no daring rescues, no running away and living happily
ever after. Just people, trying to survive. You start thinking life is
really like the stories and you end up . . .

Someone is missing, I realize. I go over to Gene. "I'll be back
in a little bit," I tell him.

"Where are you going?"

"I want to see if I can write something like a happy ending."

The Shore Club doesn't change. The blue velvet curtains still fall
like shrouds, the cigarette smoke still writes eulogies in the air. I
haven't heard from Merle since he got in the elevator and left the

Ruby two weeks ago, but I'm not surprised to find him singing here. He's singing "How Long Has This Been Going On?" again. Merle's not moving like he was at the Ruby—he's still, almost a streak of charcoal in his tuxedo, his voice low and masculine. But he's singing it. He looks different. Maybe his hair has changed a little. Maybe it's just his eyes. They seem harder, somehow. He doesn't seem to see me, so I go the bar. Bridges is there, and smiles when I sit down next to him.

"Haven't seen you in a while," he says. "You considered my offer?"

I shake my head. "I'm still getting set up, you know."

He smirks. "If you don't want to work with me, you can say so, I won't be offended."

"No?" I ask, looking at him. "It's really asking, not demanding?"

He smiles. "You . . . you're a nice guy, Andy. You wouldn't do well working for us anyway. I saw how you rushed to help me when Merle fell. And Merle says you helped him out on something else."

I don't say anything, not sure what Merle gave away.

"He didn't say what you helped him with, though. He never used to keep secrets."

"Well . . . I'm a private eye, so it's private."

"I'm not prying," he says, watching Merle. "But he did ask me the strangest favor after."

"Oh?"

"And I'm not saying I did it. But he asked for me to reach out to some friends in Vegas and find a little old lady, and then take her fishing."

I swallow, and my eyes go back to Merle. He looks stronger, but emptier, too, I realize.

"Fishing?" I ask. My voice comes out hoarse.

"You need a drink, Andy?" He waves the bartender over, who puts a whiskey soda in front of me. I take a long sip.

"He asked me to take a friend in town fishing, too, but she's . . . done a lot of good by us. We like her. So I told him no."

I nod, staring at my drink, wondering if I should warn Rose. But it sounds like she's protected. More than DeeDee was. I tried to save Merle. I set up the offer with Joe. But he . . . saved himself, I guess. If this is what goes for saving these days.

"Merle had never been interested in the other parts of the business before. Or since. But . . . he's been less afraid lately. Stronger. Hasn't fainted. Auditioned for a producer just a few days ago—haven't heard anything but maybe he'll get on the radio."

"He's good, I bet he will."

"He seems different . . ." He turns to me, and I watch him pause for a moment, then he carefully drops the mask. His eyes go softer, and the usual stiff smirk he wears falls into something sadder. "Is he all right, Andy? Really?"

I shake my head. "I don't know. I'm sorry. I can say . . . I had to give him some bad news."

"About Howard?" he asks, his eyes drilling into me. "That's who you were asking about last time. The bookstore guy. Merle's biggest fan. I hear he washed up just a few blocks from here."

I nod, not sure what to say.

"We didn't do that, though. Merle knows that, right?"

"He does. He knows everything that happened."

"I know they were . . ." Bridges looks up at Merle. "Close."

I don't say anything.

"But you know, I love that kid like a son, Andy. I don't mind him having . . . close friends. Long as no one else finds out."

"Does he know that?" I ask.

"How do I . . . I don't know how to say that."

"I think if you can figure out how, he'll be grateful."

"Yeah," he says, looking down at his drink. When he looks back up at me, the mask is back. "Do you have close friends, Andy?"

I smirk, put my own mask on, and sip my drink.

"All right," Bridges says. "None of my business. But thanks for . . . talking to me. And for whatever you did for Merle. He's been . . . I don't know. He sings new songs. Different ones, some sung by women. But he sounds so good no one cares, y'know? But I guess he's sad, too. He's got reason to be. But you helped him out. So thank you. If you ever need a favor, Andy . . ."

He lifts his drink to me, and I tap my glass on his. "No offense, Bridges, but I hope I never will."

Merle stops singing to a round of applause, and then comes offstage. When he sees me, he smiles the way Pearl did when I went back to Lavender House. Another bookend. Another little reminder of sadness.

"Hi," he says softly, his eyes darting to his uncle, who turns away. "Why are you here?"

I speak low enough Bridges can't hear. "A lot of us are . . . celebrating Howard tonight, over at the Ruby. If you want to come."

Merle looks away, then shakes his head. "I . . . need to stay here, Andy. This is my family." He pauses and looks over at Bridges, who is watching the roulette wheel. Merle smiles a little. "They care about me, even if . . . And I belong here. I'm one of them. It took me a while to realize it. But I belong here, not in some happy . . ." He looks around, letting the words fade.

"You belong wherever you want."

He shakes his head. "My uncle did something for me. Something important. And the fact that I even asked it means that I—"

"Merle—"

He puts his hand up to stop me. "I'm going to pay him back. It would break his heart if I left. I know what that's like."

"But what about you, your story?" I ask. "It could be different—"

He shakes his head and I stop speaking.

"What's the point of stories?" he asks, eyes locked on mine. I can't see anything in them, like he's wearing a mask. His words hang between us, wrapping around the cigarette smoke, and he shrugs, slowly, lazily. Then he gets up and walks back to the stage.

I sigh, but nod at Bridges as I walk away. He nods back, an odd look in his eye. When I'm in the crowd, I turn back, and they're talking. Bridges has his hand on Merle's shoulder at the edge of the stage, leaning in, and Merle is starting to smile. That's something. It's not fairy tales. But it's something.

The party is winding down by the time I make it back to the Ruby. Elsie is dancing with Pat. Gene is waving goodbye to people, Lee is still singing, but everyone is happy. And drunk. Gene looks up at me when I come in, then takes my hand and leads me to the dance floor without saying anything.

"You went to see Merle?" he asks, as he pulls my body close to his.

"Yeah."

"But he didn't come back?"

I think about telling him everything, about what Merle did, how he's changed. But that's not my story to tell, I decide.

"He's working tonight," I say instead.

"Yeah, I should get back to it, too."

"All right," I say. "I should probably go lock up, too. But don't forget, we have lunch tomorrow at Lavender House." Mrs. Purley's last visit had been ten days ago, and the family invited me over again the moment it was over. Rina was officially part of the family now, and they needed my help hanging the good portrait up again.

Gene laughs. "I'm actually very nervous about it."

"It'll be fine," I say, kissing him. "Better than fine."

"I hope so."

I watch him go behind the bar again, then go upstairs, to lock up. Last week's paper is still on my desk, opened to Rose's story—murdered bookstore owner, a real loss for the community, police chief says drug use in the neighborhood on the rise, leading to crime. I read it five times to make sure there were no hints, suggestions, but she kept up her end. But next to it is something new—a letter. Addressed to me. Here, at the Ruby. Elsie must have brought it in earlier. I don't get mail much. I tear it open. Inside is just a slip of paper—a private investigator's license. Evander Mills. I break out in goose bumps, like a wave of ice over me. The chief knows where I am. Knows where I live, work. But he's giving me this. He's saying I'm allowed to keep living . . . for now. That's something.

I open the safe in my desk, and put the license in there, with Rose's article, my gun, and the last copy of Joe's book. It hadn't actually been hard to find. I remembered the name of the printer from the accounts ledger, and stopped by there. They had some copies that hadn't come out right—the glue on the spine had leaked. They'd thrown them away, never read them—they print so many, they never really bother. So I rummaged through their dumpster until I found one: *Crimes I've Done and Been*, by a Former Mobster. The other copies were ruined, the glue seeped too far, but this one is only a little off. The cover is simple. Two men, in an alley, one lighting the other's cigarette, both wearing gun holsters. I read it alone, at night. No one else even knows I have it—it's too dangerous, I think. But it's a good read.

I close the safe, and lock up. Outside, Gene is in the hall, leaning against the wall next to my apartment door.

"Hi." I smile at him. "I thought you had to work."

"Yeah . . . I asked Eileen to take the rest of the shift, and Elsie is still down there, she can close up." His hands are behind his back, but he brings them forward now, holding my copy of *The City and the Pillar*. "I don't know if you were kidding, a few weeks ago, when you said you wanted me to read to you, but . . . I saw you'd left this book by the bar. The cover flap is only a few pages in . . ."

"Yeah." I turn away to lock my office door. "I . . . it's hard to read in a bar. The noise."

He comes up close behind me, his hand around my waist. "So let me read."

I turn to him. "Really?"

"I mean . . . I've never done it before . . . I could be a bad reader. Weird voice." He smiles. "I don't know. But I wanted to do it for you."

I kiss him, grateful. "Okay," I say. I open the door to the apartment and watch as he takes off his shoes, his shirt, trying not to worry about the chief's message, trying not to save Gene from the dangers he has to live with, we all have to live with.

In bed, I lay my head down on his chest, loving the warm stone smell of his skin, and he opens the book, restarting at the beginning. I curl up in his arm and listen to his heart, his breath. He turns the page, and he reads.

ACKNOWLEDGMENTS

Books! In the fifties, having a small press wasn't so hard: an editor, a contract with a printer, the printer handled the typesetting, etc. Just a few people to make a book. But today is different; today we have huge teams supporting authors like me and making sure these books are reaching their full potential. And I'm lucky to have one of the best teams out there working on the Evander Mills books. And I'm going to thank them now.

First, as always, my amazing agent, Joy, who has stood by me for so many years and so many books. She's amazing, she's family, I couldn't do any of this without you, Joy, so thank you.

Second, also as always, my spectacular editor, Kristin, who is so smart about how she thinks about my work and makes me think about it. I love working with her because I feel as though every book makes me a better writer, as every book I get to learn something new from her insight and intelligence. Andy is who he is because of her. Troix, who also edits me, is likewise so incisive and smart with her comments. I'm so lucky and grateful to be working with both of you.

My publicists, Laura and Libby, who have set up tours for me to places I never thought would want me to come, and also do their best to keep me sane while I'm on them (an impossible task). Their encouragement and nonstop work are what really makes these books succeed—I can write something wonderful, but no one will buy it if they don't know about it.

Which is why I also am so grateful to my marketing and sales teams: Eileen, Lucille, Arianna, Anthony, Jennifer, Ben, Lisa, Melissa, Gwyn, Christine, and probably many more I haven't met. Thank you so much for everything you do. You not only make sure people know about my books but make sure every ad you see is beautiful and smart, and every bookstore knows exactly what people will love about the books.

And speaking of beautiful, the cover! Katie and Colin have once again worked together to make something stunning and evocative, lush and historical and mysterious all while jumping off the shelf. And they're so welcoming and generous, talking to me about the design and the choices and just about how covers are made in general. I'm so lucky to have you both.

Thank you to my amazing audio team, led by Emma, who is so creative and clever. And my fantastic narrator, Vikas, who just gets these characters with so little directing from me, and now probably has to read this aloud, which is hilarious for me—me meaning Lev, not me meaning Vikas, who is currently thanking himself on behalf of me, Lev. Vikas, I think you should laugh here.

The entire Forge family is truly second to none. I feel so supported by them, valued, like I'm part of a team. The best team, really, led by Linda, who has been so welcoming and kind and leads this amazing imprint with such smart guidance and kindness. I am so, so lucky to have you and your team. There are probably countless more members I haven't met—thank you to all of you, too.

I also want to thank folks from outside Forge: SallyAnne, who continues to give me advice and guidance, and whose words have guided me since we first met years ago. I know how to talk about my work because of you. My authenticity reader, Cath, who graciously gave me feedback on the nuances of Gene and Andy's relationship. My writing group, Robin, Laura, Jesse, and Dan, for always keeping me going. And all my writing friends, new and old: Dahlia, Alex, John, Hank, Chantelle, Dan, Dawn, Sara,

Deborah, Sujata, Steve, Nekesa, Wanda, Robyn, Margot, Jeffrey, Catriona, Karen, Rachel, PJ, Adam, Caleb, Cale, Julian, Adib, Sandy, and everyone over at Queer Crime Writers. I'm so thrilled to have this community to keep me motivated and . . . closer to sane than I would be otherwise.

And of course, because this book is about booksellers, I have so many of you to thank. John, especially, for being my first supporter, and for always welcoming me when I go to Murder By The Book. Leah and Bea for giving me a home in NYC. Krysten and Julie for giving me a home in CT, and also promising me ice cream—I'm holding you to that. Barbara, for her wisdom and kindness, and so many others I've met over these years; Jenni, Mariana, Ryan, David, Bill, Laynie-Rose, Susan, Emily, Liz, Beth, Kaitee, Derek, Elizabeth, Laura, Kinsey, Sophie, and so many more who I've probably met in passing, or even never met. You are all doing the most important job, and I'm so grateful to all of you. And I'm pretty sure only a few of you are murderers.

Finally, as always, I need to thank the authors of those books I turned to when researching for this one. This is a book about books, and how books and stories create worlds and communities—I don't know any of these authors personally, but their work has helped me to create this world, and has made me feel closer to my community and my history. Nan Alamilla Boyd's *Wide-Open Town* continues to be a key text for this series, the spine on which I'm allowed to build a body. I turn back to it for every book in the series, to remind myself of the queer community of San Francisco in the fifties. For information on the Mafia in San Francisco, I must thank Christina Ann-Marie DiEdoardo and her delightful book *Lanza's Mob*. For research on queer book services of the time, I have to thank David K. Johnson and his book *Buying Gay*, and Michael Waters for his article in *The New Yorker* "The Book Club that Helped Spark the Gay-Rights Movement." Both were so helpful in helping me imagine and craft Walt's book service and the community it formed. And finally, for information about all those gay books of the fifties, I must thank Michael Bronski and his book *Pulp Friction*, which chronicles so many queer pulps. Not every book mentioned in *Rough Pages* is pulled from *Pulp Friction*, but a lot of them were. I knew I wanted to name as many real titles as possible, and to know at least something of every one mentioned, and that would have been impossible without Bronski's fantastic compendium.

So thank you to all those authors and books, not only for helping me to tell this story, but for creating a beautiful tapestry of a community and a history—our literary history. Books, I hope, entertain and educate, but the best thing they can do is bring people closer. Everyone who reads these books will become closer to queer history and the community that springs from it. I'm lucky to be part of it.

Obviously, the idea of books being banned resonates today, especially with me as the author of a book that's been banned all over the country. But as DeeDee points out, this happened back then, too, and we got through it. The American Library Association released their Freedom to Read statement in May of 1953. Six months later, in Indiana, a Mrs. White proposed the banning of *Robin Hood*. Five students at Indiana University started the Green Feather Movement in protest, dyeing feathers green and spreading them across campus to speak out against the banning. Despite the papers disparaging them and supposed FBI investigations, the movement spread to colleges across the country. *Robin Hood* wasn't banned. We forget the things we've been through, even when we're going through them again. It started with just five students. I want to thank them, too: Bernard Bray, Mary Dawson, Edwin Napier, Blas Davila, and Jeanine Carter, as well as everyone who has spoken out against those who want to make sure only some stories are told, both in the past, and today—librarians, booksellers, people who show up at school board meetings. I know how hard it is, I know the work you're all doing. Thank you.

And to Chris, for being Chris.

ABOUT THE AUTHOR

Rachael Shane

LEV AC ROSEN writes books for people of all ages, including the Evander Mills series, which began with the Macavity Award–winning *Lavender House* and continued with *The Bell in the Fog*. His most recent young adult novels are *Emmett*, *Lion's Legacy*, and *Camp*. Rosen's books have been nominated for Anthony and Lambda Literary Awards and have been selected for best-of lists from *The Today Show*, Amazon, *Library Journal*, *BuzzFeed*, *Autostraddle*, *Forbes*, and many others. He lives in NYC with his husband and a very small cat. You can find him online at LevACRosen.com and @LevACRosen.